MANIAC MENAGERIE

CURSED MANUSCRIPTS

IAIN ROB WRIGHT

Dedicated to my Patreons.

Michael Pearse, Mark Ayre, Virginia Milway, Suzie Roush, Katrice Tuck, Adrian Shotbolt, Minnis Hendricks, Kelli Herrera, Terrie-Ann Thulborn, Phil Brady, Steve Haessler, Jackie Grocutt, Darrion Mika, Karen Lewis, Suzy Tadlock, Kaarin Chadwick, Mari Meisel, Jayne Smith, Susanne Stohr, CJMac, Stacey, Amanda Shaw, Connie France, Gillian Moon, Robin, Armando Llerena, Stephanie Everett, Linda Heafield, Ali Black, Elizabeth Thompson, Stainedglasslee, Stacey Guitarmangrg, Angela Richards, Diane Rushton, Stephen Moss, Jean Geill, Elizabeth Auclair, Adrianne Yang, Joy Perry, Linda, Leslie Clutton, Sarah Chambers, Sylvia Camposano, Kat Miller, Susan Crouch, Sara Boe, Carole, Nigel Crabtree, Becky Wright, Claire Taylor, Caryn Larsen, Leigh Hickey, Jenny Ibbs, Steve Griffith, Diesta Kaiser, Fiona Thompson, Cherise Fugue, Mark Horey, Gian Spadone, Mark Stone, Rachel LaFraniere, Deborah Shelton, Pauline Stout, Angelica Maria, Katie Potter, Jordan Rasmussen, Deirdre Lydon, Bobbie Kelley, Vicky Salter, Melissa Potter, Debbi Sansom, 44bats, Nicole Reid, Bruce W Clark, Carrieanne, Chris Viehman, Mark Harvey, Kristina Goeke, Mark Simpson, Graeme McMechan, Jacqueline Coleman, Vanda Luty, Ruth F Phelps, Donna Twells, Katie Warburton, Susan Kay, Nick Brooks, Stewart Barnes, Nigel Jopson, Gemma Ve, Steven Barnett, Andrew Moss, Sally Jayne Dainton, Tania Buss, Steve Irvine, Lee Ballard, Clive The Moose, Xya Marie, Robert Smith, Oscar Booker Jr, Trevor Oakley, Leona Overton, Susan Hayden, Jennifer Holston, Kelee S, Terence Smith, Michelle Chaney, Roy Oswald, Paul

*Weaver, Linda Robinson, Chris Aitchison, Michael Rider, Deborah Knapp
Bread, Beth Thurman, Cass Griffiths, Debbie Ivory, David Lennox, Zoe Lloyd, William Matthews, Hazel Smith, Gary Harper, Laurie Cook, Margaret McAloon, Paul, Neil Grey, Catherine H, Sherrie, Brian McGowan, Pam Felten, Carol Wicklund, Mary Meisel, Deborah, Lady Aliehs, Rachel Mayfield, Erica Lewis, Mary Stephenson, Maniel Le, Tara Enright, Andre Jenkin, Lawrence Clamons, Gary Groves, Mike Prankard, Dorothy Rushforth, Dan Garay, Lynn Mcvay, Rona Trout, Mark Pearson, Mary Kiefel, Emma, Karen lewis, Eddie Garcia, Caronda Bourgeois, David Humphries, Tracy Putland, Laura Monaghan, TheWeelou23, boy stio, Emily Haynes, Pam Brown, Sharon Campbell, Scott Menzies, Deirdre Gamill-Hock, Allison Valentine, Marika Borger, Joe Wardle, Kellie Collins, William Cahill, Candee Vaglica, Kristin Scearce, Lisa McGlade, Jay Evans, Janet Wilde, Mark Junk, Rafael Montes, Sarah Atherton, Trudy Bryan, Joanne Wheatley, John May, Stacie Jaye, Kirsty Mills, Louise, Kenneth Mcintire, Adam Thayer, Jonathan Emmerson, Susan Rowden, David Greer, Becki Sinks, Carole Wilson, Richard Sorden, Becki Battersby, Derek Titus, Phil, Clare Duncan, Julie Peacock, Rebecca Strouse, Stacie Denise, Sarah Powell, Paula Bruce, G. Stella, Michael J. Mulkerin, Sandra Lewis, Hawaii Lynn, Windi LaBounta, Stephanie Hardy, Janet Carter, Lisa Kruse, Gillian Adams, Lauren, Clare Lanes, Jacqueline Scifres, Cindy Ahlgren, John Best, Stacey Arkless, Nate Stephenson*

PROLOGUE

POLICE SERGEANT ROBBIE MASON banged a fist against the door one last time and spoke into the Airwave radio fixed to his lapel. "Control, this is Phineus One. Suspect appears not present. Requesting forced entry. Over."

"All received. PSU incoming with Big Red Key. Over."

"Standing by. Over."

Mason stood on the third-floor landing of Morris House and awaited the support team. The concrete beneath his feet was pitted and stained, littered with cigarette butts. He looked left, right, checking if any neighbours had been disturbed, but the coast was clear. Most of the flats were empty or in a state of disrepair. London was a rat-infested corpse with a fancy hat, and the Tower Hamlets estate was that corpse's festering bowels.

The depressed state of the building was at odds with the weather. It was a bright afternoon, with blue skies and a beating sun. In the streets below, kids that should've been at school rode their bikes back and forth. It was a pleasant day. But Mason had a feeling it was about to spoil.

In order to avoid spooking the suspect or attracting unwanted civilian attention, Mason had volunteered to make first contact. If the suspect came to the front door, he would claim to be investigating a missing child in the area. Meanwhile, he would surreptitiously press the squelch button on his radio and summon an arrest team. The element of surprise was a police officer's best weapon.

But the ruse had failed. Either the suspect wasn't home or he was refusing to answer. Time to make good on the warrant and force entry.

Mason waited two minutes until a pair of officers from Bethnal Green appeared on the concrete landing beside him. One of them carried an 'enforcer' battering ram that was a mainstay of British emergency services up and down the country. Sixteen kilogrammes of red-painted hardened steel, it was light enough for a single person to use, but heavy enough to handle all but the toughest residential front doors. Mason took a step back and got on his radio.

"Control, this is Phineus One. Proceeding to force entry to flat thirty-three, Morris House. That is flat three-three, Morris House. Over."

"Proceed. Over."

Mason gave the two officers the nod.

The first blow from the Big Red Key dented the door and splintered the frame. The second shattered the lock and sent the door slamming against the interior wall. Mason would have managed it in one, but two blows was respectable.

The officer not holding the battering ram – PC Jaskil – immediately buried his nose in the crook of his elbow and groaned. "Jesus Christ, it stinks!"

"I'm gonna spew," said his colleague, PC Lewis, who turned around and leaned over the balcony's pebble-dashed wall.

Mason swallowed a lump in his throat and steeled himself. Foul stenches in empty flats were never a good sign. He'd lost count of the days-dead pensioners and shit-covered druggies he'd had the displeasure of discovering over the years. But this stench was worse than that.

He told the other officers to stand back and they obediently complied. Neither had the years on the job he did and with the way the force headed, they probably never would.

If you want to be unpopular and underpaid, join the force.

And forget about marriage, because there's only so many late-night shifts and deep bouts of depression a good wife can take. There's always a better-paid, better-looking accountant ready to steal them away.

Mason stepped up to the threshold of the flat's broken doorway and peered down the gloomy hallway. It was like staring into a cave, the sunlight reaching only a few feet inside. Who knew what terrors lay within?

It was time to find out.

Mason got on his radio again and updated the chief inspector, who was leading the operation from a nearby greasy spoon called Oscar's Place. Three dozen police officers lurked in Tower Hamlets, covering every escape route while also trying not to draw attention to themselves. The estate could be antagonistic towards authority, so drawing a crowd was an obstacle they didn't need. Things had to happen fast or people could get hurt. The suspect was highly dangerous.

And probably highly insane, Mason thought to himself, suddenly wishing he hadn't volunteered. *Okay. I'm going to have to go inside and find out what's causing that smell.*

Mason gave the two other officers a nod and they returned the gesture. Jaskil placed the Big Red Key on the ground and flanked the doorway opposite Lewis.

Mason took a step forward and entered the flat.

It was like walking through a dense fog. The cloying odour was so thick, so visceral, that it seemed to attach itself to the bare skin of his forearms. His eyes stung, and a swelling took root in his throat as his gorge rose. Only the fourteen years in uniform kept him from spewing that morning's McDonald's hash browns all over his boots.

This ain't gonna be good.

The hallway was bare, any wallpaper or paint having long since peeled away. Dark stains covered the crumbling plasterwork in places, but it was too gloomy to tell what they were: blood, faeces, or just plain old filth. Mason unfastened his baton and slid it free from his belt. With it, he inspected a pile of rubbish on the mouldering carpet: food cartons and plastic drink bottles. Fast food.

They'd tracked the suspect to this address, but it was clearly abandoned. With luck, they might still find something of use for their investigation. The victim's families were depending on it.

Checking his fellow officers were still at his back, Mason proceeded along the hallway.

A small kitchen filled a space to the right, its door frame missing a door. He ducked inside and immediately winced at the odour. Grease and grime caked an old cooker unit in the corner, and more food containers littered the floor. Cupboard doors hung askew on their hinges, hiding God knows what inside. The stench was eye-watering, like rotten meat.

There was a sense of movement in the room, and a shiver ran up Mason's spine as he imagined maggots and beetles wriggling, unseen, in the shadows. How could such a hive go unnoticed and uncondemned?

Stepping back into the hallway, Mason rejoined Jaskil and Lewis as they entered a stuffy lounge. A sliver of sunlight spilled in through a slender gap in the curtains, but most of the room was cloaked in shadow. A single two-seater sofa – badly stained – sat beneath the room's window. The wooden coffee table in front of it had a leg missing. Perched on a wooden cabinet against the wall was a television old enough to have shown Charles marrying Diana.

Not quite the festering pit the kitchen was, but still unfit for human habitation.

"What is causing that reek?" asked Lewis, almost to himself.

Mason shook his head. "I don't know, but we haven't found it yet." He pointed a finger at a door on the other side of the room. "The bedrooms must be through there. Jaskil? Get ready to jump on the radio if anything transpires."

Jaskil nodded anxiously, suddenly more like an unsure teenager than the thirty-year-old family man he was. Mason was sure his colleague had just welcomed his third child.

Mason trod on detritus of varying textures as he made his way across the room. There was a light switch on the wall, but when he thumbed it, nothing happened. The reason being that there was no lightbulb attached to the ceiling rose. Lewis produced a torch and lit the way for them.

The other door led into another hallway, with three more doors leading off from that. Two bedrooms and a bathroom, most likely, but there was no way of knowing without checking.

What's behind door number one? Certainly not a star prize.

Mason barked a warning. "This is the police. If anyone is inside this property, surrender yourself immediately or you may be subject to forceful action."

The three officers tensed, eyeing each of the closed doors as if a rabid gorilla might suddenly leap out and maul them. But once several seconds had passed without incident, their shoulders lowered and they let out a collective sigh. Mason gave them another nod to communicate he was still taking the lead. The perks of seniority.

The stench grew worse, the atmosphere more oppressive. Jaskil and Lewis looked ready to pass out or throw up – or both. Mason didn't blame them. The creeping dread that had been in the pit of his stomach since they'd first bashed open the front door was now in full bloom – a rancid tulip pollinated from nightmares. Death and suffering dwelt in this dingy London flat six miles from Buckingham Palace. Misery. Rot. Decay. The question was: to whom did the stench belong? A victim? Or the man they had come to arrest?

Mason nodded to the first door in the hallway, then reached out with his left hand to take the door handle. He held his baton fully extended in his right.

He opened the door.

And found the source of the odour.

All three officers gagged. The stench was beyond description – like urine-soaked meat – and no amount of job experience could keep Mason from coughing up bile that burnt at his throat and sought a way out of his mouth.

"G-God help us," he muttered as Lewis swept his torch back and forth across the bedroom. The curtains were closed, so the three hanging corpses came in and out of view sporadically, like ghost train cadavers, their rictus grins gleaming in the torchlight as it passed over them.

Mason felt afloat, unable to feel the ground beneath his feet. He put away his baton and replaced it with his torch, needing to be in charge of what he saw. His hand shook terribly, but he kept the light more or less steady as he examined each victim in turn. The killer had sliced out their eyeballs and cut off their lips. Shrivelled breasts revealed their gender to be female – the suspect's favoured prey – but they were barely human. One corpse had limbs missing below the knees. The next had only a single arm. The third was little more than a head and torso. A pile of human debris festered in the corner, fusing with the threadbare carpet. Engorged flies buzzed lethargically around the room.

"This is it!" said Jaskil, his voice thick with saliva. "Th-This is Boxcutter's lair. We've found him. Fuck. I can't... I can't breathe..."

"This isn't a lair," muttered Mason, unable to look away from the horrific tapestry of human suffering. "It's a goddamn abattoir. We need to vacate immediately."

Time to send in the forensics, the coroner, and whoever else had the stomach to deal with this shit. *Because it ain't me,* thought Mason.

No one argued. In fact, Lewis and Jaskil were already back in the hallway.

A bump sounded. It came from one of the other rooms.

Mason pulled out his baton with his free hand and cast his torch forward. Tears stained his cheeks, summoned by the hellish stench and the utter misery hanging inside the room behind him. This was an evil place.

"What the h-hell was that?" asked Jaskil like a child about to scream. "Are we leaving or what?"

The bump sounded again, this time accompanied by a muffled whimper.

"Shit," said Mason, his whole body quaking. "C-Call in the response team. We've got a live one."

Jaskil reached a shaking hand towards his lapel radio. "Jesus Christ, I think I'm going to…"

Mason strode forward, his colleague's voice turning to jumbled static in his mind as fear and urgency – and a deep, sinking dread – flooded his brain.

The muffled whimper came again. It led him towards the room next to the one with the hanging bodies. He flung open the door, desperate to end this nightmare – not just for himself, but for whomever was still suffering inside this wretched place. "This is the police!" he yelled. "Is somebody in need of…"

His words trailed off. He stumbled sideways against the door frame, legs deserting him. A squall blew through his mind, a screeching voice yelling at him to get out of there. But he was stuck, standing in a pan full of increasingly hot water, skin blistering inch by inch. The longer he stayed inside this flat…

Unlike the other rooms, this one was lit by a floor lamp placed in the corner. It threw a yellow spotlight over a young woman strapped to a wooden chair. Someone had sliced into her eyeballs and blinded her. Both of her lips were missing, exposing her front teeth. She thrashed in the chair, clearly aware of Mason's presence but unable to speak. The remnants of a tongue waggled in her mouth, leaking puss and infection. Two fingerless hands flapped against the chair's armrests.

The latest masterpiece of the Boxcutter Killer.

But it's unfinished, thought Mason. *She's still alive. He never leaves them alive.*

"I-It's okay," he spluttered. "My name is Officer Robbie Mason and I'm—"

A loud crash sounded behind him as one of the hallway doors flung open and hit the wall. Mason heard Lewis scream and then Jaskil gargle.

He's here. We're in his home.

Mason leapt out of the room, baton and torch both raised. He saw Lewis racing down the hallway in terror. Running for his life.

Jaskil was slumped on the ground, clutching his abdomen and dragging himself along the carpet like a slug. His radio squawked irritably on his lapel, as if he'd been about to make a broadcast.

Did he call for backup? Mason asked himself, trying to make sense of what he was seeing – still standing in that hot water about to reach boiling point. *Is help coming?*

A hulking beast of a man stood over Jaskil, so wide that he filled the entire hallway. But he was also stooped over as if unable to support his own weight. The witness description had been right. The Boxcutter was a freak.

As the killer shuffled along the hallway, he sported a wide, sideways limp, but it didn't slow him down. He grabbed Jaskil by his collar and yanked the screaming man to his feet. The officer bled from his guts, his white shirt dyed red, but he was fully conscious as he gawped at his tormentor. He tried to get away, a rabbit caught in a snare, but it was useless. His flailing foot struck his torch where he had dropped it and sent it spinning on the carpet. Shadows danced on the walls.

"P-Please…" Jaskil begged. "I have—"

Something in the killer's massive right hand captured the light as he jabbed it at Jaskil's face. The officer wailed as his left eye made an audible pop and trickled down his cheek.

Mason's torch rattled as his hand shook more and more. "P-P-Put him down now! Get back!"

The killer obeyed his command, tossing a gibbering Jaskil against the wall and turning to face Mason. His face was a horror.

A patch of puckered scar tissue covered the maniac's left eye, while his nose was a bulbous swelling in the centre of an uneven face. Only his mouth was normal: two plump lips pressed together in a baleful grimace. But his grotesque face was nowhere near as ugly as his crimes.

The Boxcutter. Twenty years of killing and I'm the one to find him. No. I'm about to be his latest victim.

Mason whipped his baton and struck the beast on top of his head. The impact sent a shockwave up Mason's arm that numbed him from fist to shoulder, but the damage to the killer was non-existent. The Boxcutter glared at Mason, a devil made flesh, and struck him across the face. A streak of white-hot lightning seared Mason's cheek and sent him stumbling backwards. He tried to keep a hold of his torch but it slipped from his grasp.

Things grew darker.

My eye. Mason's vision had folded in on itself like a sheet of paper, only half the size it had been. *He cut my eye.*

Mason screamed, his senses disappearing into a dizzying whirlpool of dread. All the fight left his body and he collapsed onto the dirty carpet, rolling himself into a ball like a feeble toddler. "D-Don't hurt me."

The Boxcutter stood over Mason, one evil eye focused upon him. It was enough to make him release his bladder, but embarrassment was the furthest thing from his mind.

I'm going to die. Victim number...

I don't even remember how many this monster has killed.

Mason closed his eye to shut out the horror. He tried to imagine himself away from there; tried to convince himself he wasn't lying on a dirty carpet inside a devil's lair. It didn't work.

"On your knees now!" someone shouted from the other end of the hallway. "Comply immediately or I'll shoot."

"Get down," a second voice shouted.

Mason clutched himself tighter. *Thank God. Just shoot the bastard. Do it now!*

Please...

There was a split second of silence, followed by an animalistic roar and gunfire.

Mason's traumatised mind could take no more. He passed out on the bloodstained carpet, piss still leaking out of him.

CHAPTER ONE

"AND SO WE may never solve the mystery of Rose Glendale and the brutal murder of her children. Was she a witch, as some claim, or merely another victim of a cruel, adulterous husband? And finally, are we truly to believe that her vengeful spirit haunts these woods behind me? The anxious youths of Redsow housing estate certainly seem to think so." Simon turned to his guest so that his girlfriend, Chrissy, would know to turn the attention of the camera. He always liked to end his videos with a closing comment from somebody else – someone involved in whatever grizzly topic he was covering that day. "Ricky Dalca, before we go, do you have anything else you would like to add about the mysterious disappearance of Lily Barnes?"

The youth was apparently coming up on his seventeenth birthday, but he already looked to be in his twenties. With a subtle hint of an East European accent, a shaved head, and a thick scar across his eyebrow, he looked like a thug, but the interview he'd given about Devil's Wood had been thoughtful and insightful. Even now, the lad seemed to consider his words before speaking them.

"Well…" Ricky scratched at the wispy hairs on his chin. "I suppose there's not much else to say, other than Lily was my best friend and I miss her, you know? I just want to know what happened to her so that her family can have some peace."

Sim nodded to his guest and thanked him before looking at the camera again. "As stated, no sign of Lily Barnes has been found, and Rose Glendale's farmhouse, once nestled within these woods, has since been demolished, leaving behind no clue as to what truly happened here last summer. Perhaps we'll never know, and that might be the most unsettling thing of all. This is your boy, Sim, signing off on another grim tale. Hope you liked it, and, as always, like and subscribe if you want to help me understand evil."

"That's a wrap," said Chrissy with a bright, red-lipped smile as she switched off her tiny G7X Mark 2 camera. It was lightweight and easy to pull out on a whim, so she favoured it over something larger and more temperamental. "I love it when we film on location," she said, tucking her blonde hair behind her ears as a breeze disturbed the air. The sky looked like it was preparing to rain.

Their guest, Ricky, chuckled. "You make it sound like you're in Hollywood. This is just for YouTube, right?"

Chrissy tilted her head and frowned. "And a few other places online. But don't get confused, there's money to be made from uploading content. It pays the bills and then some."

Sim nodded. "We take what we do seriously. This isn't just a hobby."

"Which is why we have one of the most successful true crime channels on the internet," said Chrissy, with the merest hint of bragging.

Ricky nodded appreciatively. "For real? Fair play then, innit? Whatever gets you a life worth living. Most of us never make it out of shitholes like this."

Sim looked around, taking in the nearby playground and the leafy trees and bushes that lined both sides of the path. "I dunno. Seems like a nice enough place."

"Looks can be deceiving, mate. Redsow has a dark side, trust me. And I don't just mean what's inside Devil's Wood."

Sim turned to stare at the wall of foliage behind him. The thorny bushes, trees, and stinging nettles were like nature's KEEP OUT sign. He pictured the sunshine disappearing a few feet inside, blotted out by the thick canopy of leaves and branches. Was a bloodstained Rose Glendale somewhere here, stalking the gloom, searching for virgin prey?

"The police searched every inch of this place, right?" asked Sim.

Ricky shrugged. "So they say, but the woods are so thick they could've stepped right over her body without seeing. Like you said, we might never find her."

Sim turned back around and smiled sympathetically. Lily Barnes was dead. No one turned up alive after nine months of being missing. "You really have no idea what happened to her?"

Ricky folded his arms and looked down at his scuffed trainers. Bird droppings and crushed acorns dirtied the pavement. "No idea. Lily just up and disappeared one day. Shit thing is, I lost another mate a few weeks back. Kid named Jude. He's gone missing too. Maybe I'm next. This place is cursed or summin'."

"Really?" Sim folded his arms, feeling a chill. "I didn't hear about another disappearance. Do you think it's related to Lily Barnes?"

"Maybe. Jude was a good kid, but too trusting for his own good, if you know what I mean? Anything could've happened to him."

"Can we do anything to help? Maybe we can ask our viewers if they know anything. Whatever you need, man. We're here."

"Yeah," said Chrissy.

Ricky grunted. "Nah. Better you just forget this place if you ask me. I don't even know how you do it, making videos about dark shit like this. Don't it mess with your head?"

Sim shrugged. *Yes, very much so.* "Someone has to report on these things."

"Why?"

"Well… because people want answers. They want to know why people do the things they do. Especially bad things. There has to be a reason."

Ricky seemed to consider this, but he then pulled a face. "Maybe there ain't a reason. Maybe bad stuff just happens."

Sim let out a sigh. He didn't want to believe that, but he had no argument for it either. He knew better than anyone that bad stuff just happened. "Who knows?" he said with an air of finality. "Maybe you're right."

"I usually am." Ricky clucked his tongue and turned away. "Anyway, I got shit to do, innit? This was all right though. Cheers for asking me."

"Yeah, no problem." Sim smiled, unsure whether the lad was being sarcastic. "Thanks again for being on camera. I'll email you when everything's live. And if we can do anything to help find your friend, let us know. Jude, right?"

"Look after yourselves, yeah?" Ricky was already walking away, but he turned back and winked at Chrissy. "And if you two ever break up, call me."

"Will do," said Chrissy with a dismissive wave. She was barely listening, turning away and checking her camera.

Sim watched Ricky Dalca shuffle off to join his friends, a set of twins dossing at the nearby playground. A massive half-empty bottle of cider sat between them. It was three in the afternoon.

The youth of Britain. Building the alcoholics of tomorrow.

Some things never change.

Sim went and touched Chrissy on the arm to get her attention. She was smiling and nodding at the footage on the camera, evidently pleased by what she saw. Sometimes, he wondered if she liked his on-screen persona more than the real him.

"Cheeky sod," said Sim, nodding after Ricky Dalca. "Hope you're not tempted."

Chrissy rolled her eyes and chuckled. "Think I'll settle for what I have. Hey, you want to take any more footage before we go?"

"No. I'm not even sure I like what we have. Witches. Curses. Magic. It feels a little beneath us. I don't know what our audience will think."

Chrissy reached out and squeezed his hand. Her long nails bit into his palm, but it was a good pain – like scratching an itch. "I think it's good to mix things up from time to time. True crime is great, but a little imagination lightens things up. Anyway, how d'you know Lily Barnes wasn't taken by a witch? Nobody's found her."

Sim shrugged. "Evil is human, not supernatural. Whatever happened to Lily Barnes, I'm sure there's a sicko involved somewhere down the line." He nodded after Ricky Dalca, who was leaving the park with his mates. "Maybe he did it."

Chrissy tutted. "That's so unfair, Sim. You have zero evidence that he had anything at all to do with it. He seemed genuinely upset about her going missing."

"We've done enough of these videos to have pretty good instincts by now, Chris. That kid knows more than he's letting on. I reckon he did it. Or at least knows who did."

"You're so judgemental, babe. Do you ever give people the benefit of the doubt?"

He wasn't able to answer that, so he shrugged.

She gave him a shrug of her own. "Perhaps you're right, but we're not the police. We can only report what we know. Anyway, let's get going. I want to celebrate tonight."

Sim flinched as something touched his shoulder, but it was only a leaf falling from one of the trees behind him. He brushed it off and frowned at Chrissy. "Celebrate? It's just another episode. We've done a hundred."

She looked at him for a moment, as if waiting for him to

realise his mistake, but he didn't think he'd made one. Their anniversary was last month and her twenty-fourth birthday was in December. What else could he be forgetting?

A lot. I spend most of my day trying to forget things.

Eventually, Chrissy grunted and shook her head at him. "We passed the two million subscriber mark today. That's huge! In fact, it's unbelievable. I want to celebrate how far we've come in the last three years. This channel… it's like our baby."

Sim fidgeted and turned his focus on the trees rustling behind him. A sudden urge to run started him walking. "Yeah, okay. We'll grab dinner, then."

Chrissy hopped to catch up with him and, as they walked together, she gave him a gentle shoulder barge. "It's okay to be proud of yourself sometimes, you know? You've made a success of yourself."

"As a YouTuber. Not exactly curing cancer, is it? And we're still way behind our competition."

"God! You're hard work sometimes, do you know that? Screw the competition. We're not doing it for them." She sighed and shook her head. "Well, *I'm* proud of you, okay?"

They walked a few seconds in silence until Sim forced out the word: "Thanks."

Truthfully, he was just the face on camera. He had a raspy voice that held people's attention, and a serious expression that suited the subject matter. But other than that…

Chrissy, meanwhile, was a year from qualifying as a forensic criminologist, and it was her research and study that had helped launch the channel in the first place. Not to mention all the work she'd put in behind the camera tickling Google's fickle algorithms. As much as people associated *Grim Tales* with Simon 'Sim' Barka, he felt like he had gained success on his girlfriend's shoulders.

"You're thinking," said Chrissy, staring at him as they walked back towards the car. "I don't like it when you're thinking. If you just stopped for a while, you'd be happier."

Sim chuckled. "Okay, I'll try to stop. I'm, um, sorry for not being more excited. You're right, we've done something to be proud of. I love running the channel with you."

She put her arm around him and rose up to place her head against his shoulder as they continued to walk. "You know, if it ever gets too much, we can take a holiday, right? I see this stuff gets to you. It would affect anybody. Sutcliffe, Bundy, Dahmer. We surround ourselves with psychopaths every day. So why don't we bulk film a load of content and set it to drip feed while we go away for a while? Don't you have a cousin in Kenya? We could go on safari!"

"He lives in Chad, and I've never met him."

"Well, we can still go on safari, can't we? Or backpacking? Anything to get us out of the flat and open up our world a little more."

"I don't even have a passport. I've never been abroad."

"But that doesn't mean you can't. Eyes open wide, right?"

Sim nodded. It was their mantra for trying new things and not being afraid. "Eyes open wide."

A break sounded good in all honesty, as things *had* been getting a little dark lately, but they might end up squandering the momentum the channel had gained during the last eighteen months. Success on the internet was built atop cyber quicksand. The moment you stopped kicking, you sank. "Maybe we can get away for a bit after New Year," he said, "but I want to get your student loans paid off before we do anything rash."

"Taking a holiday isn't rash, Sim. I just want to spend some quality time together without a camera involved. Sometimes, it feels…"

He stopped walking and turned to look at her. "What?"

She brushed her blonde hair behind her ears again and turned her green eyes downwards. "It's just that, in front of the camera, you come across as so compassionate and understanding."

"Am I not those things?"

"What? Yes, of course you are. It's why I love you, Sim. You just seem to find it easier to show what you're feeling when you're talking to an invisible audience. Lately, whenever I switch off the camera, it's like you deflate. I'm worried about you. It's coming up on the anniversary of—"

He started walking again, this time faster. "Don't be worried, okay? It's an act. On camera, I'm someone else. If you don't like the real me then—"

"Don't make threats, Sim. I get that what I'm saying sounds bad, but I don't mean for it to. I just wish you'd open up a bit more. Trust me, okay? I won't let you drown." She put a fingertip against his temple and delicately drew a circle. "Whatever you've got going on up there, I can take it. We're a team and I love you."

"Look, can we just get in the car and drive back to the flat?" He suddenly felt a pressure on his chest. Perhaps it was claustrophobia from walking down the heavily wooded path. Nine out of every ten steps had been in shadow. "It's a long drive home to Reading and I want to take a shower if we're going out later."

"Okay… sure." Chrissy cleared her throat and looked away. Suddenly, she didn't seem so excited any more.

Sim knew that it was his fault.

They reached the car where they'd parked it, alongside a kerb in a cul-de-sac of modest houses with single garages. Again, Redsow appeared to be a pleasant enough place, but Sim had believed Ricky Dalca when the lad had warned about a dark side. Three years of running a true crime channel taught you that every place had one. So did most people.

He looked at Chrissy, her blonde hair now floating beside her face in the breeze again. *But not all. Some people are as beautiful inside as they are out.*

I want to step into the light with you, Chrissy. I wish I could just let go.

But I'm not sure I can. I'm afraid of what might happen.

The dark blue Audi Q3 was in Chrissy's name, but it was the channel that paid the lease. For the first time in Sim's life he had money, and it scared him. Most of the time, he was reticent to spend it, certain it would all suddenly disappear, or that it wasn't even real to begin with. Chrissy had the opposite problem. Her philosophy was that money couldn't do you any good once you were too old to spend it, so enjoy it while you were young. Sim saw the sense in that, but it felt instinctually wrong.

But he had found happiness by trusting in Chrissy and ignoring his own self-defeating instincts. His life had changed since the day he'd met her at a local horror movie convention and dared to buy her a coffee. In the whirlwind weeks that had followed, she had dragged him out of his solitude and shown him parts of life he'd ignored: like foreign food, swimming in the sea, and going to see a show – things that were hard to enjoy alone and in misery. Suddenly, the world had become a little brighter, and a whole lot bigger.

It had even been Chrissy's idea to start a YouTube channel. When most people their age had been down the pub at the weekends, Sim and Chrissy had been trekking the north of England to retread the steps of the Yorkshire Ripper, or profiling the victims of Dennis Nilsen. It was a macabre life, but one to which Sim was inexplicably drawn. However much Sim might hate it, he navigated better in the dark.

It's where I belong. Where people can't see me.

But two million subscribers... all looking in my direction...

Why am I doing this?

Answers.

Sim got behind the wheel and put on his seatbelt. Chrissy did the same, then reached over and fondled his thigh as he started the engine. The warmth from her hand spread into his muscles and relaxed him. Despite it only being afternoon, he wanted to tip his head back and take a nap. He often felt that way after a shoot. His *Grim Tales* persona left the real him drained.

"Sorry," said Chrissy, next to him. "I didn't mean to get at you."

"You didn't." *In fact, I should be the one who's sorry.* "I'm just being grouchy." He pulled down the visor and looked at himself in the small mirror. His brown eyes were bloodshot around the edges and his cornrows needed redoing. He looked tired. Maybe a holiday really was in order. "So, um, where do you fancy eating later?"

"How about Mexican?"

"Yeah." He licked his lips. "I could go for a big fat burrito." He shifted into drive and started to pull away. "And a big bowl of nachos covered in— Shit!"

He slammed his foot down on the brake and gripped the steering wheel tightly. The Audi had barely been moving, but the inertia was enough to rock both of them forward against their seatbelts. By accident, Sim pressed on the horn, making his heart beat faster.

"Where the hell did *he* come from?" said Chrissy, growling. She was rubbing her chest where the seatbelt had caught.

Parked inches in front of their bonnet was another vehicle: a black SUV of a kind Sim didn't recognise. In fact, it was so large that it could only have been an American import. Two men occupied the front seats, glaring straight ahead.

"Reverse and go around them," said Chrissy, shaking her head in annoyance. "Probably a bunch of drug dealers."

"Yeah, probably." Sim put the car in reverse and crept backwards along the kerb before turning the wheel and manoeuvring forward.

A second SUV appeared and blocked the centre of the narrow road. It also had two men sitting up front, glaring ahead.

"What are they doing?" Chrissy now sounded scared. She clutched her hands tightly in her lap. "What do they want?"

Sim shook his head. "I don't know. Just… stay in your seat." He pressed the central locking button on his armrest and the doors clicked. If the strangers outside wanted to do them harm, they would have to bust their way inside before Sim could call the police. While he didn't want to test the theory, he was confident the windscreen was tough enough to buy him enough time to dial 999 on his mobile. *And for plenty of people to hear the commotion.*

"They're getting out," said Chrissy. She pressed herself backwards, as if trying to dissolve into her seat. "Why are they getting out?"

"I don't know!"

Four suited gentlemen appeared in the road while the drivers of each vehicle remained behind the wheel, making six men in total. One man differed from the others, though. He wasn't wearing a tie and his suit jacket was unbuttoned. His slicked-back yellow hair and rosy cheeks gave him the appearance of a ventriloquist's dummy.

The other men looked like bodyguards or hired thugs. Their impassive, joyless expressions gave them away.

The blond man flashed a smile and raised a hand to wave at Sim. There was a confidence about him, but not necessarily anything dangerous.

"I recognise that guy," said Chrissy, leaning forward. "Why do I recognise him?"

Sim raised an eyebrow at her. "Will you stop asking me questions I can't answer? I have no clue what is going on or who he is."

"All right, jeez!"

"Sorry."

The blond man stepped around the side of the Audi. Two of his bodyguards followed, as if attached to his elbows. Whoever the man was, he was either rich, important, or both. And he was now tapping on the driver-side window.

What is going on?

Sim swallowed a lump in his throat and half turned to Chrissy. "Should I open the window?"

Chrissy's eyes were wide, and when she opened her mouth, no words came out.

Sim took a breath and pressed the button to unwind the window. "C-Can we help you?"

The blond man smiled. "Yes, Mr Barka, I believe you can. Allow me to introduce myself."

Sim had almost been too nervous to drive when the blond man had bid him to follow along behind the two black SUVs. He was astonished he'd even agreed to it. Perhaps it was the shock of learning who the man was, or the insistent glare of his bodyguards. It hadn't felt like there'd been a choice.

That he and Chrissy were now sitting, ninety minutes later, inside the private lounge of a five-star hotel in Oxford, did little to calm his nerves. Sim had never heard of the *Chateau Clyde*, but it was so large and imposing that he couldn't fathom how it wasn't world famous. For the first time in his life, a valet had taken his car. He'd been reluctant to hand over the keys.

This is insane. It has to be a prank.

Chrissy sat back in an ornate, brass-legged chair and shook her head. "I can't believe I'm sitting in a room with Evers Nealy. Is this real?"

Evers Nealy had taken off his suit jacket and rolled up the sleeves of his pale blue shirt, but he continued to wear that authentic, disarming smile. "There's no need for fuss," he said with a charming Irish lilt. "I'm probably little like you no doubt think of me."

Sim took in a breath. *What? An obscenely rich member of the elite, building a tech empire on the backs of cheap foreign labour and stolen ideas?* "I, um… I'm a big fan of what you're doing with hydrogen jet fuel." He felt he should be polite. "It's the future, right?"

Nealy's smile grew wider. "The very near future, my boy. By twenty-forty, accessible, economical, supersonic air travel will dominate our skies. It'll be the end of borders as we know it. We'll finally be one world."

Sim nodded. Getting from Heathrow to California in only a few hours sounded amazing, but he was sure profit margins and politics would somehow get in the way and spoil it for the ordinary guy. Men like Evers Nealy thought of themselves as benevolent demigods, but their power came from their fortunes – and no man ever made a fortune without keeping it from someone else.

"That's so cool," said Chrissy, beaming. "I bet life will be so different in thirty year's time. Things move so fast."

Nealy grinned wider. "Don't they just? What we've achieved as a species in the last—"

Sim sat forward. "What do you want with us?" He eyed the bodyguards standing around the opulently appointed room and wondered if any of them possessed guns beneath their blazers. "Why did you ask us to follow you here? How did you even know how to find us?"

"Your phones. They run on the network I own."

Sim glared. "And you used it to track us? Is that even legal?"

"Read your small print." Nealy chuckled. "As to why you're here, I'd like to ask for your help."

"Our help?" Sim shook his head. "What could we possibly help *you* with?"

Evers Nealy crossed his slender legs and relaxed back in his chair. He reached out a hand and a waitress appeared as if out of thin air to place a tumbler of brown liquid in his hand. He took a sip and smiled again. "I would like your endorsement for a project I'm about to go public with. I would love to tell you everything, but I suppose it's what you might call top secret."

"Exciting," said Chrissy, with no hint of mockery. Her cheeks were glowing with enthusiasm. "Can you give us a clue?"

"All I can say is that it's something you've never even dreamed of, and it'll blow your minds."

Sim's anxiety was fading away, replaced by a concerned defensiveness. Nobody knew he was here, in this place, with these people. Nealy was a powerful man who probably thought of everyone else as lesser mortals – disposable, at the very least – and Sim was in no mood to be used or manipulated. Or worse. Secrets also didn't interest him. Only answers. "Why us? We're nobodies. How do you even know who we are?"

Nealy finally stopped smiling and instead frowned. "You do yourself a disservice. Your YouTube channel is one of my favourites."

Chrissy gasped. "You watch *Grim Tales*?"

"Habitually. I travel so often that YouTube is one of the few ways for me to enjoy ten minutes of downtime here and there. On planes, between meetings, I'm sure you get the picture. If there's one thing I hate about success, it's that it leaves little time to read and watch the things I enjoy. At heart, I'm quite the couch potato, but my business keeps me too busy to indulge my lazier side. Nonetheless, true crime is a favourite of mine." He shrugged, appearing embarrassed by the admission. "I have an interest in people, I suppose you might say. The best and the worst of us." He looked at Sim, almost admiringly. "You really have a talent for ascribing meaning to the vile actions of broken people, son. You have an insight the rest of us lack. I envy you, truly. If I have any weakness at all, it's that I struggle to understand people. I see problems and solutions, but you… you see the needs of the soul. You recognise the pain and the fear that drives us."

Sim shifted in his chair, unable to sit comfortably.

"He doesn't like praise," said Chrissy. "Even when he

deserves it. I tell him all the time how great he is on camera. Our audience really connects with him."

Nealy put his hand out and passed the empty glass to the magical waitress, who took it obediently. He then interlaced his fingers across his knee and sat forward to look at Chrissy. "Ah, but I believe you're the brains behind the operation, correct? The beautiful criminologist behind the scenes?"

Chrissy turned so red it was almost farcical. The only thing a brighter shade of crimson was the velvet floor-to-ceiling curtains around the room. "I'm not fully qualified yet," she said modestly, "but I do most of our research. I'm like you. People fascinate me, but I don't always understand them. Do you ever wonder what would have happened if Ed Gein had been raised by a normal, loving family, or if Jeffrey Dahmer had got therapy before he killed Steven Hicks? How much of evil is built and how much of it is born?"

"The age-old question, my dear. Some scholars have even put forward the notion that psychopathy is evolution. A shedding of hindering emotions like empathy and guilt. Who knows for sure, but it's incredibly interesting to think about. It's those kinds of questions that enamoured me to your channel in the first place. There are many other channels, of course, some bigger than yours, but few are as authentic or earnest. That's why I chose you."

"Chose us for what?" asked Sim, still feeling under threat. Still feeling like he was somehow being manipulated and made vulnerable. He had no place being in this room with this man. This was not his world. His hands did not feel right wrapped around the brass armrests of antique chairs.

Nealy waggled a finger. "I really can't tell you any details yet. Not until all the paperwork has been signed and we have you squared away."

"Then we're not interested." Sim went to get up. "Can we leave?"

Chrissy shot him a glare and grabbed his wrist. "Sim!"

"Chrissy, this is dodgy. I don't like secrets and I don't like dramatic back-room meetings in posh hotels. Most of all, I don't like—"

"Rich bastards like me," Nealy finished for him, although Sim wasn't sure those were the exact words that had been about to leave his mouth. "I admit I'm a capitalist, through and through, and that hasn't always led me down the most virtuous of paths. But I'm about to turn fifty, and as a man ages he starts to consider his legacy. Money is a great tool, but it's not what I want to be remembered for. People remember Caesar; they don't remember Crassus."

Sim grunted. "Caesar was a warmonger who considered himself above his own nation, and the fact you're mentioning Crassus shows that *he is* remembered."

Nealy raised an eyebrow. "Only by those who know their classical history, Mr Barka. Colour me further impressed."

"Unlike you, I still manage to read. My point still stands. Caesar or Crassus, both men served only themselves."

"I suppose they did, didn't they? Look, believe me or don't, but I would honestly like to do as much good as I can before my soul departs for the stars. That's the truth."

"Why should we trust you?" Sim's confidence was returning. Speaking his mind to one of the world's most powerful men felt pretty good. No one appeared behind him with a garrotte or threatened his family. No lawyer appeared and promised to sue him. Evers Nealy was just a man. "Like you said, you haven't exactly lived a life of kindness. How many companies have you bought and dismantled? How much pollution have your factories caused? How many yachts do you own while people starve all around the world?"

Nealy seemed aggrieved. "Son, I own a single yacht. Just the one. Yes, it might be a hundred and twenty metres long, but that's beside the point. All the other billionaires laugh at me." He broke out in a smile and put his elbows on his knees, his gold-ringed fingers laced together in front of him. "That was a joke. Look, I know you don't want to take me at my word – and I suppose I can understand that – but I'm not the man you think I am. Other than being very rich, of course. That is very much true."

"What exactly do you want from us, Mr Nealy?" asked Chrissy.

"Just a weekend of your time. Give me that and I'll sponsor your channel for an entire year."

"We don't want your sponsorship," said Sim. He was still ready to get up and leave, and wondered why hadn't he done so already. *Why am I entertaining this nonsense?* "We're not interested."

"Yes, we are!" said Chrissy.

Sim looked at her, surprised they were on such different pages. She was ready to throw herself into whatever this was without caution.

Nealy sighed and flopped back in his chair, as if he had suddenly lost the will to live. His eyes remained on Sim. A smirk grew upon his lips. "Okay, fine, I'll give you fifty grand for one weekend. One weekend, and after you've signed an NDA, you'll see what I'm offering. Refuse and you'll never hear from me again. One of the less-deserving crime vloggers will no doubt help me instead, but that would be a tragedy, I assure you."

Sim shook his head. He glanced at Chrissy and then glanced away. "I... don't know."

"For heaven's sake, son. I'm no supervillain or member of the illuminati. My life is mundane, trust me. But what I'm offering to show you is anything but. I promise that what I am absolutely dying to show you is right up your alley, and you do not want to miss it."

Sim chewed at his bottom lip and sat back in his chair. His mind had hit a roadblock, and he didn't know what to do or say. The words would not come and there was no clear path to take. "No. I'm sorry. I think we're going to have to leave it."

Nealy let out an exasperated sigh. "Son, I've negotiated with kings and heads of state less stubborn than you. How much will it take then?"

"Money doesn't interest me."

Nealy huffed. "Then you're a better man than me. If money really doesn't interest you, then how about answers? That's what you always say you're looking for in your videos, right? You want to understand evil. Well, what if I promised I could help you with that?"

"Then I would ask you to be more specific."

"Ah, that's the one thing I can't be right now, son. What if I beg? Would that seal the deal?"

"You don't have to beg," said Chrissy. "We agree. We want to take you up on your offer. Sixty grand, right?"

"No, I thought I said…" Nealy raised an eyebrow and grinned. "Ah, I see you're a smart one. Okay, you have a deal. Sixty grand for one weekend. Hell, make it seventy because I'm such a fan of your work. And Sim, you won't regret this. I give you my word, and if nothing else, I'm good for that."

Sim glared at Chrissy, but she wilted him with a scowl. He had to remind himself that life had been better since he'd met her four years ago, and that her instincts were very often far better than his. Following her lead had not let him down yet, so why was he so reluctant to take a leap now into what could be a life-changing opportunity? Evers Nealy was offering them seventy grand and the chance to see something… *cool?* What was there to think about? It would be unfair on Chrissy to say no, and that he could not bear.

"Okay," said Sim. "One weekend."

"And eighty grand," said Chrissy, beaming. Then she gave Nealy a wink and said, "Just kidding."

Nealy cackled. He reached out an arm and another tumbler of liquor appeared in his hand. "Excellent!" he said, taking a sip. "You'd best get home and fetch a change of clothes, then. We leave first thing in the morning."

CHAPTER TWO

"*PICKTON-49* EN ROUTE TO BERTH TWO," said Palmer, watching over the CCTV monitor bank with his arms folded. The weather outside was dreary, the unsettled sea casting an icy spray that merged with the drizzling rain, but the bright orange ferryboat came into port and lined up alongside the temporary jetty without issue. "Okay, Gibbons, call down to the docks and have transport arranged. Eagle has landed."

There was no reply. Currently, the operational security team was low on numbers, as well as pulling double duty as porters and handymen where needed, but in a few months' time, Palmer's team would triple in size. For now, he was forced to rely on a handful of hastily hired men and women. One of those men was presently asleep at his desk.

Palmer marched across the freshly painted control room and kicked the back of Gibbons's high-backed chair with his heavy work boot. The twenty-five-year-old former corporal, fresh out of the Royal Signals, jolted awake and yelled out. His ankle slipped off the desk and took a gaudy Che Guevara mug with it. It clunked on the tiled floor and lost a triangle of red ceramic flesh. "The hell? Ah, bugger it, that were me favourite mug to drink outta." He leaned down and grabbed it, examining the damage to the Argentinian troublemaker's face. "My sodding luck."

Palmer cared little for the man's loss. "Wake up, Gibbons, or so help me... Nealy is about to debark and you're in the land of nod. Snap to it!"

Gibbons shook himself and sat up straight. He placed the cracked mug down on the desk beside his two-button mouse and rubbed at his face. "I only closed me eyes for a minute, boss. Right, what was the problem again?"

"The problem is that it's raining, and our employer is about to step off a boat and get wet. Send transport down to the docks and do it now."

"All right, all right. No need to be an arse about it."

Palmer grabbed Gibbons's chair and spun the younger man around. He leaned over and glared, his brown eyes in a war against Gibbons's blue. "Can you just do your job for once without a running commentary?"

"Okay, okay, don't blow a blood vessel. I'm on it." Gibbons looked away and turned his chair back to his desk. Without further ado, he got on the phone and dispatched a pair of golf buggies down to the docks. Eventually the island would have a working cable car system to take people back and forth from the docks to the top of the hill, but for now, the cost of running one was unwarranted – not for a smattering of guests and a skeleton crew. For the time being, those travelling around the island could get by just fine with golf carts and buggies.

Palmer moved back to the CCTV bank and checked over the monitors arranged in three rows of three. He observed various staff members going about their duties and kept a careful eye on some of the island's more *notorious* residents.

This whole place is a bad idea.

But nothing stands between a rich man and his dreams.

Palmer turned his focus back to the docks, watching Nealy step off the ferry and onto the floating jetty. Next week, a specialist construction crew would arrive to start work on a six-berth quay, as well as a reception building, coffee shop, and souvenir store. All had been pre-fabricated off site, with the entire project slated to complete within three months. In fact, Nealy had constructed everything on the island in less than two years, which was insane.

To rush a thing like this...

Cut corners and eventually those corners will come back to cut you.

Palmer had won the head of security job on account of a twelve-year career in the Royal Engineers as a sergeant, but he had initially joined a crew of ex-military filling in as cheap, reliable labour for the building firm that Nealy had hired to work on the island. That firm had needed to increase the size of its workforce in order to cope with such a large project, but once construction had completed, the new hires had been let go. Nealy, however, deigned to interview some of the ex-military men to add to his security team, and Palmer had got the top spot because of his extensive experience in the field, along with the fact he didn't suffer from PTSD like some of his colleagues. Nealy had said he needed a steady mind in charge of security. *Someone who won't let the darkness in,* had been the man's exact words.

That had been four months ago, and back then Palmer hadn't known exactly what he was signing up for. Everything had remained top secret until just nine weeks ago, when Nealy had called a briefing with every member of staff on the island. Palmer had almost caught a ferry home that very night, but Nealy had increased his pay by forty per cent and shook on it. Palmer wanted his kids to go to university without getting into debt. The risk was worth it.

Nealy bought men and women like most people bought bread. Palmer just hoped he didn't end up as burnt toast.

Nealy was currently standing out in the rain, which didn't bode well. The Irishman was not an unfair or abusive boss – which had surprised Palmer – but he didn't suffer failure either.

Palmer had already seen a handful of people sacked in the last few months for sloppy performance, and it was abundantly clear that every person on the island was expendable and easily replaced. Do your job and get paid well. Mess up one too many times and you went home. It didn't help that Nealy had somehow wrested control of the island away from the UK government, which meant no one had a legally enforceable employment contract. Not quite off the books, but shady, to say the least.

"Buggies have arrived," said Gibbons over his shoulder. The younger man had pulled a plain black baseball cap over his head and yanked his mousey ponytail through the back. He seemed to have woken up properly now, his eyes no longer half closed. "Sorry about the delay, boss."

Palmer gave only a grunt. He'd now worked with Gibbons for over a month, but the man was getting increasingly feckless about his work. It was like he'd been more eager to get the job than to actually do it once hired. Perhaps he had expected something different.

But that wasn't Palmer's problem.

He watched Nealy usher his guests into the two six-seater golf carts before hopping inside himself beside the driver. It was hard to tell for sure, even on a 4K all-weather camera, but Nealy appeared to be in high spirits. Hopefully a little drizzle would go unnoticed. *He wears so much gel in his hair, he's probably waterproof.* "Okay, Gibbons, standby for further orders."

"Righty-o, boss."

Palmer sighed and picked up a bundle of papers from his desk. Each page contained a short bio of Nealy's guests. Only five in total, which should be easy enough to handle, but you could never guess how a stranger might behave. The more Palmer knew about them, the better. Especially with an under-manned crew.

Nealy shouldn't have waited this long to recruit. We need people now, not tomorrow.

The island was operating at a limited capacity until the grand opening in nine months' time, so today's guests would receive only a taste of what the place offered. It would be more than enough for any sane person.

"Looks like we've got a storm incoming, boss," said Gibbons. He brought up a weather map on his monitor and tapped the screen. A swirling mixture of blues, greens, and reds. "Just got an alert through."

Palmer nodded. "Wait until Nealy enters the Keep, then bring everyone inside. No reason for them to get wet."

"Ah, ain't you nice!"

Palmer growled.

Gibbons shrugged innocently and adjusted the peak of his cap. "Hopefully it'll pass us by in an hour or two. No big deal."

"And fingers crossed that a bit of inclement weather is the only bad luck we have this weekend. We need to be on our A game, Gibbons."

"Worried about losing your job, boss?"

"I worry about a lot of things, but not that. Are you going to be a help or a hindrance?"

"Probably both."

Palmer folded his arms and shook his head, painfully aware of the Glock 17M in his holster and how easy it would be to yank it out and pull the trigger. "Just try to stay awake, okay? I'm heading down to greet everyone, so keep an eye on things here. Bring everyone inside before the storm hits and get me on the radio if anything needs my attention."

Gibbons leaned back in his chair and stretched out his arms above his head. "You can count on me, boss."

There were two exits to the control room, and Palmer marched out of the one at the rear, thinking, *Only to let me down.*

Sim and Chrissy had sat at the back of the ferry during the trip, keeping to themselves while enjoying the relaxing to and fro of the sea. Nealy went up top with the captain to enjoy the view. It was eye-opening to see how a man like him lived, and more than a little disorientating to get a taste of it.

At 8AM that morning, Sim and Chrissy had been chauffeured directly from their flat down to Portsmouth in an imported Chevrolet Suburban. Then they had been escorted, via an awaiting Tesla, down to a private marina, where a private ferry boat was waiting to board them.

That the ferry boat was named *Pickton-49* hadn't escaped Sim.

Robert Pickton. Confessed to murdering forty-nine victims in Canada.

The boat is even bright orange, like a prison jumpsuit.

Where the hell is Nealy taking us?

It turned out that Nealy was taking Sim and Chrissy, along with two other guests, to an island in the English Channel. The trip took about an hour, and no one except Nealy and his bodyguards seemed to know anything about anything.

Now they were climbing aboard a pair of golf buggies at the bottom of a muddy hill just in time to avoid a downpour. The sea had got pretty rough towards the end.

The bodyguards grabbed everyone's bags and loaded them onto the buggies and also insisted that Chrissy give up her camera, which didn't go down well. Nealy then ushered his guards to go sit in the golf buggy up front and then sat beside the driver of the other. He patted the man on the back and told him to get going. Today, Nealy was wearing a navy blue cardigan and beige trousers. "Excuse the modest transport," he told Sim and the other passengers. "The dock still needs to be built, so we're not fully ready to receive guests. Be assured that things only get better from here on in."

"What is this place?" Sim asked from the rear of three benches. He had to grip the safety rail to keep from bouncing right out of the buggy as it picked up speed.

Nealy looked back at him and smiled, his elbow propped up

on the front bench's backrest. "We're on the Isle of Durne, a craggy outcropping twenty miles from the Isle of Wight. I flattened the peak and built the first manmade structure here in over a hundred years. I actually laid the first brick with my own bare hands."

A large-backed man in a cowboy hat whistled from the middle bench. In an American accent, full of enthusiasm, he asked, "How big is this rock, Nealy?"

"A mere nine hundred acres, but that's plenty big enough for our purposes."

"Our purposes?" asked a slender redhead in her forties. She was sitting beside the big American and spoke with a melodic French accent. "And what are those, I ask you?"

"To entertain," said Nealy with a smile. "To learn and study and try to understand the very fabric of what being human means. But more about that later."

Sim groaned. He wanted answers now.

Chrissy tapped him on the knee and scowled at him. "Cheer up, you! This is exciting. Also, seventy grand!"

"I know, I know," he muttered. "Things just keep getting weirder, though." Truth was, his heart was drumming in his chest and he could barely wait to see what all this was about. He half expected the whole thing to be some kind of surreal prank. At least his fellow guests were equally dumbfounded. Ignorance in numbers made him feel a little better.

"Allow me to introduce you to one another while we drive," said Nealy, and he pulled himself around so that he was sitting fully sideways on the seat next to the driver. The buggy was slowly climbing a steep hill, clinging to a gravel path. It was impossible to see anything ahead except for the grey sky above. Nealy pointed to Sim on the back seat. "This here is Mr Simon Barka, and his lovely partner in crime, Christina Wise. They operate what I believe to be the very best true crime channel on YouTube."

The American and the French lady turned back and smiled

at them both. Chrissy waved a hand and blushed. Sim nodded awkwardly.

"Can't say I watch a lot of stuff on the internet," said the American. "Live sports is more my thing. You ever watch the Cowboys play? No place like the Cotton Bowl."

Sim shook his head. "I used to watch a bit of NHL."

The American waved a hand and grimaced. "That's no sport for a real man."

"Allow me to introduce Mike Rondon," said Nealy, shaking his head as if in apology. "All the way from Austin, Texas. He owns more golf courses than Trump and is an expert in opening and running resorts. I'm hoping this little venture of mine might pique his interest enough to get him to come onboard as an investor."

"And one o' these days I hope to be half as rich as you, Nealy."

Everyone laughed. Sim nodded hello and Chrissy shook the man's hand.

"Pleasure, young lady."

"And finally," said Nealy. "We have Gerry Trezeguet from the fine port of Marseille. If you lived in France, you would have seen her award-winning television show."

"You're on TV?" said Chrissy, her eyes wide like a child's. "That's so cool."

The redhead smiled in a lopsided, arousing fashion. Her lips were either naturally plump or full of filler. "It's crass," she said. "I conduct family therapy sessions for a twice-weekly programme on French national television. I 'ate it, but it pays the bills and furthers my research. You might call me... what is the word? Ah, *oui*, a sell-out, no?"

Sim chuckled. There was something about Gerry's manner that made her instantly likeable. A dry wit, further enhanced by the accent.

"Still sounds cool to me," said Chrissy, grabbing the safety rail as the buggy suddenly hit a divot. "I love psychology." She side-eyed Sim. "Maybe you can help me understand this one a little better."

Sim rolled his eyes. "Don't start."

Gerry studied Sim for a second and grinned that lopsided grin again. "Ah. He is a closed book, *oui?* Emotions make him vulnerable, so he holds them inside because he fears what might happen if they were to ever spill out. There is something in the past holding him back from the future. If only he could let go, he might finally be happy."

Chrissy erupted in laughter. "How did you know all that?"

"She doesn't," said Sim, feeling a burn at the back of his neck and an aching in his teeth. "You're just guessing, right?"

"*Oui*, of course. You are typical man, so is easy to guess. To know you better, *Monsieur*, I would need to get you on my couch."

Chrissy pointed a finger playfully. "Hey, you! He's taken."

"My apologies, *mademoiselle*." Gerry winked and smiled.

Sim shook his head and looked away, hating the fact that the discussion had turned to him. Why did Chrissy need to know every thought inside his head? Was it not better to keep certain things to himself? Wasn't it safer? Nobody enjoyed hearing the truth unfiltered. That was why people lied.

But I'm not lying. I'm just… trying to forget.

They were coming to the top of the hill. Soon, they would see what was on the other side. The anticipation caused Sim to sit up straighter, to rise a few millimetres in order to get a view just that split second sooner. Would it be a secret lab? Satan in chains? What exactly had Nealy put on this island that was so secret?

The answer turned out to be…

A castle?

"There she is," said Nealy, lowering his head so that he could see beneath the golf buggy's roof. "What I like to call 'the Keep.' I was inspired by a book I read as a teenager with the same name. Built to contain ancient horrors during World War Two, it was."

"Which one?" asked Mike Rondon. "This Keep or the one in the book?"

Nealy turned back and chuckled. "The one in the book, of course. The Keep in front of you came into being a mere twelve months ago, built from fibreglass, steel, and cement. It's just a facade for a very modern facility. The horrors inside, however, they are very real."

Sim didn't like the sound of that. "Horrors?"

Nealy ran a hand over his slick hair and turned to face the front again. "Answers are almost upon us, my friends. Just a few more minutes."

Sim sat back impatiently while the golf buggy crested the hill and picked up speed. The Keep was fifty metres ahead, at the end of a cobbled courtyard. Its architecture was foreboding, all twisted spires and oddly shaped stained-glass windows, but it was indeed clearly a facade. The roof shingles were a freshly painted black, and the brickwork was a subtle mix of purples interlaced with dreary greys. The structure itself seemed to tower hundreds of feet into the air, but Sim suspected forced perspective was at play. Trickery or not, the place was big.

"Is it a hotel?" asked Chrissy.

Nealy nodded. "There are twenty-five suites in the Keep, but there's a contemporary hotel at the rear of the island with three hundred more. That's where most of the paying public will stay."

"Paying public?" Mike sat up and cricked his neck left and right. "That's my kind of public. This is a resort, then, Nealy? An attraction?"

"Like no other." Nealy had a glint in his eye. "It's a brand new, one-of-a-kind experience, and you lucky folks are about to be its very first guests."

"The suspense is killing me," said Chrissy. She elbowed Sim softly in the ribs and pulled an excited face at him.

"A fine choice of words," said Nealy, "for reasons that will soon become apparent."

Sim could not understand what he was about to see. Clearly, Nealy had plans to open some kind of exclusive resort on the island, but what was the draw? A haunted castle? It seemed so… underwhelming.

All this for a silly scare attraction? A bunch of waxworks and animatronics? A few live actors sprinkled here and there to get the pant wetting started? It's already been done.

It made little sense. The expense to build a place such as this must have been monumental. The Keep looked plucked right out of Transylvania, with a huge and intricate stained-glass window at the front. And how much did it cost to rent an island from the government? There had to be something bigger than what he was seeing.

The two golf buggies came to a stop in a small parking bay alongside the courtyard. A dozen thatched-roofed huts gave the impression of a tiny village existing in the ominous shadow of the Keep. One hut had a poster of roasted turkey legs in its window, while another showed pictures of doughnuts. A food court.

Nealy hopped off the buggy and waved a hand to beckon them. It was raining, but he didn't seem to notice. Behind him, about thirty metres away, four men rolled a large crate along on a trailer, heading for the Keep. Sim was relieved to see people working. It dispelled a lot of his apprehension. It also added to his disappointment that whatever this was would be mundane and pedestrian. The world didn't need another theme park. Especially not one accessed by an hour-long ferry ride.

Nealy dismissed his bodyguards, who zoomed off in their golf buggy. He then turned to his guests and waved at them excitedly. "Come on, come on. The sooner we get inside, the sooner we can sign those NDAs and get started."

Sim slid out of the buggy and helped Chrissy step out behind him. "He's acting like bloody Willy Wonka."

Chrissy chuckled, but then she shivered and pulled her denim jacket tightly around herself. Sim pulled his own jacket closer, too, trying to keep out the rain. The weather was just right for the setting: miserable and unsettling.

"What do you think this place is?" asked Chrissy.

"Probably just a house full of crappy rides designed to scare us. We should've known it would be something like this."

Chrissy didn't seem to buy it. "Then why bring *us*? Our channel has nothing to do with theme parks and attractions."

Sim didn't have an answer to that. It was true, they weren't a good fit to endorse something like this. But Nealy didn't seem like a man who made mistakes. *So if this place isn't what I think it is, what is it?*

"Let's hurry before this drizzle becomes a downpour," said Nealy, ushering them to follow him through the cobbled courtyard that was bordered by flowerbeds and saplings. "The heavens are about to open."

Sim looked up and saw a dark grey sky chasing away the last remnants of blue. A morning gale howled in off the sea and billowed through the women's hair. Gerry held hers down with both hands.

The small group, including two chauffeurs and four bodyguards, shuffled along the courtyard towards the Keep. They all looked up at the great stained-glass window, and Sim noticed that there was an image of a screaming woman's face hidden within the stained glass. 'Tacky' was the only word he could think to describe it.

The Keep's front entrance had a pair of elaborately carved wooden doors, ten feet high, with great brass knockers and iron hinges. Their authenticity was betrayed when they opened automatically upon their approach.

"Ah," said Nealy. "We're expected."

A grey-haired man wearing an all black uniform covered in pockets stood in the entryway, holding a clipboard in one hand

and giving a casual salute with the other. Nealy shouted out to him and asked if he had the forms.

"Got them right here, sir." His voice was booming yet polite. "Standard NDAs as you requested."

"Fantastic! Thank you, Palmer."

They were still ten metres from the entrance, but Sim had to halt to let the men pushing the trailer go by. The crate they were transporting was more like a cage, with boards covering each side and held in place by hooks. "Pardon me," one man said. "So sorry."

"No problem," said Sim.

"O'Brian!" Nealy turned back and shouted, causing the four men to flinch. "Can't you wait a moment? You're pushing right through the middle of my tour group. Jesus wept!"

The man who must have been O'Brian stuttered. "Er, yes, sir. Sorry, sir. I, er, wasn't thinking."

"It's fine," said Sim, unsettled by Nealy's yelling. "Don't sweat it, man."

But Nealy ignored Sim's placations and kept his focus on his employee. "Just get it moving – and take it around back, for heaven's sake. Guests shouldn't see you pushing crates around like this. They wouldn't allow it at Disney, and I won't allow it here."

"Yessir." O'Brian and the other men panicked, placing their shoulders against the trailer and shoving it out of the way as quickly as they could. As they did so, one of the trailer's wheels hopped up over one of the raised flowerbeds bordering the courtyard. It caused the crate to tilt, and one of the boards came loose from its hooks. The slab of wood crashed down right on top of O'Brian's head and caused the man to yelp in surprise, but despite his obvious pain, he quickly ducked out from underneath the board and attempted to lift it back in place.

But it was too late.

A shackled stranger sat in the middle of the cage on a fixed chair.

Sim's jaw fell open. A moment later, so did Chrissy's. "I-Is that Montez Sidwell?" she asked.

No doubt about it. Sim had done an entire episode on the man last year. An NFL player from Ohio who went on a coke-fuelled frenzy and slaughtered his party guests with an illegal AK47 he kept under the bed. Apparently, he'd been convinced they were all out to steal his money and fame. Probably he'd been right, but that was no excuse for killing nine people, including his pregnant wife. The crime had rocked the United States and given Nancy Grace an entire month's worth of material.

And that mass murderer was now staring out at them with a dazed look in his eyes, like he didn't know where he was. Up close, his size was even more astounding. Six foot five. Three hundred pounds. A monster of a man. He could probably have killed nine people with his bare hands if he'd wanted to.

Mike Rondon took off his cowboy hat and held it by his side. He was completely bald. "What the heck is going on here, Nealy? And how many folks know about it?"

Nealy gritted his teeth, staring daggers at the four mortified workers holding the trailer. O'Brian, in particular, had turned an unnatural shade of pale. His hands were shaking as he shoved the board back up and locked it in place. "Sir, I'm so sorry. I didn't—"

Nealy put a hand up to silence the man, then began shaking his head with a smile on his face. "Well, that's the cat out of the bag, I suppose." His anger faded, and he became excited once again. Turning around, he waved a hand up at the Keep. "Ladies and gentlemen, welcome to my Maniac Menagerie."

CHAPTER
THREE

NEALY, along with his security man, Palmer, led the group into a vast entrance hall that took everyone's breath away. The ceiling was three storeys high, with black-painted beams and a bright red pentagram at its centre. An extra-wide staircase climbed the rear of the room to a galleried landing where limestone statues with contorted faces peered over twisted handrails. The entire area was lit by mock oil lamps, flickering realistically, as well as the multicoloured light spilling in through the stained-glass window above the entrance. Most impressive of all, however, was the baleful colossus towering over them in the centre of the black-and-white tiled floor.

Jack the Ripper was twenty feet high with the sharp-toothed grin of a great white shark. In the classic depiction, he wore a stovepipe hat and the flowing black cape of a Victorian gentleman. In his right hand was a scalpel as big as a sword. Nealy had constructed a giant serial killer to greet his guests as they entered the Keep.

And Sim had to admit it was pretty damn cool.

Nealy must have seen Sim's expression, because he came and clasped a hand around his shoulder. "He's something, isn't he? This is the image that will stay in people's minds – the icon for what we're selling here."

"Serial killers?"

Nealy nodded. "In the flesh."

"What does that mean?" Sim eyed a plaque at the base of the statue, picking out a bold heading followed by a brief passage of text: THE DEMON OF WHITECHAPEL. "And why is Sidwell here? He's dangerous."

"All in good time," said Nealy. "No one is in any peril, I assure you. Sidwell is in my care, and I will explain why shortly."

"Guy was a hell of a player," said Mike. He shook the raindrops from his hat and placed it back on his head. "Shame what he did. Could've made a fortune."

"Yeah," said Chrissy, her eyebrow raised. "Shame."

Gerry put her hands on her hips and was shaking her head as she stared up at the massive Victorian slasher statue. His cape seemed to flow slightly in the wind. "It is vulgar."

"It's supposed to be," said Nealy, not at all discouraged. In fact, he was beaming with pride. "Jack the Ripper is the epitome of a boogeyman. Unknown, unexplainable, and hiding in the shadows of the very civility we are naïve enough to think protects us. He was one of the first celebrity killers. The first grizzly headline grabber."

Chrissy pulled a face. "Celebrity? I don't think that's a good way of looking at it. He killed five women, maybe more."

"Only prostitutes," said Mike with a shrug. "He was cleaning up the streets."

Gerry folded her arms crossly. "Some might call *you* a prostitute, Mr Rondon. How many unsavoury things have you done for money?"

Mike chuckled, clearly amused by the accusation. "It's only unsavoury if people find out about it, but I take your point, ma'am."

"I've been in the boardroom with you, Mike," said Nealy.

"At least hookers know they're being shafted up front. It's more honest than what we do."

"I'd have to agree with you there, buddy."

Both men laughed, but Sim shared a look with Chrissy that told him she'd also found Mike's comment more than a little gross. *I wonder how many marriages the guy's had? Or, more to the point, how many divorces?*

Chrissy took Sim's hand and squeezed. It recentred him and allowed him to focus on his concerns again. "Why do you have Montez Sidwell in a cage outside, Mr Nealy? He's supposed to be in Chillicothe Correctional Institution, last I heard."

Mike rested a hand on his oversized belt buckle – stamped and shaped into a curled-up armadillo – and nodded. "I'd quite like to know that myself, Nealy. That was a strange turn of events, even for you."

Nealy was staring up at the Jack the Ripper statue, almost like it was his first time seeing it as well. When he realised they were waiting on him for an answer, he shook himself and frowned. "Huh? Oh, yes, I suppose we should sit down and get things moving, shouldn't we? Palmer? The NDA, please?"

The security man stepped forward with his clipboard. He handed a pen to Gerry and asked her to sign. She didn't even bother reading before putting her name at the bottom. The woman gave the impression that it mattered very little to her, that she was a woman who would do what she wanted, legally bound or not.

Mike examined it a little more closely. "What is this you want our John Hancock on, Nealy? I don't have my lawyer here with me."

Nealy responded evenly, suddenly all business. "You have my word, Mr Rondon, that it is nothing more than a promise for you to keep the secrets I am about to share with you. You've already seen more than I would've liked, but everyone is still free to leave if they wish. In order to proceed, however, I must insist upon a signature. It's a boilerplate non-disclosure agreement."

Mike let out a sigh and seemed to think about it for a moment, but then he took the pen from Gerry and signed the form. "I've known you long enough to trust your word, Nealy. At this point, I'm just dying to know what the heck you've got here."

"Me too," said Chrissy, signing the form without hesitation. It left Sim in a choiceless situation. He couldn't exactly refuse now she had signed, could he? They were in this together.

He took the pen and hovered it over the signature box at the bottom. He glanced at the form briefly, but it was a bunch of legalese that hurt his brain. The only thing giving him confidence was that people more successful and probably smarter than him had already signed it. He eyed Gerry's curly signature above Mike's short, square one, and then he saw Chrissy's familiar criss-crossy scrawl. He put his own name right below hers.

It's done. I've just signed my life away.
Why do I not feel good about this?

"Okay," said Sim, his stomach suddenly unsettled. "We've all signed, so now you can tell us why you have a mass murderer locked up outside in a cage."

"He's being transported to comfier confines," said Nealy. "He'll be more than comfortable, I promise you. The trolley cages are only temporary until we get proper road access to the Keep."

"That's not what I'm worried about. How is Sidwell here? And why?"

Nealy took the NDA from Palmer and gave it a once over. After a moment, he handed it back. "Sidwell is here for a variety of reasons. For instance, he'll be made available to documentarians such as yourself, as well as scientists like Ms Trezeguet and, of course, Ms Wise."

Chrissy blushed. Even though she was only a matter of

months away from qualifying, Sim knew she still thought of herself as nothing more than a student. "I could interview him?" she asked. "I could sit in a room with Sidwell and speak with him?"

"Of course," said Nealy, opening his arms wide. "I meant it when I said I wanted to do good before my days expire. This is part of that. I want to unlock the secrets of the murderous mind, to help understand what makes us violent on the most basic of levels. Perhaps then we can one day euthanise murderous impulses from the human condition."

Gerry gasped, and then actually staggered on her heels. It must have been for effect. "You wish to cure… violence? *La vache!*"

Sim almost staggered, too. Nealy had promised him answers, but Sim hadn't even known what the questions were. Could it really be that he hoped to learn something by speaking with serial killers and madmen? What could he uncover that countless experts in the FBI, Scotland Yard, and other agencies around the world had not?

"Boldness has never been an issue of mine," said Nealy. "In today's world, we imprison madness and barbarism, but I wish to try something different. I wish to study it, observe it, and… defang it."

Chrissy frowned. "Defang it? What do you mean?"

"I want to take away people's fear of the unknown. If people can identify men like Bundy or women like Wuornos, then they can better protect themselves. Perhaps we can even wheedle out the malformed minds at a young age and treat them before the worst happens. Like Ms Wise said to me just yesterday, what if Jeffrey Dahmer had been given mandatory therapy at a young age? Would he have killed? Would any of the serial killers of the past or present?" He turned a circle, lifting both arms. "Think of this place as a university of evil. Here we will master our understanding of murder in the same way we did mathematics and biology. It is within our grasp, and it will save countless lives. It's time to unlock the secrets of the beast inside of mankind."

There was silence in the massive entrance hall. Jack the Ripper towered silently over them, his scalpel pointed at the ground.

"So why is this place decked out like a haunted house?" asked Mike. "This don't look like no university I've ever been to. There's more to this than what you're saying, isn't there? You gunna charge these eggheads for access to Sidwell and his like?"

Nealy gave a lopsided grin. "The details are still being ironed out, but there are two sides to this place, and education is one."

"So what is the other?" asked Gerry, her arms still folded, and now she was tapping her foot. She wore a pair of very high blue heels that matched the colour of her silky blouse, but even with their added height she was short.

Nealy ignored the question and turned away. He walked towards the staircase but then veered over to a set of double doors on the right. "Follow me, folks. I have prepared something for you. It'll explain everything."

Sim looked down and checked he was still holding hands with Chrissy. It felt important not to let go. Together, they followed Nealy.

But Sim couldn't help thinking about Sidwell.

Nealy didn't build this place to house a single killer.

Which begs the question: how many more does he have here?

CHAPTER FOUR

THEY STEPPED through into a cafeteria with dozens of tables: a mixture of booths and freestanding pedestals. The surrounding chairs were all brand new, still covered in plastic wrapping. At the back of the room, a row of self-service buffets carts formed a line that led to a pair of cashier stations and a separate area stocked with condiments and cutlery. Pretty ordinary for a cheap eatery, but there was also something about it that was very much not ordinary.

Placed around the room was a collection of recognisable faces. In just one glance, Sim spotted the grimacing statues of Harold Shipman, the Delhi Butcher, and what he guessed was Elizabeth Báthory – if her blood-soaked lips and gore-soaked bathrobe were anything to go by.

"Eventually there'll be live actors," said Nealy, "but I think this gives an overall flavour. When I initially conceived this room, I intended to pursue licensing deals for famous horror movie slashers, but somewhere along the line I decided it would only cheapen the experience. Reality is far more terrifying than fiction, don't you agree?"

"Yes," said Sim without hesitation. His channel had taught him that most fictional serial killers were based on real-life monsters, and that the movies often had to tone things down. If people got even the merest hint of the true suffering caused by the likes of Bundy, then they would be anything but entertained. *The man had sex with dead bodies. How many good-looking Hollywood actors would be willing to portray that?*

Nealy pointed to a group of chairs ahead. As he did so, a pair of chefs appeared behind the buffet carts, rattling tins and making a racket. Instead of chef's whites, they wore grubby butcher aprons. Heady aromas filled the cafeteria, causing Sim's saliva ducts to open. Salt, garlic, and the unmistakable scent of fried chicken.

Chrissy licked her lips and gave him a pained look. They had skipped breakfast in all the excitement.

"Ah," said Nealy. "Lunch is on its way, but our stomachs can wait a while longer. Please grab a chair and relax. This won't take long." An electronic squark came from the ceiling and caused him to grunt with frustration. "Just ignore that. This place still has the odd hiccup. It's only the intercom system playing up."

Chrissy giggled. "Don't you own a tech company?"

Nealy chuckled. "Ironic, I know."

Sim strolled forward and grabbed a chair from those arranged around a trolley with a flatscreen television. He pulled it back for Chrissy to sit on and then grabbed another for himself. Gerry and Mike sat to his left while Nealy slid past and made his way to the front. Palmer went with him. The tall security man picked up a television remote from the trolley and pushed a button to switch on the flatscreen.

Nealy pulled a phone from a pocket and tapped its display, casting an image across to the TV.

-MANIAC MENAGERIE-
By
Everstech & Le Grande Mar

The logo was stylised in red, black, and purple, with each letter formed from slices and slashes.

Nealy held his phone by his side but kept his thumb hovering over the screen. He watched his guests for a moment, smiling. "I've done a lot of things in my life," he eventually said, and then let it hang there for a few moments. "At twenty-four, I found success with a small telecoms company that eventually came to service a third of the UK's communications infrastructure. I then leveraged those profits to start a tennis equipment company that grew to become a sports brand second only to Nike. Alas, neither of those businesses did anything except make me rich. They were never my passion. My passion began with the company I am currently best known for: Ecohamlet. By twenty-fifty, half the Western world's housing stock will have environmentally friendly power, insulation, and water capture technology. Every home will be self-sustaining: growing food in their gardens, balconies, or even attics. I want to change the world for the better, and when you strip away the headlines and corporate mud-slinging, that is my singular truth. I want to make the world a better place. And do you know why?"

Everyone shook their heads, except for Chrissy, who played along and asked, "Why?"

Nealy nodded, as if to thank her for interacting. "Because my mother died giving birth to me, and my father's impact upon my upbringing was about the same as the milkman's. He was little more than a drunk." Nealy looked away for a moment, a slightly haunted look coming over him. When he spoke again, he started quietly and slowly raised his voice. "My mother's life. That was the price of my admission, and it's placed a heavy burden upon me. One that has compelled me to make my life worthwhile. Ecohamlet is my biggest effort towards that goal, but this island is another. I have already explained my intention to make this a place of research and understanding, but there are, of course, questions of funding to be raised. A place like this is not cheap to run."

"So you're going to let paying guests come here?" said Sim, under no illusions any more of what this place was. "To what? Get autographs and selfies with Sidwell and a bunch of other psychopaths? Will you be paying Sidwell a wage, or throwing handfuls of peanuts to make him perform?"

Gerry smirked, but she didn't seem particularly amused. "How many *killers* do you have here, Mr Nealy?"

"We're jumping ahead," was his reply. He tapped his thumb and the logo on the screen disappeared, replaced by a set of graphs. "Worldwide attendance for theme parks across the globe is up, but the UK lacks a truly worldwide attraction – its Disneyland Paris, if you will. Well, this island is it, folks. The Maniac Menagerie will bring people in from multiple ports and eventually put them up in one of three resort hotels. There'll be fine dining, private tours, VIP access to various facilities, and offsite activities such as sea fishing and parasailing. With the expansion of London's Heathrow Airport, the UK government hopes to increase tourism by seven per cent."

"Which is how you sold them on the leasing," said Mike. "*Quid pro quo.*"

Nealy shrugged. "This island was a useless rock earning them nothing. They were more than willing to hand it over to me with a promise I would increase tourism to the UK."

"Your own little fiefdom, huh, Nealy?" Mike took off his hat and scratched the top of his freckled dome. "Been thinking about buying an island myself. Would need to be a lot sunnier than this one, though."

"The weather is of little consequence, Mr Rondon. Eighty per cent of what we have on the island is indoors. The Keep will include many attractions, several of which you will experience today, but the biggest draw, of course, is—"

"Real-life killers," said Sim. He gripped the sides of his

chair, trying to ground himself as things became more and more surreal. "This can't be a good idea. I mean, who thinks that it is?"

"How did you even get them here?" asked Chrissy. She had lost a little of her enthusiasm now and was sitting with her arms folded. Sim reached over and put his hand on the back of her chair. "I can't believe you've even done something like this."

Nealy clicked through a few frames on his phone until a set of familiar corporate logos appeared on the television. "I have some very influential sponsors on board, many of whom were instrumental in persuading various governments to hand over their most notorious criminals."

"What do you mean by 'persuading'?" asked Sim.

Nealy shrugged and made an open-palmed gesture with his hands. "A few brown paper envelopes here and there." He chuckled to himself. "Needless to say, the island will operate under a banner of civic duty, safeguarding some of the world's most dangerous criminals while taking that cost burden away from the individual states, nations, and private security firms. The Keep is a certified penitentiary with the same obligations as any other prison, but it will be funded privately. Tourism will support a majority of its facilities, while various schools and universities will bankroll the research that takes place. It's a win-win for all involved."

"And how much of that money will go to shareholders?" asked Mike. "Because I'm not hearing a lot about profit margins here."

Nealy grinned and bought up another set of graphs. "Up to fifty per cent of profits can be—"

"How many killers do you have here?" Gerry interrupted. "How many murderers have you brought to this island that you intend to open to the public?"

Nealy stopped mid-flow and seemed to deflate. He'd been on a roll, giving a display of his boardroom prowess, but it seemed to hold little sway with Gerry, who offered him the withering stare of a headmistress. It caused Nealy to clear his throat awkwardly. "Um, well, that depends on how you categorise—"

"How many murderers are on this island? A simple question, no?"

Sim sat forward, wanting to know the answer, too. For the last three years, he'd reported on wickedness from a distance, always telling other people's stories while recounting horrors from the past. But today he had breathed the same air as Montez Sidwell, had gazed upon the man with his very own eyes. He'd had his own encounter with evil. It turned his mind back to a time when...

"The current inmate count stands at thirty-eight residents," said Nealy, flashing a smile, but only briefly. "The Keep has a capacity for over a hundred across four cell blocks."

"*Merde!*" Gerry shook her head. "This is madness, *mon ami*. Evers, my friend, you cannot do this. It is folly."

Nealy took a deep breath and turned to his security man, who was standing amongst the tables nearby. "Thank you, Palmer. You may return to your post."

"Yessir." Palmer switched off the television and strode away through the cafeteria, sidestepping a statue of John Wayne Gacy in full clown garb. The statue was so real, Sim feared it might reach out and grab him.

Nealy smoothed back his blond hair and perched against a table. "I understand your concern, Ms Trezeguet, but the prisoners on this island are far more secure than they would be in the overcrowded cells of the UK and America. I have implemented the most up-to-date security protocols here. One guard for every three prisoners. All inmates tagged with GPS implants. Automatic lockdowns if there's even a hint of trouble."

"Not enough," said Gerry. "That is not enough if you intend to bring the public here. But that is beside the point. It is wrong!

Men like Sidwell might have done terrible things, but they are not animals. You cannot make a zoo of human beings."

"Serial killers," said Nealy, his cheerful veneer slipping for the first time. "Some of whom came here voluntarily in order to escape death row. I offer every inmate here a better life than what they would have anywhere else. In exchange, they can provide something of value instead of simply draining money from taxpayers. Not just entertainment, but answers. Answers to whatever questions respected scientists like you might have, Ms Trezeguet. I can give you unfettered access. You can even be involved in the treatment regimes. This place needs experts like you. People who can add to the legitimacy of what we are doing."

Gerry took in a breath and held it. She seemed unhappy but offered no more words of argument. The offer of interviewing psychopathic minds appeared to interest her enough to consider it.

"Well," said Mike, rubbing his hands together in his lap and fidgeting with his enormous gold rings. "I like it. The guards you have here? They're armed, right? Please tell me this island isn't like the UK mainland?"

"No," said Nealy. "We've been granted status as an unaffiliated island, which means the law is whatever I decide it is. As it pertains to guns, I'm about to ink a contract with a French arms manufacturer to supply us with everything we need, but in the meantime, I have procured a few toys via the grey market. If the worst were to happen – which it won't – then we are a-go to use lethal force." He pinched at the bridge of his nose and grunted, like he was fighting away a headache, but when he looked at them again, he was once again wearing a reaffirming grin. "But I state, once again, that the worst will not happen, because I've been planning every detail of this bloody place for the last three years. It's all been covered. Whatever you might worry about, I've already thought about it and fixed it. Trust me."

Mike nodded, clearly satisfied. "I will want to go through your projections in finer detail, but so far you have my interest."

"Glad to hear it," said Nealy with a sigh. "What about the rest of you? As I said, you'll receive full access to whichever inmates you wish. Think about the things you could learn. Sidwell is just the tip of the iceberg."

"I do not know yet," said Gerry. "I need to think on this."

"Me too," said Sim. "This is... pretty nuts."

Chrissy put her hand on his knee and squeezed. "I agree. Being here and knowing what this place is... I'm not sure how I feel about it."

Nealy appeared a tad disappointed, but he quickly recovered, slicking back his hair and saying, "I'm certain the tour will change your minds, so perhaps we should waste no more time and go take it. Ladies and gentlemen, once again, I implore you to follow me."

CHAPTER FIVE

SIM AND CHRISSY strolled along at the rear of the small group. Nealy had led them back out into the main entrance, seeming to enjoy their awed expressions as they once again looked up at the giant Ripper statue and the vast stained-glass window in front of it. Now they were heading up the main staircase. Nealy mentioned that a lift was available for disabled guests, as well as a VIP lounge for those who wished to sip champagne before the start of the tour.

"This is crazy," said Sim, staring up at the high ceiling as he walked along the landing.

Chrissy nodded. "I know. Of all the pictures I had in my head, a serial killer theme park wasn't one of them."

"How did Nealy even get this place approved? Is he really that powerful?"

"Not him, his money. Still, it's kind of exciting to be here. Nealy could improve our lives with the change in his pocket."

Sim frowned at her. "What do we need to improve? I think our lives are pretty great."

"Our lives are great, Sim, but that doesn't mean they can't be even better. Imagine what we could do with the channel if we had the money to travel the globe or access high-security prisons. We could hire staff and have more time for ourselves."

Sim nodded. The channel certainly had room to grow, but the thought of changing what they had unsettled his stomach. Travelling the globe, hiring staff, and dealing with prison wardens... it was a lot to deal with. A lot that couldn't be predicted.

A lot that could go wrong.

Nealy walked so fast that his tennis shoes squeaked on the polished floor, and everyone had to take a couple of jog steps to keep up. They passed through a double doorway at the top of the staircase and stepped onto a concrete walkway a little like a train station platform. But instead of a train, there was a line of themed passenger cars with prison bars constructed around the sides. The intended effect was obviously for each guest to feel as though they were getting inside a cell. One that trundled along on wheels.

"I don't see a track," said Mike. "What system you running these things on, Nealy?"

Nealy beamed. "We're completely trackless, allowing us to adjust the route as needed. The cars are laser guided and linked to a control room. We can even adjust the ride intensity."

"Nice. Got something similar myself in a few of my parks. Cheap to make and with a nice small footprint."

"Indeed, although cost was a minor concern when I built this. Okay, all aboard." Nealy yanked open a cell door and hopped onto the back bench of the front car. He picked up a walkie-talkie that had been left there and waved a hand for everyone to join him. "Time's a-wasting, folks."

The hair rose on the back of Sim's neck. Amusement rides didn't usually bother him, but he had an inkling this one would be like none he'd ever experienced. Going ahead felt like stepping off a diving board. Once he took the plunge, there would be no way to keep from hitting the water.

"I'm not sure I want to do this, Chrissy." He was suddenly unable to take another step. "Th-This feels like a bad idea."

She stopped and faced him, reached out and took his hand. "It's just nerves. The way Nealy has built everything up has us on edge. But there's no way he would risk us getting hurt. He's a businessman. Last thing he wants is to get sued. Everything will be fine."

"But he has real-life serial killers here. Is that something we really want to see?"

Chrissy raised an eyebrow and chuckled. "Our jobs are literally to document serial killers. How is this not something we want to see? I'm anxious, too, babe, but can we really pass this up? You're always telling me you want answers, that you need to understand what makes one human being kill another. Well, this is the best chance you're ever going to get at finding those answers. We can't judge this place until we know the full story. Eyes wide open, right?"

He nodded. "Eyes wide open."

She stepped forward and held him around the waist. "I've got you."

He nodded against her shoulder. That sense of vulnerability was back, but he willed it away. He should be the one looking after Chrissy. She needed him to stand tall and be confident. Just for once.

"Come on, lovebirds!" Nealy shouted. Mike and Gerry had already joined him in the car, and now they were all staring at Sim and Chrissy.

"Coming," said Sim. He smiled at Chrissy to show he was good, then the two of them jogged down the platform and squeezed into the cell-car. There were four benches, and they slid into the front.

Nealy slammed the cell door shut behind them with an ominous *clang!*

Sim swallowed a lump in his throat and sat back. The bench was surprisingly comfy, with a padded contoured seat. In front of Sim was a net for stowing belongings, but all he had was his phone. He switched it on in case he wanted to take some photographs of whatever he was about to see, but someone hissed at him from behind.

"No pictures, my friends," said Nealy at the back. "An NDA doesn't prevent careless leaks from misplaced mobile phones."

Sim grunted and put his phone back in his pocket, but left it switched on.

"Okay," said Nealy. "Arms and legs inside the vehicle at all times, and absolutely no exiting the vehicle until permitted to do so. Tour will begin shortly."

Sim turned back and gave Mike and Gerry, behind him, a thin-lipped smile. At the very back of the car, Nealy spoke into the walkie-talkie he had picked up. It sounded like he was talking to Palmer.

"You ever visit one of my parks?" Mike asked Sim. "Got four of 'em in the great state of Texas alone."

Sim shook his head. "I've never been out of the country."

"No lie? Son, you got to see the world. Get out and place your flag."

Sim looked at Chrissy and chuckled. "I've been trying my best, right?"

Chrissy put her arm around him and smiled at Mike. "I've been dragging him out of his shell, little by little. He's not what you would call a natural adventurer, but give him time."

Mike winked and said, "Behind every good man are several ex-wives, but this one might be a keeper."

"There's no doubt in my mind," said Sim, gazing at Chrissy.

Gerry wrinkled her nose in a gesture of cuteness. "*L'amour*. Ambrosia for the soul."

"Here we go," said Nealy, putting down his walkie-talkie. "Hold on to your butts, folks."

The car jolted forward, and everyone turned to face front. Ahead of the platform, Sim noticed, for the first time, a giant skull with a wide-open mouth. They were heading right for it.

MANIAC MENAGERIE   61

About to enter the mouth of madness.

Sim didn't hold on to his butt, but he did hold on to Chrissy.

The car slid forward slowly, almost frictionless. Sim tried to relax, even as he moved steadily closer to the ravenous skull large enough to devour them all. Chrissy was beaming beside him, fully in the spirit of things.

But then the car halted.

Nealy's walkie-talkie chirped. He put it to his ear as someone relayed a message. He huffed and puffed, but then he chuckled.

"Darned thing's broken down," said Mike.

"*Oui*," said Gerry, looking bored.

"The e-ticket curse," said Mike. "The more you spend on a ride, the more likely it is to break down. I had this one in my Dallas park called the Final Frontier. It was an indoor rollercoaster with a top speed of sixty-five. Full of bright lights and theming. I let a smaller firm build it, and I quickly learned my lesson. I put up with the blasted thing for two years before finally having it dismantled. Stuck a cheap boat ride in there last year instead."

Chrissy pulled a face. "You really think the ride is broken? What would that mean?"

"Don't sweat it, miss. I'm sure Nealy will get the show back on the road in a few minutes. Either that or he shopped around for this system in all the wrong places. If he'd come to me, I would've set him with the guys at Verkoma. Best of the best. Dutch engineering. Almost as good as American."

Sim had never heard of Verkoma, and he was pretty sure American engineering wasn't as great as Mike thought it was, but all the same, he found himself at once relieved and disappointed that the ride might not be working.

Maybe we can skip it and just get straight to the point of this place.

And how exactly do Chrissy and I fit in.

Nealy was still on the walkie, mostly listening and nodding

along. He didn't seem concerned. Perhaps he was listening to a mechanic already working to get them moving again.

"I wonder if I could move my television show here," said Gerry. "I could hold meetings between murderers and the families of their victims." She frowned, her wrinkling forehead betraying her age that she obviously tried hard to disguise. "Is that unethical? Would it benefit only me? I don't know. *Merde!* It is so difficult to decipher the needs of one's ego, no?"

Chrissy shrugged. "Nothing wrong with indulging in a little egotism. I think having your show here would be great. You should talk to Nealy about it."

"*Oui.* I will do this. Thank you, Chrissy."

"Ooh, my name sounds so sexy when you say it."

Gerry smirked. "*Everything* sounds sexy when the French say it."

Sim nodded. It was true.

Nealy finished his radio conversation and let out a sigh. "Sit tight for a minute, folks. We have a late addition to the tour."

"Who?" asked Chrissy. "Is it someone famous?"

"You might say so. He arrived on the island yesterday and stayed the night in the staff barracks, but unfortunately he decided it would be a good idea to wander off and try to film some footage without me knowing. I don't blame him – he's a journalist – but he won't be forgiven twice. He's en route to join us now."

Sim sat back and gave his arms a rub. It was a little chilly. *A journalist? A journalist with an interest in killers?*

And no doubt their victims…

Everyone sat and waited. Minutes passed and Sim found himself gazing into the voids that made up each of the giant skull's eyes. Was such a macabre thing truly entertaining? Did people watch Sim and Chrissy's channel because they wanted to learn or to be titillated? Was he a documentarian, or was he profiteering off of death? Could both be true?

I should never have said yes to Nealy. This man occupies a world I want no part of. A world where profit comes before people, no matter what he says about wanting to do good.

Sim felt heavy in his seat. He wanted to get off, but it felt too late.

Nealy started clapping a minute later, startling everyone. "He's finally decided to join us. How was your illicit snooping, sir? Did you get much footage before my security grabbed you?"

"I saw a few things," said the stranger with a chuckle, "and I'm not off the island yet."

"Well, allow me to show you the things that aren't off limits. Then we can talk. Welcome aboard, Mr Dreadful."

Chrissy gasped.

Sim spun around in his seat. This was no stranger. No journalist either. This was Jason Dreadful.

One of the biggest pieces of shit Sim had ever met.

Sim stood up. "I'm getting off."

CHAPTER
SIX

JASON CLICKED his fingers and pointed at Sim. "Hey, Sim, when Nealy invited me to this place, I thought he must be crazy. But when I heard he invited you, too, I knew it for sure. How's the channel? Must be five or six mil by now, yeah?"

Sim sneered. Just the sight of this idiot, in his red baseball cap worn backwards and his ripped jeans, stoked his anger – a rare emotion for him. "I don't care about numbers, just so long as I come by my subscribers honestly. How many times have you been banned lately?"

Jason was grinning inanely. "It's almost a daily occurrence, mate, but the irony is that it only makes me more viral."

Sim looked at Nealy and tutted. "*Grim Tales* is your favourite channel, huh? So what is *he* doing here?"

"I meant what I said," Nealy replied. "But launching this place is going to be a massive undertaking, so the more people shouting about it, the better."

"Some voices are better left unheard."

"I take it you gentlemen know each other?" said Gerry wryly. She flipped her red hair over her shoulder. "We are all ears."

Jason waved a hand. "Sim and I started making content at

around the same time. We used to co-create now and then. Long time ago now."

"So what happened?" asked Gerry.

"One of us became successful, and the other... didn't. Resentment is a horrible thing."

Sim rolled his eyes. "No one is resentful of you, Jason. You hound innocent people and make snuff films."

Mike grumbled. "What's that now? Snuff films? There's a market for that, but not one I'm interested in."

"He's being dramatic," said Jason, folding his arms and pulling his hands inside the sleeves of his neon green hoodie. "I did a live report on a hostage situation once and happened to capture a woman being stabbed to death. I didn't know it was going to happen, but I was live-streaming." He shrugged sadly and almost seemed sincere. "Bad things happen. Pointing a camera at them doesn't change it."

"You are a voyeur," said Gerry. "Was your mother a sexual woman? Did she change her clothes in front of you as a child?"

Jason frowned at her. "Um... what?"

Sim rattled the cage door, wanting to get out. Chrissy tugged at him, trying to get him to sit down. "Believe me, he's more than a voyeur. Why don't you ask him about Daniel Jacobs? Poor guy committed suicide when Jason's channel presented *'evidence'* – he used air quotes around the word – "that the guy abducted a six-year-old girl from the school he taught at. Jason was so certain of his facts that he mobilized his online troops into hounding the guy. Seventeen days after Daniel Jacobs hung himself, they found the little girl alive and well, kidnapped by a mad auntie."

Jason stared at the ground. "Not my finest hour, you've got me there, Sim. But I learned some lessons, and I still maintain that Jacobs had a sinister side we never found out about."

Sim gritted his teeth and hissed. "Now you're going to speak ill of the poor guy? Jesus. Nealy, I want out of here. I can't be around this... this *ghoul*."

"Don't be so hasty," said Mike. He turned around in his seat and looked up at Sim. "If you leave now, this other guy gets an opportunity and you don't. That's not how you get ahead."

"I don't care about getting ahead."

"Well, you should. Look, son, if you're good at what you do and you do it for the right reasons, then stay and fight for it. Otherwise, your competition wins and you have to watch them in their glory."

"He's used to that," said Jason. "My channel just passed the eight million mark on YouTube, and I just got offered a television deal from a major US network. Don't get much bigger than that, mate."

"Well done," said Gerry. "You must be very proud."

Jason frowned, appearing confused about how to take the comment.

Mike was still looking at Sim. "You seem like a good kid, so stick around."

Chrissy pulled Sim back down onto the bench. "Don't let him run us off, babe. You'll be upset about it later if you do."

True. If Sim fled now, he would forever rue the memory of Jason's gleeful face. Jason would also rub it in his face at every opportunity. He already made digs at Sim and Chrissy's channel on his own, often referring to them as 'that boring channel'.

"Sit down," said Nealy. It wasn't a command, more a plea. "If Mr Dreadful plays up, he'll be the one who leaves. You have my word."

"His name's not Dreadful. It's Jason Middleton."

Jason rolled his eyes. "Give me a break, *Simon*. It's a stage name."

Sim's heart was beating in his chest, so he slowed down his breathing and tried to chill out. Chrissy rubbed his leg, but it only put him more on edge.

Stop being dramatic, Sim. You can't run off every time there's the threat of confrontation. Sooner or later, you have to start facing your problems.

Jason crossed the platform and approached the cell-car. "I come in peace, okay? I'm excited to be here with everyone."

Nealy reached over from the back seat and opened the cell door. "Mind your step, Mr Dreadful."

Jason hopped in and settled in the third row between Nealy and Mike. Gerry turned back to him and said, "*Bonjour*, I am Gerry."

"Yeah, *Bon Jovi*," he said back. "Pleased to meet you."

Mike didn't bother to introduce himself, which Sim found comforting. Was the American picking sides?

Should there be sides? I'm being petty.

No. Jason is everything I don't want to be. He profits from people's suffering.

Jason cleared his throat. "It's nice to see you, Chrissy. You must be qualified by now, huh?"

Chrissy turned and gave a half-hearted smile. "A few more months. How's, um, Janelle, is it?"

Jason gave a shrug and pouted. "The Jason and Janelle show is no more. She left me about nine months ago now."

"Oh, I'm sorry. What happened?"

"She got tired of me sleeping with other women."

Mike gave a huff of laughter, but Gerry sniffed disapprovingly.

Chrissy groaned. "Yeah, some women don't like that."

Nealy tapped a hand on the back of his seat. "Everybody ready to take two?"

Everyone nodded, so Nealy spoke into his radio and the car got moving again, edging towards the open-mouthed skull. Soon, they passed into darkness.

Sim listened to his own breathing in the darkness: deep, slow, and drawn out. The car made very little noise. Even the pretend jail bars around the sides failed to rattle, and it left him wondering if there was more purpose to them than mere theming. Were they meant to keep guests inside? Or something else out?

A floodlight switched on suddenly and bathed the car in a cone of warm yellow light. A siren sounded. Voices yelled. "Prisoners escaped. Prisoners escaped."

Sim blinked and tried to adjust his vision. "What the…?"

The noise turned deafening, the light disorientating. A wind blasted from somewhere, whistling through the bars and blasting everyone's faces. Jason hooted with laughter. Chrissy gaped at Sim in shock, her green eyes shining in the spotlight.

Sim chewed the inside of his cheek. *Is this part of the ride?*

The car bucked suddenly to the right, making everyone yell out. Then it bucked to the left. Next, it picked up speed and launched forward, hopping up and down as if it were bounding over rubble.

A van sped towards them in the darkness, its headlights piercing the shadows and merging with the overhead spotlight.

The sound of squealing tyres.

The acrid stench of burnt rubber.

The speeding van turned sideways and tipped over, sliding across the ground and throwing up sparks. The cell-car narrowly sped around it.

"Prisoners escaping from transport," said another voice in the darkness. "Officers responding."

Laughter cackled in the shadows to Sim's right as they passed by the overturned van, and he let out a scream as an arm shot out from around the side of one of its open rear doors.

Jason howled with laughter. "Easy there, Sim, it's just a special effect."

Sim was panting, but the adrenaline spike left him smiling. Chrissy, too, was enjoying the experience. It was just a ride.

Everything is under control.

The cell-car twisted and changed speeds, skidding almost to

a stop in places as it dodged around flashing police cars and barricades, before speeding up into a sprint. Several times, lunatic faces emerged from the shadows to scream at them. Mock gunfire barked and flashed, making everyone yelp with glee.

"Inmates have taken over the prison. All personnel exit immediately. Code Black. Code Black."

The cell-car turned a blind corner, presenting its riders with a breathtaking sight. Ahead of them was a prison yard with a guard tower rising behind it. In the yard, two dozen animatronics staged a riot, officers fighting orange-suited inmates with batons. Overhead, lights flashed along with the sound of a chopper. A sweeping wind blew down on them from the ceiling.

"Get those people out of here," a recorded voice yelled, and the car suddenly picked up more speed than ever, throwing Sim back in his seat. Chrissy pressed her head against his shoulder, laughing hysterically.

The car hopped up into the air and crashed back down again, then skidded sideways, almost tipping over. Finally, it sped in a straight line towards another police barrier, this one flanked by a pair of leering maniacs pointing knives at them.

Chrissy squealed

At the last moment, the cell-car skidded around an S-bend and sped on by. The sounds of the riot faded behind them.

"Prison locked down. Well done, Governor."

The cell-car burst its way through a set of double doors hidden in the darkness, and suddenly they were beneath the light of a hundred spotlights. A purple-robed figure met them, an animatronic with shining, lifelike eyes peering out of a hood. Sim wasn't sure how the effect was achieved, but it was uncanny.

"Welcome to my lair," said the imitation killer. "I am the Zodiac, and I shall be your host for the nightmares to come. Follow the rules and you may yet live. Disobey, and I will add you to the rest of my slaves in the afterlife. Keep your arms and legs inside your cell at all times. Do not attempt to escape. If you require assistance, pull the cord you see overhead."

Sim looked up and saw a red cord running along the top of the cage. It didn't fill him with confidence that such a thing existed.

The Zodiac lifted an arm and pointed behind him with a vicious-looking knife. They were in a 'between' space: the prison riot behind them and a pair of double doors ahead. To either side was a platform and fire exit. "Be gone with you," the killer roared, "before I get angry."

The car trundled forward and the Zodiac slashed his knife at them, inches from the bars. He growled like a demon.

"That is some fine engineering, Nealy," said Mike, nodding appreciatively.

"Thank you. I thought you'd approve. Did you enjoy the first part of the ride?"

Mike shrugged. "I've seen better, but I've also seen a lot worse. It passes muster."

"Good to know. With your involvement, perhaps we could look at further improvements."

"No doubt."

Sim was confused. "The Zodiac shot most of his victims. Why is he holding a knife?"

"Research showed that a gun would be too likely to cause panic," said Nealy. "Also, the Zodiac did stab two of his victims, if my facts are correct?"

"They are," said Sim, cursing himself internally. *How did I forget about Bryan Hartnell?*

"Good to know. It's important to me that this place is authentic. While also scaring the bejesus out of people, of course."

Gerry groaned. She seemed bored, slumped to one side and running a fingernail over her plump bottom lip.

Nealy sniffed. "I take it you're not impressed, Ms Trezeguet?"

"Boys and their toys. I prefer things of the flesh."

"I bet you do," said Jason.

"Okay," said Nealy. "On we go."

The double doors ahead opened up, and the car passed through, entering an unlit airlock – an empty corridor with another set of double doors ahead. A light in the gloom shone red but then turned green as soon as the doors behind them closed with a bang.

"What's next?" asked Jason. "I want to see the good stuff."

"All in good time, Mr Dreadful. These things need to proceed in a certain order."

"Don't want to blow your load too soon, huh?"

Nealy groaned. "For want of a better phrase."

Mike leaned forward so that his head poked between Sim and Chrissy. "Is this guy really a journalist?"

"He barely qualifies," said Chrissy, "but yes."

"Hey," said Jason. "I am very much a journalist. Why don't you tell good ol' boy Mike here about how I helped crack the case of Lee Christie's murder?"

Chrissy shrugged. "You got lucky."

"Did I heck. Hey, Mike, listen to this. Two years ago, in Wigan, a young lad named Lee Christie was stabbed by someone in a white hoodie. Everyone wrote it off as a gang-related murder, but I dug and dug and dug and found no evidence that Christie had ever so much as littered. No way could I let it lie, so I got everyone on the internet searching for clues. I got sent so much evidence to sift through that I was barely sleeping, but eventually I came across a video someone sent to me of Christie's former best friend bragging about how he was going to kill Christie over some girl he was sleeping with. A threat by itself wouldn't have been enough, but he happened to be wearing a white hoodie when he said it. I forwarded it on to the police, and what do you know, they got a confession. Because of me and my channel."

"If that's the case," said Mike, "then good work, I guess."

Jason nodded. "Some channels just report on the cases, but my channel actually does something to help."

Sim tensed. He wanted to say something, but Chrissy told him not to waste his breath. Jason would only wind him up more.

She's right. I'll just lose my cool and say something I regret. I don't even know why the guy gets under my skin. Maybe I am *jealous?*

Or maybe it's the injustice of a guy like him doing well.

The next set of doors opened and the car passed through. Sim had no idea what was coming, but he knew he wouldn't enjoy it.

CHAPTER SEVEN

AS THEY PASSED through into the next room, Nealy's walkie-talkie buzzed. He answered the call and sounded concerned. "What? How the hell did that happen? Handle it now, do you hear me? Right now!"

Mike turned back. "Everything all right, chief?"

"Yes, yes. Everything is under control. Just enjoy the tour." Strangely, Nealy reached out then and rattled the cell door, almost as if to test it.

Sim looked at the others, but no one else had noticed.

Is Nealy nervous about something? He doesn't look right.

Sim put a hand on Chrissy's leg, feeling an urge to protect her. But from what?

The car passed forward into what looked like the security checkpoint of a prison. There was a glass-windowed desk next to a walkthrough metal detector and an X-ray machine. Directly ahead of the cell-car was a barred gate. A prison gate.

The car came to a halt. The lights overhead died and were replaced by the red glow of emergency lamps.

"Okay," said Jason. "This ain't good."

"What's happening?" asked Chrissy, her voice a little shrill.

"Just a technical hiccup," said Nealy. He still held the

walkie-talkie in his hand, and Sim realised the man was trembling. "Just stay inside the car while my people fix it."

Sim bit down on his bottom lip. *Something's gone wrong. Why is Nealy—*

Someone cried out beyond the pretend checkpoint. It didn't sound like a recording. The shouting was accompanied by a clatter of disruption, of things being knocked over.

"What the hell is that?" Mike demanded. "Is there a problem here, Nealy?"

Nealy didn't seem his usual confident self. No hint of his gleaming smile. "Everything's fine. No cause for alarm, I assure you." He got back on the walkie-talkie and requested an update, his expression fixed in place as he listened to the answer.

Chrissy started shifting in her seat. Sim kept a hand on her leg but was transfixed by the shouting and the kerfuffle coming from nearby. Something was happening.

What is all that noise?

At first, Sim saw only a dash of movement, but then a half-naked man in his fifties appeared from around the side of the check-in desk. Bare-footed, he stepped forward, framed by the metal detector and coloured red by the emergency lighting. He glared at the guests inside the cell-car, while raising a hand to rip at his dank grey hair. No question who the man was: an inmate. His bright orange trousers made that patently obvious, along with the countless number of tattoos marring his naked chest.

Gerry cried out in horror. "An escapee!"

"It's okay!" Nealy urged. "Stay inside the car and everything will be okay."

Sim didn't know who the inmate was, but if he was locked up on this island, then there was no doubt he was highly dangerous. A maniac on the loose.

And he's staring right at us.

A brief moment followed where time seemed to stand still.

No sound. No movement. The only light was that of the flickering emergency lamps. The escaped lunatic screeched like a deranged ape.

Then he sprinted right at them.

Everyone inside the car panicked and screamed, Mike and Nealy included. This was clearly not part of the ride.

I knew I shouldn't have come, Sim scolded himself. *I should've listened to my gut.*

"Nealy!" Jason shouted. "Get us the hell out of here, man."

"Help is on its way. Just… Just stay inside the car."

The lunatic launched himself into the air and landed on the side of the car. His dirty hands gripped the cell bars. He yelled, spat, and spouted vile threats. Several of his teeth were rotten and brown. The car rocked from side to side under his shifting weight. The flickering red lights made his tattooed flesh appear bloodstained.

Chrissy threw herself against Sim and wailed in terror. Mike made threats, trying to warn the psychopath away.

"Welcome!" the lunatic bellowed, "to the Maniac Menagerie."

Sim frowned. *What?*

The killer leapt off the bars and backed away, then turned and ran back to where he had emerged, whooping and hollering and hopping up and down.

At the back of the car, Nealy let out a cackle.

Sim was the first to realise it had all been a prank, but Jason soon realised it, too. He grabbed his chest as if he were in pain. "Jesus, mate. I nearly had a heart attack. That was awesome!"

"It was grotesque," said Gerry with an unamused sneer. "A poor imitation of mental illness."

"Wait," said Chrissy, pulling her head away from Sim's shoulder. "That was… a joke?"

"Not a joke," said Nealy. "Part of the experience. Something no guest will ever forget."

Mike shook his head and grunted. "You got me there, Nealy. You got me! Thought I were gonna fill my briefs for a second."

Chrissy leaned forward and put a hand against her mouth. "I feel like I'm going to be sick. My heart is beating so fast. That was too much. Way too much."

Nealy put his hands together in a prayer gesture. "I promise that was the only jump scare of the tour. No more. You have my word."

Crissy put her head in her hands and leaned forward. Sim rubbed her back and glared at Nealy. "You should've warned us."

"I wanted you to get the full experience. Future guests will be warned to expect live actors, but I apologise for not offering you the same courtesy."

Chrissy took a big gasp of air, rubbed at her puffy eyes, then turned to scowl at Nealy. "You swear to me that nothing else like that will happen?"

Nealy nodded. "No more live actors. Just a nice relaxing tour from here on out."

Sim continued rubbing her back. "You okay to carry on? I'm happy to leave if—"

"I'm good," she said, steeling herself. "It... It was a good scare."

"That's the spirit," said Nealy. "Let's get back to it."

The car got moving again. The prison gate opened and they headed through it. On the wall, a white sign with red writing warned: **Dangerous Inmates Ahead!**

"Hey, Nealy," said Jason. "When do we get to see the Boxcutter Killer?"

Sim spun in his seat. "What? What are you talking about?"

Jason leaned around the back of Mike so he could see Sim. "Nealy told me they have the Boxcutter here. Can you believe that?"

"He's here? On this island?"

Mike frowned. "Boxcutter? That's your guy, right? UK's worst ever serial killer? A Hall of Famer?"

"The most sadistic murderer ever to stalk Britannia," said Nealy gravely, "and, yes, I have him right here inside the Keep."

Sim slumped against the bars. He tried to catch his breath but couldn't. Chrissy noticed his state and frowned at him. "You okay?"

He nodded, even though it was a lie. The Boxcutter was the one killer he refused to do an episode on. The man's crimes…

If ever a human being were possessed by the Devil, it was the Boxcutter Killer.

"The police only sentenced him a few months ago," said Chrissy, shaking her head at Nealy. "How did you even get him here?"

"It was expensive in more ways than money, I can tell you that. He is to be the island's star attraction, a truly terrifying creature. I've looked into his eyes, and I swear evil itself looked back at me."

"No shit," said Jason, shaking his head with a glint in his eyes. "He killed four police officers before they could take him down. Shot the guy twice and he still kept coming. The episode I did on him got over twenty million views. I made a shit tonne in advertising revenue."

Chrissy sneered distastefully. "He killed twenty-nine women."

Jason nodded. "And four men. A twenty year killing spree, never to be forgotten."

"How did they finally catch him?" asked Mike, adjusting his hat.

"One of his would-be victims escaped and identified him. He's all messed up, so it was pretty easy to find him after that."

"Sara Khan," said Sim. "The Boxcutter attacked her while she was walking her dog around a nearby pond one night. She leapt into the water to escape him and he didn't follow. She said afterwards that he seemed afraid of the water."

"Yeah," said Jason. "Something like that. I forget the deets, but that sounds about right."

"It is right," said Sim. He remembered it well for many reasons, not least of all because he also had a fear of water, having never learned to swim. It had made him realise, despairingly, that he and the killer shared something in common.

"You never did an episode about the guy, did you?" said Jason. "You missed a trick."

Chrissy spoke up. "We chose not to, out of respect for the victims and their families, as well as the last girl he abducted. She survived. If you can call it that."

Jason pointed a finger gun at her. "Jenny Pollack, right?"

Chrissy tutted. "*Jenna* Pollack."

"Ah, close enough."

Nealy cleared his throat. "We're about to enter A Block. I suggest you pay attention. You don't want to miss this."

Jason leaned back in his seat with a grin on his face as the car picked up speed.

But Sim couldn't grin. He felt like he was going to be sick, so he closed his eyes and held his breath. If he could have teleported himself away, he would have done so now, but the car continued forward, taking away his control. He truly was trapped inside a cell.

And somewhere on this island is a creature of pure evil.

They entered a room with a wraparound cinema screen playing a black-and-white newsreel. A silky-toned narrator welcomed them from a dozen hidden speakers.

What makes a killer? the film began. *What is it inside the hearts of men like Charles Manson, Peter Sutcliffe, and Andrei Chikatilo that makes them monsters? Which flavour of madness possessed Ed Gein when he turned his victim's flesh into furniture, or Jeffrey Dahmer when he ate and stored the body parts of murdered young men? Was it mental illness, brain damage, or is there such a thing as evil? And if so, how long has this wickedness been with us, and how do we create a world where it no longer exists? Hold on tight and see for yourselves what madness looks like up close. Perhaps you'll find the answers.*

The video changed, colourising, and the moustachioed face of H. H. Holmes – America's First Serial Killer – appeared on screen. The narrator started to recount the serial killer's crimes, starting with the construction of his 'Murder Castle,' but Sim quickly lost interest, his mind turning once again to the Boxcutter Killer. Or, to use his recently discovered name, William Kendall White.

"How do you hope to keep the Boxcutter locked up safely?" Sim found himself asking. He turned around to await an answer.

Nealy flinched. "Huh? Oh, well, I expect to keep him as safely locked up as he would be anywhere else. His cell is uniquely secured, and we feed him via a dumb waiter. No member of staff ever interacts with him directly."

"Is he allowed out of his cell?" asked Gerry. "He has a right to exercise, no?"

Nealy huffed. "That man has no right to anything, but we have it taken care of, regardless. He has access to a specially built area for physical activity."

"Like a pet rabbit," said Jason. "Cool."

"You could think of it that way," said Nealy. "Either way, the Boxcutter has what he needs, and far more than he deserves."

Mike was nodding. "So, how 'bout one of you crime experts gives me the lowdown on this guy? You got me curious."

"How can you not know?" Chrissy tucked her hair behind her ears and raised both eyebrows. "Don't you watch the news?"

"Trust me, miss. American news only cares about America. I try to avoid it wherever possible. Humour me."

Nealy spoke into his walkie-talkie and requested the car to

be stopped. He then lowered the unit onto his lap and put his hands together. "I think Mike should know what he's going to have the macabre pleasure of seeing, so someone please enlighten him."

"I wouldn't call it a pleasure," said Mike. "But still…"

Chrissy looked at Sim. She obviously wanted him to talk, but he didn't know if he could. But when he saw Jason preparing to open his mouth, he knew he had to. Jason would only butcher the details. "They call him the Boxcutter Killer," said Sim, "because he blinded his victims with a sharp, flat knife. The first murder was in 2002 in Felixstowe. They found Mary Farrier stuffed into the cupboard beneath the stairs of her home. Someone had poked out both her eyes and strangled her. This came after a recent spate of home robberies, where women had had many of their personal effects stolen."

"Perfecting his craft," said Chrissy. "Once he learned he could break into people's homes with impunity, his crimes escalated."

"Blah blah blah," said Jason. "The guy didn't kill again for another eighteen months, probably to make sure he got away with it. His next eventual victim, Chloe Paget, really had a tough time. The Boxcutter abducted her and tortured her for six days. Cut bits off of her to see how long she could last. Blinded her first, though, so she spent the entire nightmare in the dark."

Mike licked at his lips and grimaced. Sim actually liked the guy more for being visibly sickened by the story. Unlike Jason, who seemed to get a hard-on over death – the grizzlier, the better.

"Chloe Paget was found stuffed inside a fridge at the dump," said Sim. "The Boxcutter evolved his methods very little after that. His typical victim was female, of no particular type, and he abducted them late at night, taking them somewhere deserted – usually an abandoned factory or condemned house. There, he would torture them, cutting off bits of flesh or entire limbs, but always starting with the eyes. Most victims died of blood loss or the rapid onset of infection. This went on for twenty years until Sara Khan finally identified him."

"A proper freak," said Jason. "She said he had a face like dropped lasagne and that his body was all crippled and bent."

"Because his mother kept him in an under-the-stairs cupboard as a child," said Sim testily. "After they took William Kendall White into custody, a trauma specialist managed to get him talking. The tale he told was pretty grim. His mother, Barbara, used to lock him in a cupboard under the stairs for up to sixteen hours a day, usually to keep him out of the way while she had sex with men for money. As a result, his bones grew improperly and his eyesight developed poorly. His crimes are some of the worst in human history, but his mother is as responsible as he is. She raised a creature of pain and suffering."

"A monster," said Chrissy, nodding emphatically.

Sim nodded. "Barbara White went into a diabetic coma at forty-six and died, so we can't ask her to tell her side of the story. We don't know if she was mentally ill or just wicked."

Mike shook his head in disgust. "My mother was a piece of work herself, but I never doubted that she loved me. Almost makes you feel sorry for the guy, huh?"

"I wouldn't go that far," said Nealy. "But it goes to show that evil might be a consequence of upbringing. Current theories suggest William Kendall White sought revenge on his mother by blinding and mutilating dozens of women. I would ask him, but he hasn't spoken a word since he arrived on the island."

"So how did he evade capture for twenty years?" asked Mike, still looking queasy. "That's a hell of a run."

Sim shrugged, wishing he had the definitive answer, but truthfully, it was just a plain failure on behalf of the police. "The random nature of William's victims, along with the fact he moved around a lot, living off the grid, made it hard to predict his next move. Some say he struck only when he was certain of success, as cautious as a fox. Others say he was ignored because he was homeless – effectively invisible."

"He used to cover himself from head to toe in order to hide his deformities," Chrissy added, "which also made him difficult to identify. It also meant there were never any fingerprints or hair at the scene. Nor was there any sexual element to his crimes, which often leaves DNA behind."

"He's also intelligent," said Sim. "Apparently, he spent a lot of his days in public libraries, where it was warm, finding a quiet corner and reading for hours on end. He gave people the creeps, so they usually left him in peace."

Jason was smirking. "Once I get an interview with that freak, my channel is going to hit the stratosphere. In fact, I'm gonna make it the opening episode for my TV show when it launches."

Sim shuffled in his seat and let out a breath. Just thinking about the Boxcutter made him feel lightheaded. Fortunately, Jason was there to distract him with his own brand of vileness. "Do you have any trace of empathy, man?"

"I don't think he does," said Chrissy. She looked over and scowled at Jason. "I bet you celebrate whenever you hear there's been a murder. Money in the bank, right?"

Jason rolled his eyes. "It ain't even like that. You got to make light of this shit or it eats away at you. Look, just because Sim has a dark and tortured past doesn't mean everyone else has to dedicate themselves to being depressed and boring."

Sim shook his head. "No one wants to hear from you any more. Shut your mouth."

Chrissy frowned at Sim. "What is he talking about, dark and tortured past?"

"God knows." He glared at Jason, wishing he could reach out and slap him with his mind. *Just keep your mouth closed and don't talk about things you don't understand. Especially when it concerns me.*

Jason stared back at Sim for a moment, but then he cleared

his throat and looked away. "I'm just screwing around." He shrugged his shoulders and pulled his cap around so the peak was at the front. "This stuff screws with your mind if you let it, so it's important to keep your smile."

Gerry nodded. "Detachment is important in our line of work. You must keep the light inside of you shining or else the darkness can get inside and poison you. *Oui*?"

"Wee-wee," said Jason.

Sim grunted and turned back to face front. "I can handle the darkness. It's vultures like him I can't deal with. Can we just get on with the tour?"

"All right," said Nealy. "You folks want to see something cool, because here it comes."

CHAPTER
EIGHT

A BLOCK WAS EXACTLY like you would expect a prison ward to look like. Again, using forced perspective, the large space seemed to rise up four storeys, but the balconies were clearly facades, their cells empty and with no obvious way to reach them. The cells on the ground floor, however, were very much real. Real and inhabited.

The car slowed down to a crawl and moved alongside the first set of cells.

Chrissy put a hand to her mouth and spoke through her fingers. "Is that… Miguel Reyes?"

"Yes," said Nealy. "Responsible for the death of six people in the summer of 1998."

"He shot his neighbours because he thought they'd been taken over by aliens," said Sim, staring at the old man sitting on the cot bed. He looked so frail.

The cell was large, the size of a decent living room, with a television, bed, small sofa, and what looked like a kitchenette. At the back was a small door that might've led to a private bathroom. But despite the comfortable accommodation, Miguel Reyes sat silently, staring at the floor.

"I thought he was diagnosed with schizophrenia," said Chrissy. "Shouldn't he be in a hospital?"

"We have a medical team here at the island," said Nealy. "Reyes is closely monitored."

"Because he's a suicide risk," said Jason. "Right? Doesn't he have a habit of trying to kill himself?"

Nealy shook his head. "Not since he arrived here. As I say, we have the resources here that no other prison or hospital has. Reyes is well taken care of, and our facilities will only improve."

Sim studied Reyes once again and saw an empty vessel. The old man was either heavily dosed, or he had gone some place inside his own mind. The room's television played cartoons without sound.

The car moved on.

Sim saw and recognised several other inmates. Seth Markle, the Kissimmee Killer: responsible for bludgeoning four tourists in Orlando with a hammer. Abdul Achebe, responsible for abducting and murdering three young girls in Nigeria. Simon Cruz from the Philippines, known as 'the Kraken', drowned seven women in the ocean near his home. And James Sachs, the London banker whose perverted desires led to him killing five high-end escorts in various hotel rooms. His money almost bought him out of trouble until a *Daily Mail* journalist exposed him.

It was a surreal daydream. Sim had made videos about these vile men, but they had never truly been real, just boogeymen in news articles and Netflix series. Almost fictional – their crimes historical.

But here they are, right in front of me. Real-life murderers. Monsters with an urge to slaughter and mutilate. Soulless human beings.

Everyone else was equally in awe. Even Jason was silent. Chrissy shook her head constantly and gasped, and she did so now, only this time she turned and grabbed Sim by his arm. "Oh my God, look!"

Sim leaned forward and stared into the next cell. Like the others, it was kitted out with various comforts and entertainment, only this one had an easel and paint canvass in the middle of the floor. Upon the canvass was a half-painted depiction of an intricate machine – like something out of an H. R. Giger drawing. The cell's inmate was sitting in an armchair watching television, a lanky, far-eastern man with a tussle of black hair. It was Lee Chen.

An innocent man.

Like the other inmates, Lee Chen did not seem happy, but unlike them, he was no killer.

"That's Lee Chen," said Jason. "The Shanghai Spike. Wow. That guy is responsible for, what, like, nineteen murders?"

"We don't think he did it," said Chrissy. "We did a three-part series on how the Chinese Government scapegoated him because they couldn't find the real killer. The only evidence they had against him was a witness who had obviously been coerced."

Jason rolled his eyes and chuckled. "Leave the investigating to me, guys. Lee Chen is guilty. Look at him. Pure psycho."

Sim did not see it. Lee Chen had been a ship engineer and was a talented artist. It was true that the murders coincided with his time ashore, but he was an educated man with a wife and child. His upbringing was healthy, and he had been a model citizen prior to his arrest. Nothing about the man fit the profile of a serial killer. "He's been hurting himself," she said. "His arms are bandaged."

Nealy sighed. "Yes. I'm afraid he's had a tough time settling in. He barely speaks a word of English, and his mind needs a great deal of occupying."

"Smarter than your average killer," said Gerry. "I, too, have my doubts about this man's guilt. I would like to interview him, *oui*?"

"Of course," said Nealy. "I will make it happen. Anything to help manage his time here will be most welcome."

"Do you have your own team of psychologists here, Mr Nealy?" she asked.

"Not as yet. We have three doctors and six nurses, but no mental health specialists right now."

Chrissy turned around in her seat. "How can that be? You have men like Reyes who need special care. You can't pull them out of hospitals and leave them in cells without support."

"My doctors are more than capable of handling things, Ms Wise. Of course, I will continue to recruit and grow our team here as time goes on."

Lee Chen looked up and stared at the passing car as if he had noticed it for the first time. He then stood and walked over to the bars of his cell, but he didn't speak or reach out to them. He only stood there. His eyes were two inky pools of sadness.

"He shouldn't be here," said Chrissy. "He's not like the others."

"I disagree," said Nealy. "He was convicted and sentenced like every other inmate here, and without my involvement, he would be rotting in a Chinese prison. I give him as much freedom as I can allow."

"What freedom?" asked Mike. "Poor fella looks about ready to end himself."

Nealy sounded flustered as he spoke. Perhaps he hadn't expected this kind of resistance. He pointed ahead, as if seeking to move on. "Look, this is where the prisoners may leave their cells for rec time."

A circular area lay ahead, surrounded by four orderlies – men in white jackets sporting telescopic batons. In the middle of the circle, two people played chess, shackles around their ankles.

Sim edged over to the side of the bench, pushing his face between the bars. He couldn't believe what he was seeing. Dominic Woodward and Francine Mescal sitting opposite one another. One was 'the Huntsman', an Alaskan native who liked to shoot human beings for sport. The other was a French nurse who enjoyed suffocating patients with a pillow.

Gerry put a hand to her head and groaned. "*Beur!* It is only a matter of time before someone gets 'urt in this place."

"I promise you that will not happen," said Nealy.

"What if they escape? What will you do if one of these madmen attacks your guests?"

"It won't happen," said Nealy testily. "I have taken every precaution."

"You 'ave two killers out in the open playing chess. It is folly."

Mike put a hand up to calm her. "I have to say, she's right to be concerned, Nealy. Any mishaps at a place like this will be expensive. It's a lawsuit waiting to happen."

"No," said Nealy. "The island will be accessible only to those over the age of eighteen, and all guests will sign a waiver. This place is no more dangerous than a safari. Also, security will be increased threefold once the Keep opens to the public and starts generating income."

"Great," said Sim. "So you're understaffed?"

Nealy ignored the question.

Mike took off his hat and turned it in his hands while he appeared to think things over. "I'm on the fence here, buddy. On the one hand, I see the potential in this place – it truly is one of a kind – but on the other, I want to run a million miles from this island. Even I find this to be in poor taste."

"Then come on board and help me get it right, Mike. Give me your ideas. This tour is only a small part of what we can do here."

Mike nodded. "I didn't say I'm out, but my price has just gone up. We'll talk."

"Onwards then," said Nealy, sounding a little defeated.

The car rotated slightly to face the chess game. A stench wafted into the car.

Chrissy wrinkled her nose. "Eh, that's gross. Smells like…"

"Doodoo," said Jason, and he chuckled. "Looks like the Huntsman didn't bother to put his hand up."

Sim noticed, with horror, that Dominic Woodward had soiled himself. The right leg of his orange trousers had darkened, and something vile trickled down the side of his white plimsoll. It clearly wasn't an accident, because both he and his chess partner were cackling.

Nealy growled. "Dirty little..." He stood up in his seat and poked an arm through the bars. "Leon, John... get this pair back inside their cells and hose 'em down. Forty-eight hours lock-up for the both of them."

The four orderlies moved into the circle with their batons raised. This overt threat prompted Dominic Woodward, a strapping outdoorsman who had spent twelve years living in the woods, to launch himself out of his chair and rush the closest man. He had shit on his hands and immediately grabbed at the orderly's face, smearing it over his mouth and lips. The orderly sprawled backwards in disgust, spitting and gagging.

Francine Mescal shouted something in French, perhaps a warning, but she did nothing as the other three orderlies beat Woodward to the ground with their batons. The big man did not scream or cry out; he only laughed.

Two more orderlies appeared from somewhere at the rear of the prison and helped drag both prisoners away. Their cackling echoed throughout the cell block.

The stench of human shit pervaded the air.

Chrissy heaved and covered her mouth.

"You okay?" Sim put a hand on her back.

She shook her head and looked at him with tears in her eyes. "I-I need to get out. I... I'm going to—" She pushed her head against the bars and vomited through the gap.

"Jesus," said Jason. "Lunch overboard."

Gerry cursed in French, either because she disliked vomit or was angry that Chrissy had been pushed into producing some.

Sim tried to soothe her, and then he turned to glare at Nealy. "She needs to get out."

"Just take a breath," he said. "In a moment, you'll be fi—"

Chrissy puked again.

"She needs to get out now! Stop the goddamn car."

Mike grunted. "Do it, Nealy. Poor girl's turning inside out."

Nealy grumbled into his walkie-talkie and the car came to a stop. He did not look happy. Unlike everything else, this clearly had not gone to plan. "Do I need to have a nurse come, Ms Wise?"

Chrissy shook her head, holding her wrist against her nose and wiping vomit from the side of her mouth. "No... I just need to get some air. Maybe a drink. Can I... Can I get off here?"

Nealy looked around cautiously. "I can have someone come down to escort you, but the tour will continue."

"That's fine." She didn't sound like she cared even a little. "I'll catch up with you all afterwards."

Sim nodded, pinching his nose closed. "Let us off, Nealy."

No!" said Chrissy. "You stay."

"What? No way. I'm not staying here without you."

"I want you to see the whole thing. One of us needs to. I'll be fine."

Sim frowned at her. "You're still interested in this place? After what we just saw?"

Nealy hissed in annoyance. "What you just witnessed is a common occurrence in every prison in the world. Inmates play up. My staff dealt with it and no one was hurt."

"Tell that to shitface," said Jason. "I think he just unlocked a new core memory."

"He'll be fine. Now look, anyone who wishes to leave the tour can do so now, but this project will go ahead with or without your involvement. I highly suggest you consider being a part of it because, once the wrinkles are ironed out, it will be the most visited tourist attraction in all of Europe."

Chrissy looked at Sim with watery eyes. "He's right. We can't miss out on this."

"Not if you want to join me in the premier league," said Jason. "Only the big dogs survive up here."

Sim rolled his eyes. "Not talking to you, man."

Nealy grumbled. "I'll have someone come down to clean the mess. You all have one minute to decide whether or not you're staying." He lifted his walkie-talkie and requested assistance. Soon, another orderly appeared. The man reached inside the car to unlock the cell door and then stood back.

"I really think I should go with you," said Sim as Chrissy stood up from the front bench.

Once again, she shook her head. "No, honestly, stay. I'm just grossed out by the smell, that's all. I'll be fine once I get some air. Eyes wide open, right?"

Sim nodded, although he couldn't bring himself to say the words back.

Jason reached around the back of Mike and patted Sim on the back. "Come on, mate. You'll be okay without your babysitter for an hour or two."

Sim shrugged away his hand. "Stay out of it. And don't touch me."

Jason put his hands up and backed off. "All right, mate. Don't shit yourself."

Mike tittered. Gerry muttered in French.

Chrissy hopped out of the cell and quickly turned to block Sim from following. She placed a hand on the gate and slammed it closed. "Stay, Sim. Have a blast. Tell me all about it later, okay?"

"Are... are you really sure?"

"Yes! I just need to eat. I don't do well with an empty stomach. You enjoy the rest of the tour. I'll catch up with everyone later."

Nealy nodded at the orderly, who was still waiting obediently. "Take her to the cafeteria for some lunch. I'm sorry you're feeling unwell, Ms Wise."

"No problem. A bunch of free food will make everything better."

He nodded. "Enjoy all you wish."

Sim still wanted to get out. His gut told him to. But… "All right," he said. "Take it easy. Love you."

"Love you, too."

Jason went to speak, but Sim shot him a glare that kept him quiet.

"Let us leave this place," said Gerry. "I cannot take any more of this odour."

Mike waved a hand in front of his face. "Yeah, Nealy, get us moving, won't you? And what the hell are you feeding your prisoners?"

Nealy chuckled and got back on the walkie-talkie. Within seconds, the car started moving again.

Sim looked out through the bars, watching Chrissy depart with the orderly who was leading her towards a staff area at the rear of the cell block. A puddle of vomit glistened on the floor behind her.

Palmer got off the walkie-talkie with Nealy and then kicked the leg of his chair. He had chosen Woodward and Mescal because they were two of the prison's calmer inmates. Nealy had wanted a display for his guests – two killers out in the open. Lions in the wild.

How was I supposed to know they would stage a dirty protest?

Because the two of them are insane and shouldn't be on display for tourists.

Gibbons had turned in his chair and was smirking at Palmer. He pulled off his baseball cap and readjusted his ponytail before placing it back on his head. "Shocker, huh? A right shitshow."

"Not funny," said Palmer, although a chuckle escaped him.

"It could've been worse. At least Woodward didn't wipe his arse on the guests."

"Yeah, there is that." Palmer studied the CCTV feeds. Christina Wise had exited the ride and was en route to the cafeteria with an orderly. Nealy wouldn't be happy about that. Palmer had got the impression the island's project was on thin ice, and the current guests were vital in keeping Nealy's dream alive. Mike Rondon was the fifth richest man in Texas. Ms Trezeguet had one of the most watched television shows in France – her endorsement would help legitimise the Keep. The YouTubers were more puzzling, but then the internet was a foreign world to Palmer, full of teens and young adults with no idea how the world ran, or how lucky they were to waste their lives gurning in front of a camera. The future did not look bright for mankind.

"Hey," said Gibbons. "I can't get Frank on the radio. D'you know where he's at?"

Palmer frowned. Frank was floor lead, in charge of security of the prison areas. It was his duty to be contactable at all times. "When did you last hear from him?"

Gibbons shrugged. "Few hours ago."

"And you're only bringing this to my attention now?"

"Hey, you're the man in charge. I assumed you knew what was happening with your own team. Clearly not."

"Don't start with me, Gibbons. I'm in no mood."

"Woodward's chocolate factory was your fuck-up, boss, not mine."

Palmer crossed the floor and approached Gibbons. The younger man was almost lying down in his chair, legs stretched out in front of him. "I don't care about that. I care about your attitude towards your role, and that you have been aware of a missing member of staff for several hours and haven't reported it. That is unacceptable, and I'd say you've just made it onto my last nerve."

Palmer had made a career out of chewing up and spitting

out subordinates, but Gibbons showed no sign of being the slightest bit bothered by the reprimand. In fact, he sat up and leaned forward, staring impassively at Palmer. "Listen, boss. You need to realise something, right? This ain't Afghanistan or some training exercise in Belize. There ain't no civilians to terrorise here, just a rich geezer's playground destined to make the world a worser place. So relax and stop giving me a hard time. The job ain't that hard."

Palmer was without words. He'd faced insubordination a thousand times before, but Gibbons's fecklessness was on another level. How did this idiot expect to keep his job?

Too late for that. He's gone. I don't trust him.

But I need him while there are guests here this weekend.

Palmer suddenly snapped to life. He grabbed Gibbons by his shirt and yanked him to his feet. The younger man growled but didn't struggle. "Easy there, boss. Don't want someone to get hurt."

"Have you got a screw loose, Gibbons? Nealy is paying you top rate to be here, and you're going to throw that away because of laziness?"

"It ain't laziness, believe me. Let's just say you and I have different priorities."

"My priorities are your priorities, you moron. After this weekend, you're done, and if you don't do your job until then, I'll break both your arms and send you home weeping."

Gibbons's expression remained impassive until, slowly, a smile crept onto his face. "I'm just messing with you, boss. Can't you handle a little banter?"

Palmer shoved Gibbons backwards, sending him into his seat and rocketing against his desk. A split second of fury crossed the younger man's face, and that was enough to fill Palmer with satisfaction. "You finish up this weekend and I'll talk to Nealy about sending you home with an extra week's pay. Fuck with me one more time and I won't be so generous."

"All right, all right." Gibbons continued smirking. "I'll be a good little lad, okay? You don't have to worry about me. I know the systems like the back of me hand. I'm in complete control of everything."

"You'd better be." Palmer turned and stormed away, needing to take a minute to calm himself. He might not have PTSD, but his years in the army had left him less than whole. Violence was always a single heartbeat away, and he had to keep control of himself to prevent it from spilling out.

If I beat the hell out of Gibbons, I'll be even more shorthanded.
And what the hell happened to Frank?

CHAPTER
NINE

THE CELL-CAR EXITED A Block and entered a new area, one that caused a knot to form in Sim's stomach. Thunder struck from hidden speakers and an electric light flickered, its focus upon a sign on the wall:

Maximum-Security Cell Block

They were now inside a corridor with a long, featureless grey wall to their left and several square windows to their right, although the windows were actually plastic screens with images projected onto them from behind. The current effect was that of heavy rainfall and a full, shining moon. The simulated downpour was at once unsettling and soothing.

"This is lit," said Jason, wriggling in his seat and irritating Mike in front of him.

Sim might have agreed, but his mind was on Chrissy. He still felt like he should've gone with her. If she was feeling unwell, he wanted to be at her side.

But she doesn't need you at her side. She can take care of herself. In fact, most of the time she takes care of herself and *you.*

I should just do what she says and enjoy the rest of the tour.

"Here comes the Boxcutter," said Jason. "I know it."

Sim shuddered. It was only the fear of embarrassment that forced him to keep a hold of himself. He couldn't bear the thought of Jason's mockery, so he remained inside the vehicle, unable to escape his fears. Unable to know what was coming next.

Stop freaking out. Everything is under control. It has to be.

If the Boxcutter really was here, then Nealy would have done absolutely everything necessary to keep the monster secure. No reason to be afraid. At least, no more than Nealy intended for him to be.

Doors ahead opened and the cell-car passed through. What Sim and the others encountered next was like something out of a Thomas Harris novel.

The cells in this block were far bigger than those in A Block, and instead of bars, they were glass fronted. Sim half expected a Hannibal Lector lookalike to jump out at them, but everything was still.

They were being watched.

To the right was a raised platform with a booth on top of it. Inside that booth was a pair of guards in blue prison uniforms. They had been chatting between themselves but stood to attention when they saw Nealy.

"How is everything?" Nealy called out to them. One of the two men responded that all was well.

"That's good to hear," said Gerry. "But I lack confidence after what I've seen so far."

"Don't," said Nealy. "This is the area where we keep our more dangerous inmates. They are monitored continuously and the guards here are armed at all times."

Sim relaxed slightly, but not enough to feel completely at ease. He tried to count the cells ahead and spotted at least a dozen.

A dozen bloodthirsty maniacs.

They were moving up on the first cell right now. Everyone

turned to their left and peered through the bars around the vehicle. The cell behind the glass was sparsely furnished, with a bed and a desk being the most prominent features. Fixed to the top of the glass facade, a sign identified the inhabitant as 'FERAL FRED'.

Sim gasped. "Oh my God. You have Fredric Rougeau here?"

"Indeed," said Nealy. "A very odd fellow. I speak a little French, but not the kind he does."

Once again, Mike appeared nonplussed. "Feel like I should know who this guy is. Feral Fred?"

Jason was grinning. "You never heard of Feral Fred? Kid grew up in the sewers beneath Paris. His mum was a vagrant who lived on the streets. Often she would go underground where it was warm and dry, and she raised a kid there so the government wouldn't step in and take him into care. Problem was, she died of sepsis when Fred was six, and he had to survive down there all alone. They say he didn't speak to another human being for ten years until the day they arrested him."

"He killed to feed himself," said Gerry. "*Oui*? For many years, Feral Fred was an urban legend in France. Homeless people kept going missing in Paris – every month for years. It was said that a monster living in the sewers was eating them. When the authorities finally went underground to investigate, they found the bones of over fifty people."

"They also found Fred," said Jason with a ghoulish grin. "Kid came at them like a vampire. Two police officers quit the force afterwards because they were so screwed up because of it."

"*Oui*," said Gerry. "They were traumatised. Poor men."

"So where is this guy?" said Mike. He took off his hat and tilted his head towards the bars. "I wanna see the crazy little fella."

Sim looked through the bars and into the cell, but he saw no one inside. At the back was an open door leading to a bathroom. Was Feral Fred inside?

Nealy tutted. "I'm afraid our Parisian guest is a little shy, and he doesn't do well with open spaces."

"He's hiding?" said Jason. "The kid who killed and ate dozens of people is hiding?"

"He does not wish to be on display," said Gerry. "Who can blame him?"

Jason stood up in his seat and started banging on the cell bars around the car. "Hey! Hey, Fred-meister, get out here and say hello!"

Mike was knocked forward by an errant elbow and yelled out irritably. "Eejit!"

Sim hissed. "Sit the hell down, Jason."

"Yes," said Nealy. "I must insist."

Jason pulled a face. "What? I just want to see the goods. That's why we're here, isn't it? To see evil up close."

Gerry tutted. "Fredric Rougeau is not evil. He never had a chance to grow properly or develop an understanding of right and wrong."

"And he only killed bad people," said Sim, and then regretted it. It was a theory of his, not a fact.

Jason was still standing, but he looked down at Sim with a frown. "Huh?"

Sim took in a breath and let it out slowly. He knew Jason wouldn't let it lie, so it was best he just explained. "While the murders were happening, the homeless community in Paris came out and said that the people disappearing were the worst amongst them. The rapists and drug addicts. The ones who had habits they would do anything to feed."

"I also heard this," said Gerry. "Some in Paris called the killer *le Contrôleur Antiparasitaire*. The Pest Controller."

Jason nodded appreciatively. "I didn't know that."

"That's because you don't research your subject or care

about the truth," said Sim. "You only care about clicks. Whatever's most outrageous, right?"

Jason rolled his eyes. "I didn't make the game, mate. I just play it. Don't hate on me for getting a higher score than you because it just makes you seem jealous."

"I agree," said Gerry, giving Sim an apologetic look. "I think you are dealing with issues of resentment. You clearly dislike Mr Dreadful's success, when it would be healthier for you to concentrate on your own."

Jason clicked his fingers and nodded. "Nailed it. You just do you, Sim, and let me do me. To each his own, right?"

Sim shook his head and sneered. "So now you're Mr live-and-let-live? How many times have you dissed me on your channel? How many times have you invaded a person's privacy for one of your doorstep ambushes? I run my channel with integrity. I report the truth and only the truth."

Jason nodded in agreement. "Still sounds like you're jealous, though, mate."

"Enough!" said Nealy. "We're about to approach the next cell."

Sim folded his arms and gritted his teeth almost hard enough to make his molars crack. He glanced, one last time, at Feral Fred's cell, and this time he thought he saw the slightest movement from the bathroom doorway. Before he could tell, one way or the other, the cell-car moved along.

The next cell wasn't empty, but it might as well have been. Whoever was inside was lying beneath the covers on the bed, either asleep or, like Feral Fred, not wanting to be on display. The sign for this cell read **Jimmy Preswick: Brisbane Brutalist.**

The cell after that had an old man sitting at a desk reading a book, not even noticing the cell-car as it rolled by. **Edward Gotz: The Composer.**

Carlos Escoban: The Columbian Strangler was next, also barely visible, as he was slumped down on the far side of his bed.

Nealy was clearly frustrated, having said nothing for the last five minutes. Jason spewed disappointed comments in a constant stream while Gerry looked bored. Only Mike tried to be upbeat, no doubt seeing dollar signs drifting away from him and not wanting to accept the fact.

"They're never going to cooperate," said Sim. "Killers like to take control, not give it."

"They've never done this before," said Nealy. "It's... not ideal."

Jason huffed. "Course they didn't do it until now. They waited until they could shaft you. Did you forget they're sadists?"

Nealy shook his head and seemed like he was biting down on an urge to shout. Sim agreed with Jason. For all his success and money, Nealy should have seen this coming.

"Can't you tempt them out?" asked Mike. "That's how we train the sea lions at my parks. Play nice for the guests and they get a fish."

Gerry groaned. "Once again, they are people, not animals. You cannot force them to perform."

"No," said Mike, "of course not. That's why I used the word *tempt*."

"It's the right idea, Mike," said Nealy. "I'm sure I can come to some kind of agreement regarding good behaviour. They already have it good here, but I could offer further rewards."

"A deal with the Devil," said Gerry. "Start negotiating with them and you no longer hold all the power. That's a bad way to run a prison."

"But a good way to run a business," said Mike.

Sim had to admit he was disappointed. Two of the killers who had failed to show were ones he'd yet to do an episode on. It would've been an experience to see them in the flesh before filming about them. Carlos Escoban was the exception in that the third episode of *Grim Tales* had been about the cartel hitman. It was said he'd killed over two hundred people, but no one really knew. Sim considered him more dangerous than most, because he was a professional killer, not a sociopath acting upon base urges.

The cell-car continued at a slow pace. Too slow, in fact. Sim was actually feeling bored. And hungry. He thought about Chrissy and wondered what she was eating. If he could click his fingers, he would join her.

But she wants me to finish the tour, so I will.

Just got to pass by a dozen maniacs first.

The next cell wasn't empty, which filled everyone with cheer. A perverse kind of cheer when you considered what they were happy about. There was a woman inside the cell, staring right out at them through the glass, her face a blotchy, unattractive mess. Her hair was greasy and tangled. The sign above her cell proclaimed her to be **Brenda Bates: The John Killer.**

"Oh, wow," said Mike. "She ain't no looker, that's for sure. This is the dyke hooker that killed a bunch of men on The Strip, right?"

"Foolish men," said Gerry. "Those who live in vice dig a pit for themselves. Dig too deep and they never get out."

Hiring a prostitute wasn't exactly upstanding behaviour in Sim's opinion, but the five men Brenda had shot hadn't deserved to die. Two of her victims had ostensibly been guilty of little more than loneliness.

Sim studied Brenda Bates, trying to recognise something within her gaze. She tilted her head curiously at him, almost like she knew him, which of course was impossible. Perhaps, as he tried to understand her, she was trying to understand him.

Was this woman evil? Or just damaged? If he passed her on the street, would he instinctively feel something dark and repulsive? Or would she be no different from any other stranger?

What is inside her that's different from the rest of us?

Or is the capacity to kill universal?

Brenda placed a hand against the glass. For a moment, it appeared she might wave, but then she bared her teeth and bit into her wrist. The act was so sudden, so violent, that it sent Sim flinching back against his seat. "No, don't!"

The others in the car were slower to react, but when the first signs of blood appeared, they groaned in unison. Brenda had torn a sizeable chunk out of her wrist, hot blood spilling down her forearm. She smeared her wound over the glass, glaring at them as she did so. After a moment, she spat the chunk of her own flesh against the glass, where it stuck for a moment before sliding down.

"Hell's bells, Nealy." Mike shook his head. "Again? This rodeo is getting out of hand."

Nealy groaned and got on his walkie-talkie, but he put it back down when he saw the two guards rushing out of the security booth and racing over to Brenda's cell. One of them swiped a magnetic keycard over a sensor on the pillar between cells, and a section of the glass wall popped open. Both men wore handguns on their hips, but they entered the cell with batons raised.

Brenda broke her silence. She turned towards the men and screeched. "Fuckers!"

The first guard stepped up to her and barked a warning. "Brenda, calm down. We need to get that wound seen to."

"Let me die, fuckers." She spat a mouthful of blood, spattering the guard's boots. To the man's credit, he didn't react. He stood his ground, firmly and calmly. "Please, Brenda. No one wants to hurt you. You need to calm down."

"I'll hurt you, pig. Male pig! Try to put your hands on me, I'll kill you."

Nealy leaned against the bars at the back of the car. He shook his head and moaned. Sim got the impression he was unused to being an impotent observer of events outside his control.

"She likes jokes," said Sim.

Jason looked at him as though he were mad. "What?"

"She likes jokes. All the interviews I've seen of Brenda... she likes to joke around. It calms her."

"Yeah, good one, mate. You go out there and give her your best stand-up routine."

The guard with the blood on his boots took another step towards Brenda. Her wrist was bleeding badly; there was a possibility she'd torn an artery or vein. The guard had his baton raised, but he held it behind him while reaching forward with an empty hand. "Come on now, Brenda. You know me, don't you? I don't want to hurt you. I just need you to put on some ankle restraints for me so we can get you some help. It's for everybody's safety."

"Fuck you! I'm not letting you shackle me like a slave."

"Brenda, if you don't do it voluntarily..." The guard's voice suddenly had a nervous flutter, a slip of self-control. As calm as he seemed, the man clearly understood he was in a small room with a very dangerous woman.

And Brenda recognised that fear. Baring her teeth, she leapt at the guard and grabbed his head between her hands. Then, like a kid biting into an apple, she clamped her teeth down on the guard's cheek. He immediately screamed and whirled around, but Brenda didn't let go.

The other guard reacted, striking Brenda on the side of the knee with his baton. It sent her stumbling backwards, but she used the momentum to roll over her cot bed to the other side. She then used the cot as a barrier between them, raising her bloody wrist and snarling. "Come near me and I'll bite your throat."

The wounded guard clutched his face and cursed. Blood stained both his hands. His baton lay on the floor by his feet. The other guard stood on the other side of the bed, warning Brenda to get down on the ground. But the more he shouted, the wilder she got, transforming into an animal little by little. She yanked at her hair, spat blood, and kicked at the bed.

"Stand down!"

"I'll kill you!"

Nealy was shaking his head repeatedly. He got on his walkie-talkie and called for backup. Gerry had stood up in her seat but could only watch in horror. Mike muttered beneath his breath.

Jason caught Sim's eye. He'd gone pale, his expression tormented. "This is bad," he said.

True. The guard and Brenda were at a stalemate, and the danger was nowhere near done. If she got the better of the man, there was no telling what she might do. The guard with the torn cheek had got off easy. Nealy had built a keep and filled it full of caged lions.

And that guard is escalating things. You don't corner a lion.

"Stand down, Brenda, or I'll have to use force."

Sim reached for the cell door. At first it wouldn't open, but then he spotted a small red button above it. It was an emergency release, and it caused the cell door to make a clunking sound. When he pushed the door, it swung open.

"What are you doing?" Jason asked incredulously.

"I honestly don't know." Sim stepped through the door and out onto the flat walkway running alongside the cells. Nealy was distracted by his conversation over the walkie-talkie, but when he saw Sim out of the car, he immediately shouted at him to get back inside.

Sim didn't know why, but he ignored the warnings and headed around the cell-car. Brenda stood shrieking in front of him, separated only by a sheet of reinforced glass. She noticed him immediately but kept her focus on the guard, who was currently trying to get around the bed to hit her with the baton. The injured guard was by the door, blocking it, and when he saw Sim, he waved him away. "St-Stay back, sir!"

But Sim went up to the glass, peering at the bloody serial killer on the other side. A woman who had grown up in a trailer with a meth-addicted mother. A woman who had turned to prostitution in order to feed herself. Who was then subjected to rape and beatings until she finally snapped. A woman who often spoke in interviews about her childhood dream of becoming a comic book artist.

"H-Hey, Brenda." His voice was shaky, so he tried again. "Hey. My name is Sim."

She side-eyed him, still wary of the guard. "Fuck off, Sim. Unless you want to end up like the other guy."

Sim looked over at the wounded guard, clutching his face in the corner. "Yeah, that was pretty cheeky of you."

She frowned at him, her rage knocked aside for a second. "What the hell are you talking about? Who are you? I'm not into black guys, so go to Hell."

"I already told you, my name's Sim. You're Brenda, right? I know all about you."

The guard glared at him. "What're you doing? Get back inside the car before you get hurt."

Sim shook his head, maintaining eye contact with Brenda as much as he could. People often thought she hated all men, but that wasn't true. In interviews, she spoke fondly of a male teacher who had once taken an interest in her, and about a beloved boyfriend from high school who had died in a car crash. "She won't hurt me. Brenda only hurts bad men, right?"

Brenda bared her bloodstained teeth. "How do I know you're not bad?"

He moved right up against the glass, holding Brenda's gaze. "Because I don't want anything from you. All I want is for nobody else to get hurt."

She turned her glare back on the guard. "Then tell him to back off."

"He can't. His job is to make sure you're safe. He needs to get your arm taken care of, to keep you from bleeding to death."

"No. No, he's just like all the rest."

Sim shook his head. "I understand why you hurt those men. You were just protecting yourself. Michael Johnson was cheating on his wife when you shot him. Clive Hutchinson was a drug addict and a thief. They were evil men, and you were brave to take care of them. Like a superhero." That got a reaction. A slight flinch that showed the thought of being a hero meant something to her. Sim kept going, desperate to keep her attention. He nodded towards the trembling guard, who had lowered his baton a little. "He's not one of the bad men, Brenda. Let him help you, okay? Do as he says and he'll get you to a doctor."

Brenda's defiance melted and she grew teary. A serial killer about to cry. "I-I don't want to be here."

Sim nodded. "I know. You did what you had to do and now you're being punished. It's not fair. But you're safe here, Brenda. No one wants to hurt you, so stay calm and let them help you."

She stared at him for several moments, then nodded. "All right. But if anyone tries anything…"

"I know. You'll take a bite out of them. Hey, can someone get this woman a hamburger? She's starving."

Brenda let out a cackle, but as she did so, she went and sat down on the bed with her legs stretched out towards the surprised guard. He approached her cautiously, pulling a chain from a pouch on his belt and kneeling down in front of her. Her wrist bled onto the pale blue bed sheets and she was growing increasingly pale, but she kept a smile on her face and allowed her ankles to be chained together.

"Everything's okay, Brenda. You're safe."

She looked at him and nodded. "Okay."

Sim turned away from the glass and moved back towards the cell-car. He fought the urge to double over and vomit. His heart ricocheted throughout his chest. His knees were hollow.

I just had a conversation with Brenda Bates. I made her laugh.

Sim stepped silently back into the car and sat back down at the front. He was short of breath and couldn't speak, but he realised everyone was looking at him.

"That was awesome," said Jason, and it looked as though he meant it.

Mike nodded, his breathing heavy. "Nealy should put you on his staff. How did you know you could talk her down like that?"

Sim swallowed and tried to find his voice. "I, um… I did an episode about Brenda, spent weeks researching her. Suppose it almost feels like I know her, and how to get through to her."

The injured guard was moaning in pain, but he didn't take his anger out on Brenda as he helped escort her out of his cell. Perhaps if he'd been a little meaner, he might have avoided getting hurt.

Nealy was groaning to himself, his head hanging low. "Well, this is going to cost me." He put the walkie-talkie against his mouth and pressed a button. "Palmer, meet me at the infirmary. David's been hurt, and I'm going to need your help to make things right with him. I'll be there in ten."

Nealy opened the cell door and climbed out.

"Where are you going?" Mike demanded. "You gonna abandon us after what we just saw?"

"I'm off to contemplate my mistakes, Mr Rondon. The day hasn't gone according to plan, for which I can only apologise, but you're perfectly safe. Wait here, and I'll have someone come escort you to the exit. Tour's over, folks. Apologies again."

"This was inevitable," said Gerry, running her fingers through her hair as if she had knots. "Madness does not cooperate. You cannot bottle it and try to sell it."

Nealy huffed and pulled down the sleeves of his jumper. "This place will succeed, trust me. Just think of this as beta testing." He slicked back his hair and closed his eyes for a minute. Then he opened them and gave those inside the car a curt nod. "I'll catch up with you all later. Just sit tight." He rushed off to go help the wounded guard, who was still clutching at his bleeding face miserably. Brenda was being led away by the other guard down the pathway in front of the cells, shuffling in her chains. She left a trail of blood behind her on the shiny floor.

Sim sat patiently with the others and suddenly felt abandoned as he watched Nealy go one way with the bleeding guard and the second guard go another way with Brenda. As he looked back and forth, he noticed someone watching him.

Two cells down, Feral Fred was standing up against the glass, his pale skin glistening under the spotlights, his long hair bunched around his shoulders. When he saw Sim looking his way, the young cannibal raised a hand and waved. Despite his better judgement, Sim waved back.

CHAPTER
TEN

GIBBONS STOOD for the first time that day. He'd been awake in the barracks all last night, thinking things through. The tiredness had made it difficult to deal with Palmer.

Arsehole is gonna get what's coming to him. Sodding corporate lackey.

Gibbons was the island's head tech specialist. He'd taken an A level in Computer Science before joining the Royal Signals and specialising in communications. Add to that his IQ of 132, and he was an asset to any team. *Not some dogsbody to be bossed around. If Palmer understood half of what I can do, he would show me some proper respect.*

Gibbons went over to the CCTV monitors and gave things a once over. Nealy had left the tour group unexpectedly and was now inside the infirmary at the back of the prison. It looked like John had been injured, which was no surprise. The guy was an idiot. Palmer was with them, arms folded like he was the big man in the room. How wrong he was.

The rear entrance to the control room opened, and three guards stepped inside. Monroe, Ballesteros, and Jones. All three were ex-military men. They wore black uniforms and had Glocks holstered at their hips.

Monroe nodded to Gibbons. "We got a message to come up. Everything okay?"

"Yeah," said Gibbons. "Palmer wanted to do one of his team talks. Stick around until he gets back."

"We've had to leave our posts. If Palmer isn't here, we should—"

"Just take a load off, mate. He'll be a minute. Nealy's tour has hit the skids, so we'll be getting new orders."

Monroe let out an anxious sigh, but he looked at his colleagues and shrugged. "Fair enough. On your head be it, Gibbons."

"As always."

The three guards took seats around the room.

The control room had a tonne of proprietary systems from Everstech, but the prison's functioning ultimately came down to a bunch of electronically locked doors and three hundred or so cameras. That was the backbone of the island's security. Despite being a tech wizard, Gibbons would have relied on computers a little less and on manual locking systems a lot more.

But Nealy is a man willing to die upon the altar of technology. It's his power. His route to controlling the world. Every time he has to rely on a human being to do a job, it diminishes his ambition.

Gibbons crossed the control room and went over to the weapons locker. There was one in almost every backstage staffing area, accessed by a security key card. He opened the locker and peered inside. There were a couple of oiled MP5s and several Glock 17s. Also, a box of flashbangs. It was an MP5 he wanted, so that was what he took.

"What you doing?" asked Monroe, his eyebrow raised.

Gibbons looked over at the man and smiled. "Palmer wants me to give these a clean and polish. He's on me back as usual."

Monroe chuckled. "Yeah, he never takes a break, does he?"

"No, he does not," said Gibbons, and he pulled a loaded magazine from his pocket and slapped it into the MP5.

"Hey!" Monroe stood up. "What the fuck?"

Gibbons aimed the MP5 at the man and winked. "What the fuck indeed."

He pulled the trigger and put three high-powered 9mm rounds into Monroe's chest. His body armour was impotent, and he flew backwards against a bank of computers before slumping to the ground, dead.

Ballesteros and Jones leapt to their feet and grabbed for their Glocks. Gibbons emptied his magazine into them, spraying their blood all over the place. Their bodies danced a moment before flopping onto their backs. Jones had almost managed to fire off a shot, but his gun had instead gone flying out of his hand and under a desk.

Gibbons blew the smoke away from the end of his barrel and sneered. "Fascists."

He put the empty MP5 down on his desk and grabbed another magazine from the locker. He could still see Palmer in the infirmary, so there was no need to worry, or even rush. Things were going exactly as intended.

Too easy.

Gibbons had summoned Monroe, Jones, and Ballesteros to the command room because they were the most experienced members of security. With them out of the way, the rest of the plan would go easier. Only a dozen wage-monkeys left to deal with.

And Palmer, of course.

To ensure no one got in his way, Gibbons activated the control room's panic function, locking it from the inside. It would raise the alarms across the Keep, but that didn't matter now. It was too late for anyone to stop the wheels that were now in motion.

Moving quickly, he grabbed Monroe and Ballesteros's pistols and disassembled them, pocketing the slides and recoil springs so that no one could rebuild them. He spotted Jones's weapon underneath the desk but decided it couldn't do any harm from there, so he left it. The clock was ticking and he couldn't afford to delay.

He grabbed the handset for the radio that was used to communicate with the ferries at sea and put out a brief message. "Liberty. Proceed."

This is going to be fun.

Gibbons grabbed his chipped red mug and finished the water inside. He then tossed it over his shoulder and listened to it shatter on the ground behind him. "Viva la revolution."

While logging into the security system, he grabbed the intercom speaker and opened up all channels. It was time for a public service announcement.

Sim shuddered as if someone had tap danced over his grave. It was five or six minutes since Nealy had left, and no one had yet arrived to come and get them. They were stranded in the middle of the central walkway, with the empty security booth on the raised platform to their right, and the cells to their left. Up ahead, faces peered down at them from skewed angles. Behind, Feral Fred had gone back into hiding.

"When is someone coming?" said Mike. "I'm not going to just sit here like a plucked turkey all day."

"Maybe we should get out and walk," said Jason. "We just need to head back the way we came."

Sim shook his head. "The airlock doors closed behind us. They're probably locked. I think we should just sit tight."

"I agree," said Gerry. "Can you men not sit still for a few minutes?"

Jason pulled off his baseball cap and scratched at the red line it left around his forehead. "This sucks."

Sim saw movement and pointed. "Someone's coming."

"You think they'll let us complete the tour?" asked Jason, placing his red baseball cap back on his head.

"Nealy didn't make it sound that way. I think we're done."

"Sucks."

A security guard approached the cell-car with a baton in his hand, but it seemed to be a precaution because he wore a smile as he greeted them. "Hey, folks, I'm Matthew. Nealy's asked me to take you down to the cafeteria for some lunch. You want to get your things and—"

The guard flinched and looked up at the ceiling as an alarm sounded. Red lights flashed above each cell.

"What is that?" asked Jason.

The guard shook his head. "I don't know." He got on his radio and tried to call for an update, but he couldn't get anyone. When he swiped his card to open the door to the cell-car, he looked unsettled. "Okay, folks. Let's get you out of here."

Jason hopped out without hesitation and immediately started stretching his legs. Mike got out next, then reached back to help Gerry. She was reluctant to exit, peering around nervously. "This does not feel good," she said.

Sim agreed, but he didn't voice it. The alarms still sounded and the red lights still flashed. None of it felt like a good sign.

Maybe Nealy is shutting everything down because of what happened with Brenda.

There was a painful squawk, and everyone held their ears. Feedback from powerful speakers.

"Attention," said a voice. "This is the new lord of the Keep. All systems are now under my control. By being here, you have allied yourself with the evil capitalist, Evers Nealy. This place is a citadel to his ego, an abomination reflecting his ambition to play God. But today, he will be humbled. I, and my brothers of the Burning Dollar, will not allow this place to exist. The Keep will burn, along with every predator inside of it. Today, you wanted to celebrate murder, but instead you will experience your own. Death to capitalism, and death to those who revel in it."

The voice went away, replaced by electrical droning. Then, once again, the only sound was from the wailing alarms.

The guard was shaking his head. "Was that Gibbons? The hell is he doing?"

"Get us out of here," said Sim, putting a hand on the man's arm. It caused him to refocus.

The guard nodded. "Okay, everyone, follow me. We're going to take a shortcut." He hopped up onto the platform. It was three feet high, which meant everyone had to put a leg up and hop onto it. Gerry in her heels needed help, so she reached out both arms and had Mike and Jason lift her. Luckily, she was not much bigger than a child.

The alarms changed pitch, going from a *wee woo* to a deeper buzzing sound. A heavy clunk sounded from nearby, and it caused Sim to stop and look around. What he saw made no sense. It was so utterly, unbelievably bad that his brain refused to acknowledge it.

The cells are unlocked.

Sim saw Brenda's cell door slide open. He considered that it might have been left unlocked after her freakout, but then he saw Feral Fred step out of his cell and appear in the walkway. From the way he stood there, it was clearly a surprise to him, too.

"W-We need to get out of here," said Sim.

When the guard saw Fred out of his cell, he swore and pulled out his handgun. He pointed it at the teenage killer. "Back inside your cell now!"

Jason grabbed Sim's arm. "Come on. Time to leg it."

Sim nodded, and along with Mike and Gerry, the four of them dashed to a door at the rear of the raised platform. Mike got there first, faster than his age and size suggested possible. He grabbed the vertical door handle and yanked, but he ended up slipping and staggering backwards. "Darned thing's locked." His hat had slipped sideways on his head, giving him a slightly crazed look.

Sim grabbed the door handle for himself, but it was definitely locked. He then spotted the sensor on the wall and realised why. "We need a keycard."

Jason turned and pointed at the guard. "Dude has one."

Everyone hurried back down the platform, calling for the guard to help them, but his focus was on Fred. He still had his gun pointed, and he was yelling at him to get back inside his cell. But Fred only seemed confused. His speech was limited, and his understanding of English was probably nil.

"We need to get out of here," Sim shouted at the man. "Matthew!"

The guard glanced back at them and shook his head. "Lock yourselves inside the security booth until help arrives. I can't leave here."

"No way, buddy," Mike argued. "We need letting out of this place right now."

Matthew frowned. He was still aiming his gun at Fred, but he was no longer keeping an eye on him. "Look... this is a crisis. The cells are unlocked."

"No shit," said Jason. "That's why you need to let us the hell out of here."

Matthew tensed up and seemed unable to decide, but then he huffed and said, "Okay! Get back to the door." He turned away from Fred and started walking. "Quickly!"

There was a flash of movement. But Fred remained in place. It was someone else moving, someone else sprinting out of their cell.

A topless man with six-pack abs and a mane of silky blond hair dashed bare-footed down the walkway. He was fast, and he was on top of Matthew before he even knew what was coming.

Matthew's handgun fired at the ceiling before tumbling from his hand and skidding along the polished floor. The force of the tackle whiplashed him forward so hard that his neck nearly broke. His legs couldn't keep up with the momentum of his body, and he fell onto his hands and knees. Before he could recover, the Brisbane Brutalist leapt onto his back and smashed his face against the ground, again and again and again.

Sim tried to close his eyes, but he couldn't look away from Matthew's broken, misshapen face. Blood poured from his broken nose and shattered teeth, pooling on the ground in front of him. He let out a moan, a dying plea.

Feral Fred stood in place the entire time.

There was movement from the other cells.

Sim cried out as an arm grabbed him, but it was only Jason. The urgent look on his face told more than words, and it prompted them both to run.

But to where? We can't get out.

Gerry let out a scream six feet ahead, followed by a baritone yell from Mike. Sim's stomach fell to his knees, and he almost collapsed from pure terror as he saw the maniacal grins of a dozen murderous lunatics rushing towards him.

"Into the booth!" Mike shouted.

Jason grabbed Sim and redirected his run. For a moment, they were headed straight towards danger, but then Mike yanked open the door to the security booth and yelled at everyone to dive inside.

Gerry went in first, followed by Jason. Mike urged Sim to hurry, but he was already moving as fast as he could. Ten feet away, a man he recognised as the Cali Cutter sprinted towards him like a wild man.

Angel Ramses, responsible for cutting the throats of nine homosexual men. Captured in March 2012.

We're all going to die.

Sim threw himself into a dive, aiming his entire body at the open doorway. He landed inside on a patch of rough carpet, skinning his elbows and bashing his knee. But the pain was distant, his terror present, so he turned onto his back and screamed at Mike to close the door.

But it was too late.

The Cali Cutter leapt onto the Texan's wide back and started throttling him. Mike tried to punch the man, but he couldn't get an angle. Meanwhile, multiple killers amassed outside.

"Help him!" Gerry cried.

But Sim was frozen. He stared into the eyes of a serial killer and could not move.

"Fuck sake!" Jason suddenly swung a small red canister through the air and struck the Cali Cutter on the back of the head. It dislodged the killer from Mike's back and allowed the Texan to stagger inside the security booth. Jason tossed the fire extinguisher aside and yanked the door closed.

Gerry leapt forward and pushed a bolt across, locking the door in place.

The killers threw themselves against the windows of the booth, sneering and spitting and smashing their fists against the glass. Gerry screamed as they leered at her, and Mike shouted warnings at those who tried to get in. But the lunatics were dead set on getting inside.

Sim crawled on his back underneath a desk at the front of the booth. Everyone else moved into the centre of the carpet, watching the animals trying to get inside from every angle and knowing it was only a matter of time before they succeeded.

Sim pulled himself into a ball and prayed for someone to help.

We're trapped. We're helpless.
We're dead.

CHAPTER
ELEVEN

"WE NEED TO DO SOMETHING," said Mike. At some point he'd lost his hat, leaving his bald head exposed. He stepped up to the computer on the booth's desk and started tapping at the mouse. "Damn it. Password protected."

"What good would it have done anyway?" said Jason. "You want to send an email?"

"I want to call for help, boy!"

Jason shook his head. "I reckon help knows shit just hit the fan, but we'll be dead by the time it gets here."

"Don't say that," said Gerry. "I will not die here on this island. I need to live so that I can castrate that fool Nealy."

"I'll be right behind you," said Mike. "This is gonna cost that man big. I'm going to open another park with the money he's going to pay me."

Sim didn't care about money or reparations. He only cared about getting out of there alive and back to Chrissy. Was she safe?

Please, let her be.

Sim looked up and saw the Brisbane Brutalist smashing his forehead against the glass. His blond hair was flecked with blood. His perfectly white teeth gnashed together so hard it looked like they might splinter.

Half a dozen inmates surrounded the booth, all of them trying to break the windows and get inside. Fortunately, they had so far failed to make a crack, and their fists were leaving bloody smears on the glass. The booth's door seemed to be the weak point, its hinges rattling after every impact, but for now it remained in place.

"I think... I think we're okay," said Gerry. "This glass is holding."

"So is the door," said Jason. He had his back against it, bracing it, but it was enduring just fine. "For now."

Mike nodded, a trembling hand against his jaw. "So we wait. We wait until Nealy sends in the cavalry."

Sim was still tucked up beneath the desk, but he slid out slightly so that he was closer to the others. He didn't get up, though. It felt safer down on the ground. "Will the cavalry even come? Who was that on the intercom? It sounded like this place has been taken over."

"The Burning Dollar," said Jason. "I've read about them on the net. They're this group of nutcases, dedicated to the downfall of capitalism or something." He shook his head in disgust. "Guess Nealy was on their hit list."

"This place is the nadir of capitalism," said Gerry. She was staring out at the snarling psychopaths with something approaching fascination. "Nealy wants to monetise murder, make a spectacle of it. I will not be endorsing this place."

"Me neither," said Mike.

Jason shrugged. "I'm gonna see if I survive the day and then decide."

Sim rolled his eyes. "Already thinking how to use this to your advantage?"

"Life is how you look at it, mate. Keep moving forward and nothing can ever hold you back."

Sim didn't have time to argue philosophy. He wanted solutions to their current predicament. Wracking his brain, he suddenly had an idea. "I-I have my phone on me. Let me try to make a call."

"Forget it," said Mike. "We're in the middle of the Channel."

Sim pulled out his phone anyway, but he quickly saw that the Texan was right. His phone had no network. "What about Wi-Fi? This place must have it."

"Does anyone know the password?" asked Jason. "Because I don't. Nealy told me he didn't want anyone live-streaming and leaking about this place."

Sim tried to log in to the several networks showing up, but each one asked for a password. He threw his head back in defeat. "Damn it."

Jason put out a hand. "Nealy took my phone from me when I got caught snooping. Do you mind if I borrow yours for a while?"

Sim wasn't particularly attached to his phone, but he had an instinctive distrust of Jason, so he asked, "Why?"

"I want to film."

"What? Are you serious?"

"Hell, yes. Nealy will try to cover this up. If we can film this, then maybe we can protect ourselves with some leverage."

"It's a good point," said Mike. "I've known Nealy for a long time. He's a man of his word, but his survival instincts override all else. Best we start thinking about how this ends."

Sim shrugged. "Fine, whatever. Just keep the camera away from me."

"Sure thing." Jason asked for Sim's pin number and unlocked the phone. He then raised it and started filming the maniacs outside the window. "Date is Saturday 19th October and we are on, um, what was the name of this island?"

"Durne," said Gerry.

"Yeah, we're on the Isle of Durne at a place called the Keep. Evers Nealy built it and filled it with pretty much every mass murderer you can think of. Well, he screwed the pooch, and now we're trapped inside a booth with a dozen psycho dick jobs trying to kill us." He went on and on, naming those present inside the booth and giving a brief summary of what had happened. Afterwards, he backed up the video file in a separate folder and gave it a misleading name. "Okay," he said. "Let's hope that wasn't our obituary."

Sim lay back on his elbows and stared at the ceiling's spotlight. His whole life revolved around serial killers. Now it might just end with one.

The alarms sounded. Nealy turned the air blue. "What the hell is going on?"

Then Gibbon gave a speech over the intercom and Nealy swore a whole lot more.

Palmer remained in the corner of the infirmary, arms folded, silently wondering how badly he could torture Gibbons without killing the man. *Why would he do this? Is he insane?*

I knew that piece of shit was bad news.

Nealy glared at Palmer and demanded answers, but Palmer was in no mood to be cowed. After this, he would almost certainly lose his job, so what was the point of trying to keep it? "I have no idea, sir, but Gibbons was a bad hire."

"Oh, you're blaming me, are you?"

"No, sir, I'm blaming Gibbons. I don't know what he's doing, but when I find him, I'm going to beat the answers out of him."

Nealy glared for a moment before nodding resignedly. "Sounds like a plan. I need him taken care of right away, before—"

Nealy's walkie-talkie hissed. Irritably, he picked it up from the table and answered the call. What met him was a lot of yelling and screaming. "The cells are open," someone warned. "All the prisoners are free. Send backup. And be quick about it."

The call ended with Palmer unsure who had even made it. It might have been Chuck – or maybe even Fred. He was yet to hear from the man.

Nealy had turned pale. He gawped at Palmer and swallowed a lump in his throat. "Can that be true? Could the prisoners be loose?"

Palmer shook his head. "You built the system, sir. You tell me."

Nealy slicked back his hair and thought about it. After a moment, he lost even more colour as he gave an answer. "All the cells can be operated remotely one at a time, but there is no limit on how many can be open at once. If someone in the control room really wanted to cause anarchy, then… Damn it! Gibbons could have unlocked the entire prison with enough time."

"My betting is that if he could, he would. We need to assume that every inmate has escaped."

The wounded guard, John, was lying on the treatment bed and listening. He moaned now. "We need to evacuate the island before those nutcases kill everyone."

Nealy rolled his eyes. "Yes, thank you for your input, John. Let's assess the situation a little more first before we go nuclear. Palmer?"

"Yessir?"

"Get your team together and attempt to mend this situation. In the meantime, I'm going to gather as many non-security personnel as I can and get them into the panic room. If help is required from the mainland, I shall arrange it from there."

Palmer nodded. "Understood. I'll head to the armoury and gear up. What do you want me to do about our guests?"

Nealy pinched the bridge of his nose and closed his eyes. "If anything happens to them, the Keep closing down will be the least of my problems. Gather your team first, but then I need you to pull those civilians out of harm's way. ASAP."

Palmer turned towards the door. "Roger that."

"And Palmer?"

"Yessir?"

"If you encounter Gibbons, shoot him in both kneecaps for me."

Palmer grinned. "Oh, you can count on it."

CHAPTER
TWELVE

SIM FOUND the courage to stand up inside the security booth. Outside, the maniacs were going wild. They'd dragged the furniture out of their cells and were smashing it apart, wielding scraps of wood and bits of hollow metal piping. Sim watched with the same awe he had when watching a nature documentary. Only this one was set inside his nightmares.

He worried about Chrissy endlessly. He prayed the anarchy was contained only to this cell block, but he had no way of knowing. Was she aware of the danger he was in? Was Nealy with her, getting her to safety? Not knowing was the biggest torment. He could do nothing to help her. He was stuck inside the booth with no means to help even himself.

Jason stood beside Sim and was uncharacteristically quiet. He, too, was watching the chaos outside. Some of the inmates still beat at the booth's glass windows, but most had turned their attention to trying to escape the cell block. The airlocks at each end of the walkway were locked. The various side doors and fire escapes, too. Soon, one of the maniacs would think to get the dead guard's keycard, and then they would be out of there. Sim didn't know if that was a good or bad thing. It would reduce the danger to him but increase the danger to Chrissy.

"This is not how I expected this weekend to go," said Jason finally. "You okay?"

"No," said Sim. "Not at all."

"You're worried about Chrissy, huh?"

Sim frowned, wondering if Jason had read his mind. It was unlike him to show actual empathy. "I don't know if she's safe or not."

"I reckon she's fine, mate. She was heading to the cafe. No monsters there. Not real ones, anyway."

The Cali Cutter threw himself against the glass and made both of them flinch. Sim wrung his hands together and shook his head. "Where is Nealy's security? Shouldn't help be here by now?"

"Maybe they're on their way, fully armed and ready to party."

The Cali Cutter licked the glass, then laughed at them.

Sim looked away. "I hope so. I don't want to end up in one of your shockumentaries, Jason."

Jason huffed. "I'd be dead right alongside you, so how would that happen?"

"Good point."

"Hey, man. Can I ask you a question?"

Sim studied the windows, ensuring no one was about to break through. He saw Carlos Escoban stalking the walkway below, a calmness to his strut. At one point, a half-naked killer wandered into his path, and he grabbed the man in a headlock. He then broke his neck, seemingly for no other reason than pleasure. It sent a shudder down Sim's spine. Then he spotted Feral Fred, crouched at the edge of it all, watching what was going on. He flinched whenever another inmate came near, and sometimes lumbered away like a chimpanzee, but at no point did he join in the anarchy.

"I said, can I ask you a question?"

Sim turned to Jason and nodded. "Sure. Go ahead."

"Why do you have such a problem with me, man? I mean, we were almost friends once. You don't like the way I do things? Fine, I can accept that. There just seems to be more to it."

Sim let out a sigh, suddenly feeling attacked. But why did he feel like that? Jason had only asked a question.

Maybe it was because the question was hard to answer without betraying a part of himself, without removing some of the bricks from the wall he'd built around himself.

"I just don't think you get it," was the answer he gave. "I don't think you ever step back and consider that there are actually victims. You glorify the killers."

Jason nodded. "Maybe you're right. But have you ever considered I might be dragging them out of their dens and shining a light on them? The more people see the bedwetting freaks for what they are, the less frightening they become. Do you know how many murderers have contacted me from prison demanding I give them a cut, or that I show them in a more positive light? My channel drives them mad, because I'm not catering to their sick egos. I control the narrative, not them, and they hate it. Maybe I get carried away sometimes, chasing numbers and selling merchandise, but that's because I'm passionate about what I do. I take as much pride in it as you do."

Sim huffed at that.

Jason rolled his eyes. "Oh, sorry. Are you so superior that your channel is the only one of any worth? Listen, people enjoy what I do, and that's why I do it. I do it for them, the people putting coins in my bank."

"It shouldn't be about money."

"It shouldn't be, but it is, Sim. And you're not as noble as you think you are. It isn't a search for the truth that compels you to do what you do, it's something else."

Sim folded his arms and resisted the urge to lash out. It

wouldn't help the situation. There were still killers trying to smash their way in. "So you think you know why I do things now? You have no idea."

Jason looked at him with something like pity, and it was unwelcome. "You forget we worked together, mate. I know more about you than most. What happened to you in the past…"

Sim turned on him. "My past is *my* business. You shut your mouth, okay?"

Jason sighed and put his hands up. "Sure, have it your way. But get it straight, I'm not the bad guy here. You hating on me isn't my issue. It's yours." He turned away and rejoined Mike and Gerry, who were messing with the computer and trying to see if they could do something – anything – to help them. It was only a matter of time before the howling predators outside found a way in.

Sim remained at the window, staring out at the inmates. Along with the Cali Cutter, the Brisbane Brutalist was still banging his fists against the glass. The man's forehead had sliced open to the bone from headbutting the window, and he bared his teeth like a rabid wolf. Madness had struck this man at some point in his life – or perhaps he had been born insane – and looking at him now, Sim saw that the convicted murderer was not like everyone else. Evil, sociopathy, whatever you called it, this man's soul was different. His gaze was alien, almost primeval. Nothing existed inside this man except anger and hatred and a biological imperative to be at the top of the food chain. It pushed aside any room for remorse or compassion.

Sim also saw that same vacant gaze from the Cali Cutter, Carlos Escoban, and various other killers. But not all of them. He'd not seen it in Brenda Bates's eyes, nor did he see it in Feral Fred's. The young cannibal was still crouched at the edge of the chaos, and rather than empty, his eyes showed only confusion. These monsters were as alien to him as they were to Sim.

Evil took many forms.

Maybe Nealy was one of those forms. The fact he had even conceived a place like this showed a sickness – perhaps a sickness in society as a whole. That people would pay to see serial killers up close…

Or watch documentaries about them on YouTube.

Sim had the terrible realisation that he and Nealy might not be so different.

He turned back around to face the others. The booth's door had bulged slightly, its hinges finally giving way. Through the window, he saw Carlos Escoban heading towards the booth with a thick length of wood. If it was heavy enough, it might shatter the glass.

"We need to make a plan," said Sim, "because, one way or another, I'm getting the hell out of here."

Chrissy was already bored with the food. Wasn't that always the way with buffets? Everything looked so good at first, but then halfway through your second plate of boiled rice and beef stew, things just tasted… icky.

She was worried about Sim. Something was up with him lately, and her only assumption was that it had to do with his mother's death. The ten year anniversary was only weeks away, and she knew it was playing on his mind. He had no other immediate family besides a distant auntie and a senile old grandmother.

And me. He has me.

When Chrissy had first met Sim, he'd been a loner. A shared passion for horror had brought them together at a convention, but once they started dating, she had been shocked by how quiet his existence had been. He held a job with a sandwich packing company, standing on an assembly line eight hours a day for minimum wage. His home was a single-bedroom flat in a rough part of town, with his only friends being the people he sometimes gamed with online. It had been as though he'd been afraid to live in the real world – the world that required effort and interaction. Yet, somehow, even in those first days, she had sensed a kind, loving, and loyal human being. She'd been right.

But lately, Sim was drifting away from her. Increasingly, he was quiet. Perhaps just thoughtful, but then she wouldn't know because he rarely shared what was going on inside his head. She could count the number of times he smiled in a day on one hand. Was he depressed?

And if so, how do I help him?

She had hoped this weekend might get him excited again. A new adventure for them both. Meeting Evers Nealy had been surreal, and there was an atmosphere around the guy that just made you think your entire world was about to change. But Sim had done nothing but pout since arriving on the island. It had actually made her a little mad, and reminded her of her father's moodiness that had no doubt led to her parents divorcing when she had been twelve.

Are we headed the same way? I keep trying to get him to open up, but what if he just never does?

She told herself to lighten up on him. This island was enough to make anyone glum. It was one thing to make documentaries about serial killers, but a whole other thing to actually meet them. She still couldn't believe it. Sidwell, The Huntsman, and all the others she'd seen so far... It was insane. And frightening.

Chrissy had been chaperoned from the cell block to the cafeteria, and food had already been waiting. She had dived in with gusto.

Now she put down her knife and fork, fuller than she'd intended to be.

Oh, who am I fooling? I've never left a buffet without wanting to be sick. That's the whole point!

The orderly noticed she was done and gave her a nod. He

said nothing, so she assumed she could remain at the table while the others completed the tour. She swigged from her lemonade and winced as the bubbles forced their way down her throat. She'd had heartburn all day. Her stomach, likewise, was unsettled. From the moment she'd entered the Keep, she had been anxious. But, as always, she tried to remain upbeat for Sim. Sometimes it felt like she took more responsibility for his emotions than he did.

It's tiring sometimes. Why isn't he happier? What else does he need in his life? The channel is doing great. Nealy has promised us seventy grand…

Am I not enough?

At first, Chrissy didn't notice the alarm sounding – she had been too deep in her own thoughts – but then it came into blaring focus. The orderly looked around, confused. Clearly, he had no idea what was going on.

Chrissy called over to him. "What is that? The fire alarm?"

"I'm not sure, miss. Let me try to find out." He got on his walkie-talkie and tried to get someone, but it soon became clear that he was having trouble. He started tapping at the unit with his index finger. Meanwhile, the alarms continued to blare.

Sim? Are you okay? What's happening?

There was a *crackle*, and a voice suddenly sounded over an intercom. "This is… lord of… Keep. All systems… control. By being here, you have allied… capitalist… Nealy. This… citadel to his…"

Chrissy frowned. The message wasn't coming through clearly, and she didn't know what the speaker was trying to convey. She looked at the orderly. "Who is that?"

"I don't know. Damn speaker's on the fritz. I swear, half this place has bugs, but don't tell Nealy I said that."

"That doesn't make me feel better. Has something gone wrong?"

"I don't know. Wouldn't surprise me."

Chrissy stood up, pushing back her chair. "I want to speak to Nealy now. Take me to him."

"Calm down. I'm sure it's just—"

"Now!"

The orderly flinched. "Okay, okay. Let's go."

CHAPTER
THIRTEEN

THE BRISBANE BRUTALIST and the Cali Cutter stood aside as Carlos Escoban moved over to the window with his heavy length of wood. The man glared at those inside with dead brown eyes, his face expressionless.

Mike moved close to Gerry and put an arm around her. She was trembling visibly. "I got you. Anyone tries to hurt you, they'll have to get through me."

"What's your plan?" Jason asked Sim. "Because I would love to hear it."

Sim peered around the cramped booth. There was nothing of use, only a computer, desk, and CCTV system. There was a big red button to sound the alarm, but that was beyond unnecessary. Fighting wasn't an option. They would have to think their way out.

Escoban raised the length of wood over his shoulder, and then, like he was striking a baseball, he swung it.

The glass cracked.

A spiderweb appeared in the centre of the window and slowly spread. Escoban struck the glass a second time and an entire chunk came loose.

Sim stepped up to the cracked window and took a breath. "We... We need to talk our way out."

Jason groaned. "What? That's the worst idea ever."

"No," said Sim. "It's the only thing that will work. These people are insane. We need to use that to our advantage."

Gerry shook her head. She'd taken off her heels and was now barefoot – and five inches shorter. "How do we do this?"

Sim decided it would be easier to show than explain, so he sidestepped the crack in the window and stared out at the Brisbane Brutalist. "Hey, do you know who this is?" He nodded towards Escoban, who was now trying to force the wood into the crack to make it wider. Fortunately, the glass seemed reluctant to shatter. "This is Columbia's greatest killer. No one is more frightening than Carlos Escoban."

The Brisbane Killer's face contorted, the split across his forehead puckering. His blond hair was soaked through with blood. "He ain't shit. You have no idea the murders I've committed, mate. I terrified the whole of bleedin' Australia."

Sim nodded. "Yeah, you're pretty scary, but you didn't kill anywhere near as many people as Carlos."

Carlos overheard what was being said, causing him to cease hammering at the glass. He turned to the Brisbane Brutalist and rolled his eyes. "He's messing with you, *pendejo*."

"What you just call me, mate?"

"I called you *pendejo*, you stinkin' *puta*."

The Brisbane Brutalist roared like a bear and then charged like a bull. He picked up the smaller Escoban and lifted him into the air. Momentum took the two of them off the concrete platform and they landed badly on the walkway below. As they struggled, Escoban wrapped the Brutalist in a headlock and proceeded to choke the larger man. The violence caused several inmates nearby to whoop and dance. And then join in.

Sim called out to the Cali Cutter. He told the man there were demons everywhere, and that God had demanded he deal with them. Smiling in ecstasy, he set about his fellow maniacs with devastating violence, tearing at their eyes and biting into their necks.

Jason covered his mouth like he was about to be sick. "It's working. They're tearing into each other. God."

Sim nodded grimly. "Psychopaths are driven by ego, and they don't particularly care who they kill."

Gerry swallowed a lump in her throat. "You manipulated their psyches. Very clever, Mr Barka."

Jason nodded. "I forgot the Cali Cutter had delusions about hearing God's voice. You really know your shit, man."

"Thanks. You fancy getting out of here?"

"Hell, yes," said Mike. He unbolted the door and opened it.

Everyone hurried out, looking left and right and trying to avoid being seen.

Sim's entire body tingled. They were out in the open with a dozen killers. It was a similar feeling to standing too close to a bonfire. Hang around too long and they would get burned.

"How are we going to get through the exit?" asked Jason.

"The keycard," said Sim. "The guard must still have it."

"How have none of these maniacs thought to find it? They must know it's the only way out of here?"

Sim started moving. "Who cares? Let's just get it."

They hurried across the platform in a huddle, keeping close to one another to protect each other. By now, the entire cell block had erupted into a mass brawl. Some of the more timid killers were back inside their cells, but Carlos Escoban was dead on the floor with the Brutalist roaring over his body in triumph.

The dead guard – Matthew – lay on the ground ahead, his skull a bloody mush. Sim tried to control his nausea as he neared, knowing he might have to get blood on his hands. Then, to his relief, Jason hurried ahead and offered to do the deed himself.

Sim stood with the others while Jason knelt beside the body. He rubbed his hands on his shirt and then started checking the guard's pockets. His belt had several pouches, but they were all empty. His pockets, likewise, had been turned inside out.

Something occurred to Sim. "His gun! Where is his gun?"

"And his baton," said Jason, still searching the body. "I don't see any of his things. The keycard isn't here."

Gerry cried out as someone grabbed her from behind. It was the Brisbane Brutalist. His forehead had leaked blood all over his face, and more stained his naked chest from where he'd killed the guard and Escoban. He held Gerry around the throat and licked her ear.

"Let her go!" Mike demanded.

"Not until I'm done," said the killer, running his hands over Gerry's slender body.

Sim raced forward to help, but the beast of a man backhanded him so hard that he thought he felt his cheek shatter. He spun in a circle and collapsed to the ground, almost losing consciousness. Gerry screamed, and when he focused again, Sim saw that two other half-naked maniacs had joined the Brutalist in dragging her away. "N-No. Let her go."

A gunshot rang out.

Sim flinched, the explosion coming from nearby. He looked around and saw no guards.

The Brisbane Brutalist's forehead opened up in a gaping chasm. Bits of brain spilled down his cheek.

Gerry broke free, shrieking in terror. Mike ran forward and gathered her into his arms, letting her sob into his shoulder. One maniac went after her but fell down dead as another gunshot rang out. A few feet away, the Brisbane Brutalist remained standing on his feet. There was a hint of confusion on his face, but no panic, even as his brain continued to leak from a hole in his head. Three seconds he stayed upright, before his muscular body finally collapsed to the ground.

Sim got gingerly to his feet, still half-dazed from the brutal backhand. Another gunshot rang out and the third maniac fell down dead.

Who is shooting?

A guard?

Sim turned around, trying to locate their savour. It wasn't who he expected it to be. Not by a longshot.

Feral Fred was down on both knees with the handgun smoking between his palms. He held it awkwardly, but he was a hell of a shot. When he saw Sim looking at him, the scraggly teenager tilted his head curiously.

"Oh shit," said Jason. "What do we do?"

Sim put both hands up and nodded slowly at Fred. "You saved us. Thank you."

Fred said nothing, but he kept eye contact with Sim for a moment until he glanced over at Gerry, who was still sobbing into Mike's shoulder.

"You wanted to save Gerry, didn't you?" said Sim. "The only person who ever showed you love was your mother, and she obviously taught you never to hurt a woman. You're a hero, Fred."

"I don't think he understands," said Jason. "We need to find a way out."

Fred hopped forward in a crouch, but he stopped a few feet short of Sim. Sim wanted to turn around and run, but he forced himself to stand his ground and face this strange creature. To his surprise, Fred grabbed something from between his toes and skimmed it across the floor. The object glinted beneath the spotlights.

A keycard.

Sim knelt down and carefully picked it up. He kept his eyes on Fred, worried that turning his back might prompt an attack, like with a bear. "Oh, I think he understands better than you think. Thank you, Fred."

Fred turned and lumbered away, the handgun still in his possession.

"Come on," said Mike. "We need to get out of this madhouse."

Sim held the keycard in victory and sprinted down the platform. When he tapped it against the door sensor, it gave him a green light. He couldn't keep himself from cheering out loud.

They were getting the hell out of there.

Chrissy followed the orderly out of the cafeteria, wondering where everybody else was. The alarms sounded everywhere, but the Keep was oddly deserted. It led her to wonder if Nealy had employed enough staff, which then led her to worry that he'd built a prison without enough people to run it.

The orderly still hadn't managed to hail anyone on the walkie-talkie. From the concern on his face, Chrissy could tell something bad was happening. She desperately wanted to find Sim.

Rather than head back to the cell block, they headed to the main entrance. The orderly explained it was the current assembly point in case of a fire, which was his best guess for what was going on. It was also their best bet for finding Nealy.

But when they reached the open hallway with the giant Jack the Ripper statue and stained-glass window, they found the room empty. The only sound was the echo of their own voices calling out.

"Hmm," said the orderly. "The alarms have stopped. That's a good sign. I think."

"This is ridiculous," said Chrissy, staring up at the giant scalpel pointing down at her. "Why can't you contact anyone? I want to know if my boyfriend's okay."

"I'm sure he is, miss. The alarm system is new. It's probably just a bug in the system. No reason to think anything else."

"There's every reason. After what I've seen today, I think this place is an accident waiting to happen. What if an inmate has got loose?"

The orderly frowned. "That would never happen. Look, I'll get answers as soon as I can."

Chrissy was about to continue arguing, for no other reason than it kept her frightened mind occupied, but footsteps alerted her. When she looked towards the staircase, she saw a single man in a black security uniform trotting down towards them. He wore a dark baseball cap with a ponytail swinging back and forth behind it.

The orderly let out a relieved sigh, obviously recognising the man. "Gibbons? Do you know what's going on?"

"Yeah, there's no need to worry, mate. The alarm system has come on by mistake and we can't get the sodding thing to switch off. Nealy said we need to evacuate, just in case there's a fire somewhere we don't know about."

The orderly looked at Chrissy with a hint of a smirk. "You see? Exactly what I said."

"Well done, you." She turned to the newcomer, Gibbons. "Do you know where the tour group is? My boyfriend is with it."

The man smiled. "You're Christina Wise, correct? The others are being taken to the exit. They'll meet you outside."

Chrissy tried to act nonchalant, despite her heart beating a hundred times a second. For a moment, she really had feared the worst had happened. "Okay, no problem, but could you just call them on your radio for me, please? I'm worried."

He shook his head. "Don't be. I just spoke to Nealy. He said everyone is fine."

She nodded. "Okay, well, if they aren't out in a few minutes…"

"I'll call again. Right, follow me and we'll wait for everyone outside."

Chrissy and the orderly followed Gibbons through the automatic exit doors. It was raining hard, and Chrissy immediately pulled her collar tight to avoid her T-shirt getting wet. "Do we have to wait out here like this?"

"I should grab us a buggy," said the orderly. "We'll get drenched otherwise."

Gibbons nodded and pointed towards the Keep. "I saw one parked around back. You want to run and get it?"

"Sure. I'll be as quick as I can."

Chrissy watched the man rush off through the rain, but by the time he returned, she would be soaked through. She let out a groan.

"Sorry about this," said Gibbons. He stared out at the sea in the distance, almost like he was looking for something.

"No problem. As long as everyone's safe. Where are the rest of the staff?"

"On their way. Just sit tight. Everything's going as planned."

"What do you mean?"

He looked at her and smiled. "Why did you come to this island, Ms Wise? Why would you want to see a bunch of sick maniacs up close? I don't understand the attraction."

There was something accusatory about his tone, and it caused her to frown. "Well, I didn't know what I was coming here to see. Nealy was very secretive about it all."

"Offered you money, I'll bet?"

Chrissy shrugged. "Where is Nealy? I want to talk to him."

"Oh, he's going to be busy. You can talk to me."

"Um… no thanks." She looked towards the Keep, urging the orderly to reappear.

"You okay?" Gibbons asked, a slight smirk on his face.

"Just cold. I need to get under shelter. D-Do you think he'll be long?"

"He sure is taking his time, isn't he? I should go check."

Chrissy nodded, liking the thought of him going away. There was something off about this guy. The way he spoke… It was like he hated Chrissy. But why would that be? She'd never even met him.

Gibbons walked away. Chrissy let out a sigh. Maybe she could sneak back inside the Keep and search for Sim herself. It made no sense that they were the only ones out here. If there was a fire drill, then people should've been spilling out by now.

Gibbons turned back. "Actually, you'd best come with me, miss. Nealy will go mad if he finds out I left a guest alone out in the rain. Come on."

"No, that's okay. I'll just wait."

He waved a hand insistently. "Don't be silly. Follow me and we'll get out of this rain."

She wanted to argue, but she couldn't think of a reason. "Um… okay, then."

She caught up with Gibbons, and the two of them headed around the side of the Keep. It was not an area meant for guests as there were crates and boxes stacked up everywhere, as well as a huge skip full of rubbish. There was, however, a buggy, just like Gibbons had said. At least he'd been telling the truth.

No sign of the orderly, though.

"Where did he go?" asked Chrissy.

Gibbons frowned. "Not sure. Get in the buggy and I'll go find him."

Eager to be out of the rain, she complied and got in, sliding onto the rear bench and shrugging off her wet denim jacket. From the looks of the sky above the sea, the weather was only going to get worse. The rain was already biting.

Just as Gibbons was about to leave, the orderly reappeared. It caused Gibbons to pull his gun and yell. "Stop!"

The orderly put his hands in the air and yelped. "What the hell, man?"

Gibbons lowered the weapon and apologised. "You shouldn't jump out at me like that."

"I didn't. My keycard wasn't working, so I went to test it on the side access door to see if it was just a problem with the buggy. It's not. I can't deactivate any of the locks with my card."

"Really?" Gibbons chewed the inside of his cheek. He reached into the chest pocket of his vest and pulled out his own keycard. "Let me try mine." He swiped the card across a sensor on the buggy's dashboard and the electric dashboard flickered to life. He popped the card back into its pocket.

"Huh," said the orderly. "Why is your card working and not mine?"

Gibbons shrugged. "Probably because I deactivated every card of level three or lower."

"What? Why have you done that?"

"Because my card is level four, so if I deactivated anything higher than a three, my card wouldn't work either."

The orderly folded his arms and looked pissed. "Yeah, but why deactivate anyone's card? You're not making sense."

Gibbons chuckled. "I'm just messing with you, mate." He raised his gun and shot the orderly in the face.

Chrissy screamed.

Gibbons turned to her and put a finger to his lips. "Shush now. Don't want to make a scene, do we?"

"Wh-Why did you do that? Why?"

"Because he was a sodding orderly. Lowest paid monkeys in this place. It's people accepting pitiful wages that allow monsters like Nealy to become so powerful. I got no time for people who don't stand up for themselves." He reached in and grabbed her by the hair, yanking her along the bench. "Let's see how you do."

Chrissy screamed and struggled, but if she wasn't careful, she would end up without a scalp. So she begged. Begged to be let go.

"Come on now," said Gibbons. "I just told you I like people who stand up for themselves. I don't want to hear any begging."

"Why are you doing this?"

"Because someone has to. This place is evil, and you're a part of it."

She slid off the bench and fell to her knees in the mud. "No, I'm not. This place has nothing to do with me."

"It's a temple of worship for serial killers. Seems like you built something similar online."

She got to her feet but was still being controlled by her hair. "Let me go! Let me go, you fucker."

"That's more like it." He yanked her hair and sent her sprawling against the wall of the Keep. Unlike the front facade, the side was just a featureless brick wall with air con units and various entry points. Her elbow scraped on the wall's rough surface, sending a pang up her arm. The pain made her angry, and she lashed out with a kick that struck Gibbons right in the knee. It hurt him, but she knew it was a lucky shot. She couldn't fight back for long.

So she ran.

"Hey, bitch, get back here."

Chrissy screamed as she ran, never having ever been so terrified. What the hell was going on? Who was Gibbons and why was he doing this?

He's crazy. Oh my God. Is he one of the inmates? Has he escaped and disguised himself as a guard?

No, the orderly knew him.

Chrissy screamed louder as a gun fired behind her. The shock caused her to miss a step, and she staggered sideways against the wall. Desperate to keep moving, she groped along the bricks, almost paddling herself along. But it was too late.

Gibbons caught up with her and held her at gunpoint. "Nice try. Points awarded. Game still lost."

"Please…" She was out of breath. "Please."

"Too late for that. No one is leaving this island." He reached forward and grabbed her by the shoulder of her jacket. She tore at his wrist, trying to struggle free, but he spun her around and grabbed her from behind. She continued to fight, but all he did was laugh, the gun pressed against her temple. "Keep fighting," he said. "I won't tell you when I'm about to pull the trigger, so just keep going until oblivion sets in. There you go. That's the spirit. Any second now…"

She fought desperately.

He's going to kill me. He's going to shoot me in the head.

Frantic, she clawed behind herself, trying to reach her attacker's face. Instead, her fingers clutched at something else, something lower down. When she pulled her hand back, she realised she had snatched the keycard from his breast pocket.

Ahead of her and to the right was a door. Beside it, a magnetic scanner.

It was her only chance.

"Let go of me!" She threw her head back and felt something brittle give way. Gibbons cried out in pain, cursing at her. Chrissy knew he would pull the trigger as soon as he recovered enough to aim.

She had seconds.

Chrissy threw herself forward, landing on her knees in front of the door. She pressed the keycard against the sensor and yipped hysterically when it turned green. She dared a glance back and saw Gibbons clutching at his face, blood between his fingers. A hundred times she had researched serial killers and asked why the victims hadn't fought back harder. Now she knew that fear was a paralytic, and it made every movement clumsy.

She clambered to her feet and grabbed the door handle.

"You bitch!"

"Fuck you!" She yanked the door open and leapt through the gap.

A gunshot echoed off the brickwork.

Chrissy fell forward, the door swinging closed behind her and clunking as the lock reengaged. Panting and screaming, she rolled onto her back and waited for Gibbons to follow. But he only banged on the other side of the door, swearing to kill her.

He can't get in...

Chrissy lifted her right hand and saw that she still held the man's keycard, effectively locking him out. Its shiny plastic surface was stained with blood.

My blood. I'm bleeding.

She examined herself and spotted a bloody hole right below her collarbone on the left. She'd been shot.

I've been freaking shot!

Wooziness washed over her – her vision tilted all over the place – but she couldn't stay where she was. What if Gibbons found another working keycard, or bashed the door in? She had to get out of there.

Feeling numb rather than being in pain, she slowly dragged herself up off the floor and staggered down the corridor she had found herself in. Several doors led off of it, all with magnetic locks. She picked one at random, pressing the card against the sensor.

And then she entered a staff room with pool tables and a kitchenette. Unable to stay standing, she slumped against the wall and vomited for the third time that day.

This is a nightmare.
How is this happening?
Sim, where are you?

A door on the other side of the room burst open and a gun was aimed at her once again. She was too beaten to scream, so she just stayed where she was and waited for it all to be over.

But this time it wasn't Gibbons standing behind the gun. It was the other security guy.

What was his name? Palmer?

Palmer frowned upon seeing her and lowered his gun. "What the hell happened to you?"

"Gibbons," she said, and then slid to the ground. Before she passed out, she saw an angry scowl cross the man's face, but it didn't seem to be directed at her. "It was... Gibbons," she said again as she faded. "Shot... me."

CHAPTER
FOURTEEN

SIM and his terrified companions staggered down a corridor and entered the first door they came across. They had hoped to find help, but all they discovered was some kind of utility area with a sink and drain, along with a wall full of shelving and lockers. Jason immediately grabbed a mop from the corner and unscrewed the head, leaving himself with a makeshift staff. It was better than nothing. Unfortunately, there seemed to be nothing else of use.

"Help me move something in front of this door," said Mike, and he started dragging a nearby locker. It wasn't fixed to the wall, so Sim went and helped him, and together they slid it in front of the door. It wasn't impenetrable, but it gave them a little extra safety.

Sim leaned back against the locker and took a moment to catch his breath. He could already hear the maniacs outside, getting free. "D-Did anyone shut the door behind us?"

Everyone looked at each other.

"I was only focused on getting my ass out of there," said Jason.

Sim grunted. "The maniacs are out then."

They must have realised the door was open immediately

after Sim and the others had passed through. The magnetic lock must have failed to reengage. He would have to feed that back to Nealy.

Other feedback includes closing this entire place down and sending the inmates back to wherever they came from.

Sim scolded himself for even entertaining the idea that this place could work. As Gerry had said from the start, it was folly.

"We're trapped again," said Jason. "Great!"

"But safer," said Gerry, and then pinched the air with her thumb and forefinger. "A little."

The fiery-haired psychologist was rattled after what had almost happened to her, and it was obvious she was doing her best to keep herself together. Nobody needed to guess what the Brisbane Brutalist would have done to her if Feral Fred hadn't shot him. The Australian's moniker had come from more than just the damage he did with his fists.

But Fred saved us. Even after the wretched life he's lived, he knows right from wrong. At least, his version of it.

"We can survive this," said Sim. He lifted his head, even though it took great effort, and he looked each of his companions in the eye. "In this room are three experts of the broken mind. Together, we can survive this."

"How?" said Mike. "I'm asking as someone who is very much not an expert."

Sim chuckled. He could see the man was terrified, perhaps for the first time in his life. This wasn't Texas any more. It was somewhere adjacent to Hell.

"We survive by using our expertise. Jason and I have studied almost every killer in this place. Gerry, you know how madness operates. There are buttons we can press, levers we can pull."

Jason nodded, appearing enthused more by Sim's confidence than by his words. "Plus, they ain't all bad. Feral Fred helped us."

"Yeah," said Mike. "Where did that little guy learn to shoot? He would make one hell of a Texan."

"I'm thinking it was as much luck as skill," said Sim. "But Jason's right. Not every killer in here will be a threat. They all have their own MO, and some of them will be more focused on escaping than anything else. Some might even stay in their cells rather than risk what's outside."

Mike was following along, scratching at his bald head as though he wished he could cover it with his palm. "So things might not be as bad as we feared? That's good to know. Also, a few of the bad ones are already out of the way, right? That mad Australian and the Columbian fella?"

Sim nodded. "Escoban would have been a problem. We've had plenty of luck on our side so far. We just need it to continue a while longer."

"I still can't believe help hasn't arrived," said Jason. "Where the hell is Nealy?"

Gerry huffed and leaned back against the shelves with her arms crossed. "Somewhere safe, I would bet. The few guards in this place are probably protecting him rather than coming and getting us."

Mike shook his head. "Nealy wouldn't do that. Even being cynical, he would see our deaths as a massive liability. If he can get us out of here, he will."

"Then where's the cavalry?" Jason asked, lifting his arms and letting them flop at his sides.

"He hasn't hired enough people to run this place," said Sim. "It's obvious. I think this place is over budget, and I'm sure most investors don't want to touch the Keep with a bargepole. That's why Nealy's turned to a pair of YouTubers like me and Jason. We're not exactly high profile."

"Hey," said Jason, but then he reconsidered and shrugged. "Yeah, I guess you're right."

"Whatever guards are in this place likely have their hands full." Sim shook his head and grunted. "We already watched one die, and we know that another was responsible for unlocking the cells. For all we know, half the security team could be in on what's happening here."

Mike growled. "Corporate terrorists. Had to deal with a few myself over the years. Had to stop my orca shows because of them. Set fire to my place in Martha's Vineyard and almost killed the maid."

"Tragic," said Jason.

"So help might not be coming," said Gerry. She raised a foot and rubbed at her grubby sole. Her shoes hadn't made it out of the cell block. "*Magnifique*."

Sim rubbed at his eyes and realised he'd been crying at some point. When he blinked, his lids stung. "We're going to survive this. I'm going to find Chrissy and get down to the docks. Then we're getting off this island. I'll sail the ferry back by myself if I have to."

"You keep on saying that," said Jason, flapping his arms again. "But how do we get out of the Keep? What's the plan?"

Sim held the keycard up. "You need these to enter certain doors, right? All we have to do is get through enough of them to put distance between us and the inmates. Meanwhile, we remember one thing: serial killers are not supernatural. They are flesh and blood, the same as us. If it comes to a fight, they have no advantage other than our fear. If we face them head on, we have a chance of surviving. Mike, you're a big guy. With you on our side, we can make *them* afraid of *us*."

Mike chuckled and smacked a fist into his palm. "My football days are long behind me, boy, but I think I can probably crack a few skulls."

Jason tapped his staff against the ground. "And I'm ready to go full Morgan Jones on whoever comes at us."

Mike frowned. "Who?"

Sim nodded to his colleagues and smiled. "We can do this. The hard part is over."

Everyone let out a sigh, steeling themselves for what was to come. It was little more than a self-empowerment exercise, but sometimes belief went a long way. If they behaved like victims, they would be done for. The one thing serial killers did not expect was for their prey to bite back.

Jason suddenly frowned. "I, um, hate to put a downer on things, guys, but I just had a worrying thought."

"What?" Gerry frowned at him. "Tell us."

"Yeah, it's just something we haven't spoken about, that's all. In the excitement, it kind of went forgotten about."

Sim shook his head, not following. "What are you talking about?"

"Well, um…" Jason sighed. "What do we do if we bump into the Boxcutter? Nealy has him squirrelled away somewhere inside the Keep, but he's probably on the loose as well. We can fight back against some of these maniacs, but I don't think any of us has what it takes to face off against that freak."

Sim slumped back against the locker and groaned. All his new-found confidence drained away, and he wanted, once again, to crawl under a desk. "I think all we can do is pray to God that we don't bump into him. If we do, we won't make it out of here alive."

Jason nodded. "I was afraid you'd say that."

"Two minutes to catch our breath," said Sim, "and then we're leaving."

And then I'm coming to get you, Chrissy.

Chrissy came to in mid-air. For a moment she thought she was floating on the sea, but then she realised she was being carried atop the shoulders of a man. She immediately struggled and fought, but it was useless.

"Easy!" said the man carrying her, and he eased her down onto a counter high enough that her legs dangled. When she saw the man's face, it all came back to her.

"P-Palmer?"

The man nodded. "You okay? You've lost some blood, but I think you should get away with it. Bullet went in and out beneath your collarbone. I've seen worse."

She tried to lift her left arm but ended up crying out. The pain was like someone had filled her blood vessels with red-hot needles. "It hurts."

"Yeah, gunshot wounds are funny like that. Try not to move your arm, okay? I'm going to patch you up and that should help." He turned and started searching the room. It was a large area, which Chrissy quickly realised was a gift shop. But instead of plush teddy bears and plastic animals, there were rubber knives and serial killer puppets.

"What is happening?" she asked, while Palmer continued searching.

"Gibbons. He's sabotaged the Keep."

"What do you mean?"

He looked up at her from behind a display table. "I mean, he unlocked the cells and now the inmates are running the asylum. I have no idea why."

Chrissy felt woozy again, and she wasn't sure if it was just from blood loss. "Sim! I... I have to get out of here."

Palmer rushed back and steadied her just in time to keep her from tumbling off the counter. "Easy there! Look, I have something."

By *something*, he meant a Jack the Ripper tea towel and some Ted Bundy themed duct tape. "I'm going to take off your jacket and lift your shirt. Is that okay?"

"What if I said no?"

"Then you might bleed to death."

"Go ahead."

She closed her eyes and Palmer gently applied the tea towel to her wound and secured it with the duct tape. The pain was immense, and she thought she might pass out again, but fortunately he was done in less than a minute. When she opened her eyes, she saw him looking back at her. "What next?" she asked. "What do we do now?"

"Nealy should be in the Keep's panic room by now. I need to get you there, too."

She shook her head. "We have to help the others. I need to find Sim."

"Leave that to me." He pulled a handgun from his side and yanked back on the top of it. She knew nothing about guns, but he seemed to know what he was doing from the way it clicked smoothly. "I'm going to put a stop to whatever this is. In the meantime…"

Chrissy took deep breaths and tried to stay conscious while Palmer went behind the counter and bent down. She was vaguely aware of him opening a hatch in the floor, then suddenly he was upright again, holding some kind of toy-sized rifle.

She frowned. "What is that?"

"It fires CS gas canisters. Here."

She shook her head. "I don't want it."

He shoved it into her arms. "If I can't protect you, or if we get separated, aim this at the target's feet and pull the trigger. It'll make life hell for anyone in the room – probably you as well – but it'll put a stop to anything trying to hurt you. Crude but effective."

She nodded, but she really hoped she didn't have to use it. Palmer had said the cells were unlocked. Did that mean they were sharing the building with three dozen psychopathic killers? This was the Chernobyl of prisons.

We might never make it off this island.

"What is Gibbons planning?" she asked. "Why the hell would he do this?"

"I wish I knew. What was he doing when he shot you?"

"Heading outside. He was looking out to sea. Why do you think?"

Palmer shook his head and sighed. "Probably booked a ride

out of here. Cause a fire and then get the hell out. It's in the terrorist handbook. Doubt he's working alone."

"Were you in the army?" She didn't know why she asked it. Perhaps she thought it would give her confidence.

"Long enough to know what I'm doing. Try not to worry. Once I gather my men, I'll take back control of this place, even if I have to kill every inmate."

"That's... a harsh solution."

"You got a better one?"

She shook her head. "Has Nealy given you the okay to kill his tourist attractions?"

"This isn't about my job now, Christina. It's about my duty. Nealy placed you and the others in danger. I'm going to do my best to get you out of it."

"Chrissy."

"What?"

"Call me Chrissy."

He nodded and smiled at her. "Okay, Chrissy. How's the shoulder?"

"Better now that it's wrapped up."

"Good. There's a security annex through the door behind us. I'm going to log in and try to get a view of the prison. We should be able to see where Sim and the others are."

Chrissy hopped off the desk, almost into Palmer's arms. Her shoulder hurt like hell, but she ignored the pain as best she could. "Let's go, then. I need to know Sim's okay."

Palmer nodded and moved away behind the desk. There was a door behind the counter that he unlocked with a keycard. Opening the door, he stood aside and let her in first. Inside, she discovered a small back office with a desk, a computer, and some filing cabinets. Everything looked brand new.

Palmer eased her aside and moved over to the deck. The computer was switched off, so he had to press a button on top of the tower. The wait for it to boot up was excruciating, and the sudden jaunty chime it made when it was ready caused Chrissy to jump.

Palmer smiled at her. "You're safe. Relax."

She nodded, but could feel both hands trembling by her sides.

Palmer stooped in front of the computer monitor and started clicking the mouse. He logged into various programs and cursed several times as he struggled to do what he wanted. She got the impression he wasn't a fan of technology, but he kept at it until he succeeded. "Got it. Here's the CCTV feeds for the entire facility."

Chrissy stooped beside him, staring at the monitor. Dozens of tiny boxes appeared in a grid, some showing movement, others focused on empty rooms. Palmer clicked the ones with movement.

"Shit," he said as a feed showed a rioting prison block. It was A Block, one of the first areas they'd entered on the ride through. Chrissy spotted Seth Markle, the Kissimmee Killer, kicking at a door and trying to get out. Three dead guards lay in the middle of the cell block, their necks visibly broken. Miguel Reyes, the old schizophrenic, was sitting cross-legged beside the bodies, rocking back and forth. "This is bad. My men..." He flicked to another video, this one showing a guard with a slashed throat lying on a trolley bed. "Damn it, John. Why didn't you go with Nealy? Did anyone manage to survive this?" He switched back to the feed from A Block, as if he were unable to look at his dead colleague any longer.

Chrissy clutched her aching stomach. "You're not going to regain control, are you?"

Palmer glanced at her and then blew air out of his nose. "I don't know. At least the inmates are mostly contained for the moment. Without a keycard they can't—"

Seth Markle suddenly yanked open the door in A Block. Seeing a way out, several inmates flooded to join him and they all escaped in a group.

Palmer shook his head. "What? How did they…? Gibbons!"

"What? What has he done?"

"He's deactivated the magnetic door locks. When you took his keycard, you left him no choice. He must have logged into the system from somewhere to do it. Maybe the VIP lounge or the loading bay around the back of the Keep."

Chrissy stared at him. "So… every door is unlocked now? The inmates can go anywhere?"

He nodded, grave concern written all over his face. He might've been in the army, but he had clearly never been in a situation like this. Who ever had?

"I need to find Sim," she said, feeling it now more than ever.

"Okay. Okay, let me try to find out where he and the others are." Palmer started clicking on more of the feeds, chaos reigning in multiple cell blocks. Every guard they saw was dead.

Then they spotted Sim.

Chrissy sighed with relief. Sim was with Mike, Gerry, and Jason – and they were okay. Currently, they were creeping down a narrow corridor. Jason held a wooden pole and crept in front.

"They're okay. Thank God."

But Palmer didn't seem relieved. His brow furrowed and his mouth moved in a silent whisper.

"What's wrong?" she asked him.

"I know where that corridor leads to," he said. "It's not good."

"Where does it go?" she demanded. "Where does it lead to?"

"The Boxcutter's lair. They're heading right for it."

Chrissy felt woozy again. This time, Palmer wasn't quick enough to catch her.

CHAPTER
FIFTEEN

JASON OPENED the door in front of them. He took the lead, because he was the only one armed. Sim had to respect him for his bravery; he was ready to fight. Mike, too, was on high alert, both fists bunched in anticipation of using them. Gerry stuck close to him, with Sim right behind her.

When they exited the corridor into the room ahead, they found themselves inside what looked like an abandoned warehouse. The walls were dirty and crumbling, and glass panels overhead let in weak sunlight. Scraps of metal and rotting wood were piled up everywhere, and Sim wouldn't have been surprised to see tubby rats scurrying back and forth. Except that it was clearly a themed room – there were several telltale signs. The floor was freshly laid cement without the slightest scratch. Also, a fresh breeze flowed from working air conditioners and kept the large space at a comfortable temperature. On one side of the room, a small partitioned cubicle held a brightly lit EXIT sign.

"What is this place?" asked Mike. He yanked up his jeans and adjusted his belt buckle, a little less tense after finding the room empty. "Looks like somebody forgot to pay the maintenance bill."

"It must be some kind of attraction." Sim took another look around, trying to figure it out, but the warehouse was empty besides debris. Then he spotted some graffiti, so large and prominent that he wondered how he had missed it.

"Oh no." He shook his head. "Oh no, oh no."

Everyone looked at him. Gerry grimaced. "What? What is wrong, Sim?"

He pointed, because he couldn't get out the words.

Everyone turned around and looked up at the graffiti.

WELCOME TO THE BOXCUTTER'S LAIR.

"That ain't good," said Jason, and he raised his wooden staff, searching for danger.

"I don't see anyone here," said Mike. "I think we're good."

Gerry held a hand over her mouth like she was going to be sick. With her other hand, she pointed to the partitioned cubicle at the side of the warehouse. "What if he's in there?"

"Why would he be?" Jason asked.

Gerry shrugged.

"We need to check it out," said Sim. "It might be our way out."

Jason groaned. He held his staff in both hands and cricked his neck. "Let's get it over with, then. If I'm going to die horrifically, I would rather it be sooner than later. If my corpse poops itself, don't let Gerry see."

Gerry groaned. Mike moved next to her and put a hand on her back to comfort her.

As one, they crossed the debris-laden warehouse en route to the small cubicle at the back. It looked like nothing more than a tiny annex, built merely as a barrier to keep out any draughts. There seemed no reason to assume the Boxcutter would be inside. If the serial killer had been here, then surely he would've focused on escaping? No need to hang around.

They reached the cubicle and stopped. Jason held his staff and moved to the right. He gave Sim a nod, communicating that he wanted him to open the door.

Sim took a breath, grabbed the handle. "On three. One... Two... Three!"

Sim opened the door. Jason jabbed his staff through the gap. But he hit thin air. No one inside.

There was just a small space with two doors – the one they'd just opened, and another one ahead. The next door had a sign reading: EXIT TUNNEL.

Gerry let out a breath that she'd clearly been holding. "A way out! *Tres bon.*"

"You think it leads outside?" asked Jason.

Sim shrugged. "Perhaps it's a utility tunnel like at Disney. A staff route to get around the Keep unseen."

"Sounds good to me," said Mike, and he stepped forward to open the door.

"Wait!" said Sim. "Don't be so hasty."

But Mike had already moved too fast. He opened the door and gave everyone a view of what was inside. It was indeed a tunnel. And, thankfully, it was empty.

"This looks like our way out," said Jason, stepping inside and turning around. "Come on!"

They shuffled inside the tunnel. Sim's stomach was in knots, but every step he took convinced him more and more that all was okay. It really could be a staff tunnel leading to a way out. This nightmare might finally have an end.

They continued in silence.

The tunnel was long, stretching off for at least a hundred metres. The beginning was solid cement, like an underground bunker from an apocalypse movie. A little chilly, Sim felt a breeze coming from somewhere, but he could see no gaps in the cement. On one section of the wall there was a large poster, five feet high and mounted on a wooden board. It read: KEEP MOVING AT ALL TIMES!

"It changes up ahead," said Jason, and he raised his staff as if he expected danger. But none came.

The cement walls gave way to a metal and glass section with complicated struts and fasteners. A few feet beyond it, the tunnel became a transparent tube, like one of the shark walk-throughs you found at aquariums. But water didn't surround this tube, only darkness. Shadows reigned beyond the glass, like staring into a mineshaft.

At least the tube itself was lit. LED spotlights shone down from the centre of the ceiling, placed every ten feet or so.

"Not a fan of this," said Mike. "Feels like we're walking into damnation."

Jason managed a nervous chuckle. "Just another of Nealy's attractions."

"I agree," said Sim. "But what's the attraction? What is this supposed to be? What is the link to serial killers?"

"Hmm," said Gerry. "A walk through darkness? A metaphor, perhaps?"

Mike grumbled. "Let's not waste time wondering. Nealy'll have plenty of time to provide answers later, trust me."

Everyone agreed and picked up speed. Sim shivered from the cold, but also from the creeping sensation of darkness closing in on them. The tunnel was so unsettling that it could be an attraction all by itself. Perhaps it had nothing to do with serial killers. Maybe it was just meant to freak people out.

Job done.

They reached the halfway point.

The darkness seemed to move. Everyone continued, but Sim slowly came to a stop at the back of the line. Goose pimples had covered his arms, and he suddenly felt something wasn't right.

I feel like something's out there.

Watching us.

Sim turned to face the glass wall of the tunnel, almost

pressing his face right up against it. The darkness was absolute, but somehow it seemed to shift ever so slightly.

Two flickers of light broke through.

Eyes.

Sim leapt back as a figure rushed out of the darkness and collided with the glass. Lit by the frayed edges of the LED lights, the contorted, monstrous face shone with a sickly orange glow.

A misshapen nose. A fleshy patch over the left eye. Brown, rotting teeth.

The Boxcutter glared at Sim, massive hands pressed against the glass. He wore a grubby brown jumpsuit the colour of decay.

The others turned back and screamed in terror, but none of them matched the colossal scream coming from Sim's lungs. His entire body froze, like he was having a seizure. He tried to move, to get away, but his knees locked in place. Even breathing was impossible.

The Boxcutter beat his fists against the glass. The entire tunnel shuddered as the maniac bellowed and howled. A demon from Hell.

Jason rushed past Mike and Gerry and grabbed Sim by the arm, looking him in the eye and blocking his view of the monster outside. "Sim? Sim, it's okay. He can't get inside. Look at me! You're okay. We're leaving here, right now."

Sim nodded, but he still couldn't move. Jason had to tug at him and keep a grip on his arm. The wooden staff tapped against the floor with every step they took.

The Boxcutter followed for a few seconds, banging on the glass and bellowing.

Then he leapt back into the darkness, swallowed whole.

"He's gone," said Gerry, her vocal cords tight, almost strangled.

Mike grumbled. "Goddamn freak."

"Come on," said Jason. "Keep it moving."

Sim was a gibbering wreck. He fought to regain his senses, but the sudden onslaught of primal terror had rocked him to the core. The most sadistic killer on Earth had locked eyes with him.

And all I saw was utter and complete, ice-cold emptiness.

Evil exists. It's inside that monster.

The group hurried forward, reforming in a line inside the narrow tunnel. It was the opposite of a shark tunnel. *They* were the exhibit, being watched by a man who lived in the shadows outside.

A noise behind caused them all to glance back. Sim shuddered, and when Jason's hand slipped away from his arm, he moaned, missing the comfort already.

"What was that?" asked Gerry. She stepped backwards, her bare feet leaving grubby prints on the cement floor.

Mike clenched his fist. "It's nothing. Probably just a door slamming somewhere. It was… just a noise. It was nothing."

Sim realised that the LEDS at the very front of the tunnel — the section with cement walls — had turned off. It meant the glass tube fell away into a darkness as deep as the one outside. Were the lights motion activated? Nealy's eco-credentials suggested they probably were.

But what was that noise? It didn't sound like a door slamming.

"Let's just keep moving," said Mike. "The sooner we get out of this glass intestine, the better."

Everyone started moving again, but Sim walked backwards, keeping his eye on the shadows towards the beginning of the tunnel.

Something stepped out of those shadows.

The Boxcutter stared straight ahead. From inside the tunnel.

How?

How did he get inside?

Sim tried to shout out a warning, but his breath caught in his chest. He fought and spluttered until the words came out. "R-R-Run!"

The Boxcutter lumbered forward, a hunched-over beast. But despite his size and visible limp, he moved fast.

Too fast.

The others turned to see what had startled Sim, and when they saw what was racing through the tunnel towards them, they screeched in terror and broke into a sprint.

The Boxcutter bellowed. The noise rumbled through the glass pipe.

Sim crushed up against Mike, screaming hysterically. The Texan slowed in order to shove Gerry in front of him, but it caused a bottleneck, with Sim trapped at the back.

"M-Move!" Sim glanced over his shoulder and saw the Boxcutter racing towards him, a galloping, misshapen beast. "Get out of my way," he yelled. "Get out of my way."

"I'm trying!" said Mike.

He's going to catch me. He's too fast.

How is he so fast?

Sim let out a bellow from the depths of his stomach, and once again his entire body froze. This was it. The end. It was always going to be.

The Boxcutter roared, his mouth a black hole full of jagged teeth. His eyes were cauldrons of shadow and malice.

Mike started pulling at Sim from behind, trying to get him moving, but they weren't getting out of this tunnel alive. Sim tried to close his eyes, but they refused to obey him.

The Boxcutter caught up to them.

But Sim noticed something strange, a distortion of the air. Something caught the light, and the Boxcutter's pose suggested he was pushing something in front of him.

Sim was suddenly knocked backwards. He fell, landing on his rump.

In his confusion, he squinted ahead.

Three sets of caster wheels caught his eye. One set fixed against the ceiling and two on opposite edges of the floor.

The Boxcutter shuddered to a halt, smashing up against the air itself.

No, not the air. Glass.

The Boxcutter was standing behind a moving glass barrier affixed to the tunnel via casters running along thin railings in the ceiling and floor. None of the railings were easily noticeable, but now that he knew they were there, they were obvious.

The Boxcutter has stopped because the casters had hit upon a section of stoppers, preventing the glass panel from sliding any further. The monster pressed himself up against the glass partition and licked the transparent surface with a bulbous brown tongue.

Jason grabbed Sim and helped him to his feet, despite the fact he was freaking out. "What the hell? This is messed up!"

"Nealy promised no more live actors," said Gerry. "He did not keep his word."

Mike slumped against the side of the tunnel. "Is that the guy? The real guy?"

Sim stared at the sadistic killer only inches away and nodded. "That's him. This is the Boxcutter Killer."

"Ugly as a stump," said Mike, but he sounded as if he wanted to cry.

The Boxcutter stepped back from the glass and cackled. He was a gigantic human being, perhaps seven feet tall if he could stand up straight. His left shoulder was a rounded boulder, twice the size of the right. He glared at Sim, seeming to ignore all else.

Then he spoke. "You!"

Sim felt like someone had punched him. He was a fourteen-year-old boy again, facing something he couldn't understand. Something he might never understand.

Evil.

Why does it exist? How is it made?

Jason grabbed Sim around the waist and dragged him backwards. Mike helped and yanked Sim by the arm. Together, the two men pulled him along the tunnel towards safety. If safety still existed.

Sim couldn't get his legs beneath him, or even turn to face the same way as the others. He was locked in a stare with the Boxcutter, who continued to grin and cackle.

"I remember you, little boy," the killer yelled after him. "I remember you!"

The tunnel ended with a themed door, a slab of metal with a bright yellow and black warning sign stamped across the middle. No one appreciated it. They were well beyond admiring the work that had gone into the Keep.

Mike shoved open the door and helped everyone through. Gerry was limping slightly, her bare feet no doubt bruised from all the terrified sprinting.

Before Sim passed through into the next room, he took one last glance back down the tunnel.

The Boxcutter was gone.

Sim shook his head, tears staining his cheeks. He could barely keep himself upright, and he had to lean on Jason, who had to lean on his staff to keep from collapsing under the added weight.

"The hell is this?" Mike scratched at his head. "Is there no end to this insanity?"

Jason groaned, looking around in horror. "Enough already."

Sim pushed himself away from Jason and leaned against the wall. He shook his head and blinked several times, not wanting to see any more.

They were inside some kind of waxworks. A museum of horror.

Ted Bundy towered over Gerry, arm in a plaster cast, and his curly black hair so lifelike it could've been used to make a wig. Next to Bundy stood Dennis Rader, the BTK strangler. BTK for Bind, Torture, Kill. No explanation needed.

Also in the room were wax figures of Richard Ramirez, David Berkowitz, Fred West, and many more. For the first time in his life, serial killers did not fascinate Sim at all. In fact, he was downright disgusted.

"This place is horrible," said Gerry, grimacing at a bespectacled statue of Jeffrey Dahmer. "All of these killers in one place. Who would enjoy this?"

Jason put both hands on his staff and slumped against it. "Twenty-four hours ago, I would have. Now, I'm considering changing my channel to nothing but Minecraft videos. Sim, what d'you think?"

Sim didn't answer. He pressed his back against the wall and slid down onto his butt. He couldn't stand it any more. Couldn't walk or run or speak. The Boxcutter was here. His nightmares were real, not just videos on the internet.

I'm done. No more. Please, no more.

God, just get Chrissy out of this place and you can have me.

"You okay?" Jason asked him. "You don't look good."

Gerry tutted. "Are any of us? We were just chased by a fiend."

Jason shook his head, squinting suspiciously at Sim. "Nah, something's wrong. Sim, what is it? The Boxcutter… It's almost like he knew you."

Mike nodded. Sweat beaded his bald head. "He said he recognised you. How?"

Sim shrugged. He couldn't answer that. He couldn't tell them that the Boxcutter recognised him because they had met, many years ago.

Not that *long ago.*

Feels like yesterday.

"It's not important," said Gerry. "We need to keep moving, *oui*? We must be near the end of this wretched place."

"I'd love to know where Nealy is during all this," said Mike. "We've been on our own since the moment he left us. Almost makes me feel like this is all part of one big show."

Jason pulled a face. "If that's true, then the man's a genius. I'm not willing to risk it, though. That guard earlier looked pretty dead to me."

"We all saw it," said Gerry. "We know this is real. There has been too much blood spilled to assume otherwise."

A door opened at the side of the room and someone rushed in. Everybody yelped, and Jason leapt forward with his staff. "Yo, bitch! Who goes there?"

A bloodstained man in an orange jumpsuit skidded to a halt about fifteen feet away. He seemed shocked to see them, and his hands immediately shot up into the air.

"Oh, hell no," said Mike. "Quick, we need to take this guy down and lock that door."

Jason raised his staff.

The inmate kept his hands raised and started shaking his head. "Please!" He could barely pronounce the word, but he said it again. "Please!"

Sim remained sitting on the floor, unable to get up, but he had enough strength to call out to the others and inform them who they were looking at. "That's Lee Chen."

Mike glanced back at him. "Who?"

Jason answered. "The Shanghai Spike."

"He's bad, right?"

"Hell yeah."

Sim called out again. "No, he's innocent. He... He shouldn't be here."

Lee Chen nodded. "Innocent. No do crime."

"I also believe he is innocent," said Gerry. "I studied his case briefly, and there was an appalling lack of evidence."

Mike shrugged. "So what? This guy should be locked up with the rest of them, not in here with us. Hey, Mr Chung, you stay right there, you hear me?"

Lee Chen frowned.

Sim decided he didn't care enough to argue. If Mike and Jason wanted to beat Lee Chen to a pulp, then whatever. None of them were getting out of the Keep alive anyway. If help had been coming, it would've arrived by now. They were trapped, hunted, and if Lee Chen was here, then other inmates would be soon.

Maybe even the Boxcutter. He'll get a chance to finish what he started twelve years ago.

Nealy had said there were three dozen killers in the Keep. Who knew which one would be the one to kill him, and in what horrid fashion?

Maybe the Kissimmee Killer will strangle me? Or Brenda Bates will shoot me in the head.

While Mike and Jason crept towards Chen, Sim studied the waxworks, suddenly asking himself why he had spent so much of his life studying wickedness. Every shiny face he gazed upon he knew intimately from his research and from his channel. He had documented them all.

Aileen Wuornos. Killed seven while working as a prostitute.

Dr Harold Shipman. Euthanised a possible two hundred and fifty victims, making him one of the most prolific murderers in human history.

Ed Kemper. Killed six college girls and several members of his own family. A highly fetishistic killer.

Pedro Lopez. Monstrous child killer who…

Sim shook his head. He could think about it no longer. The defences he had built against such atrocities had fallen away. His soul was exposed. Raw.

And yet his eyes kept moving from statue to statue.

Jeffrey Dahmer.
Myra Hindley.
Peter Sutcliffe.
Simon Cruz.
Andrei Chikatilo.
Ed Gein.
Wait a minute!

Something occurred to Sim, but he couldn't quite put his

finger on it.

Simon Cruz? The Kraken.

All the statues were of past serial killers, or ones who didn't seem to be at the Keep. Nealy had gathered many killers here, but not all of them. The waxworks were a clever way to include the monsters who were not here in the flesh.

But Simon Cruz was here in the flesh. Sim had seen the Filipino serial killer in A Block, along with Lee Chen.

Just as the answers came, Simon Cruz betrayed his stillness by moving his eyes and looking at Sim. The game was up. The killer knew he'd been spotted.

"Look out!"

The Kraken leapt onto Mike's back and started stabbing him in the chest with a shard of wood. Mike, even as he yelled out in shock and pain, managed to shove Jason out of harm's way.

For once, Gerry didn't scream. She ran forward and started punching at the man on Mike's back.

Simon Cruz wasn't large, but he was unbelievably vicious. And wild. He wrapped his bare feet around Mike's waist and screeched like a vulture.

Mike roared and tried to dislodge the man, but he couldn't get a grip on him.

Jason swung his staff but ended up hitting Mike in the ribs and knocking the wind out of him. Blood spilled all down the front of his shirt, staining his silver belt buckle.

Simon Cruz leapt off Mike and grabbed Jason. Jason tried to bring up his staff but couldn't, so he tried to headbutt the killer instead. It almost worked, but the killer clawed at his eyes and sent him down to the ground.

Gerry shouted over at Sim. "Get up! Get up and help!"

But Sim couldn't. He remained slumped on the ground, knowing there was no point in fighting.

Simon Cruz turned his attention to Gerry. Mike was on the ground, clutching his chest. Jason was holding his eyes and moaning. She was at the killer's mercy. "Help me!" she called out.

But Sim couldn't move.

Lee Chen could.

The Shanghai Spike threw himself at Cruz and sent the man sprawling into Bundy's statue. The 'campus' killer teetered back and forth but stayed in place.

Cruz spun around and snarled. He shouted in a foreign language and then launched himself at Chen. The two men fought, but Cruz was by far the most brutal. He beat at Chen's face and bit into his shoulder. Eventually, the man had to shove Cruz away and try to retreat.

Gerry rushed over to Sim and begged him to get up. "Please. Help me. I need you. Can't you see what's happening? Open your eyes."

Sim flinched. *Eyes wide open.*

Chrissy had spent the last three years getting him to face the world, to try new things. She'd given so much of herself to him, with so little in return. If he died right now, he would never get a chance to pay her back for all the love she'd shown him. Wouldn't even get to say thank you.

Sim started to get up, but as he did so, Cruz appeared and snatched Gerry from behind. She kicked out with her bare feet, squealing, but no one was close enough to help her. Sim was still in too much of a daze to react.

Cruz moved away, holding the wooden shard to Gerry's throat. "I take her," he said. "I take her or I kill her. Choose."

"You're not taking her anywhere," said Mike, and he flung himself up off the floor and towards Gerry.

Simon Cruz released his grip on Gerry and threw her aside. He set his feet firmly to receive Mike's tackle and thrust out with the shard of wood.

Mike barked, a sudden, clipped sound, and then he collapsed to his knees. The wooden shard was sticking out of his eye. Cruz had a hold of the other end, and he shoved it hard enough to topple Mike onto his back.

"P-P-Please! D-D-Don't!"

Cruz straddled Mike's chest and shoved down on the shard with both hands, burying it into his eye socket. Mike gurgled and said words that were not words. His hands and feet rattled on the ground.

Then he stopped moving completely.

Cruz had a wide grin on his bloodstained face. He turned and looked for Gerry, who was cowering beside Lee Chen, who appeared ready to protect her.

Jason was back on his feet by now, but he was dumbstruck by the sight of Mike on the ground.

Could the colourful Texan truly be dead?

Cruz leapt to his feet and sidestepped in a circle, weighing up who to attack first. Predictably, he went for Gerry.

Lee Chen leapt in the way, but he was outmatched once again by the Kraken's ferociousness. Gerry yelled out for help, penned into a space behind them.

Sim didn't know what to do. He wanted to fight, but the thought of facing off against a killer was too much to bear.

Jason approached with his staff, but Cruz dodged as soon as he tried to hit him. The man was a shark, too quick, too lethal.

Chen fell to the ground, his face a mess from multiple scratches and punches. Jason was clumsy and unable to put his staff to good use. Cruz was grinning with the pleasure of the hunt. They could not match his ferocity. Not even close.

Sim once again became sure they were all going to die. He had survived a killer once. He couldn't do so again.

And that time I only survived by begging. I didn't fight my way out of it.

No, I didn't beg. I manipulated. I used my empathy and understanding, something no serial killer possesses. All of them are driven by impulse and subconscious desires.

"Gerry!" Sim suddenly called out, but he had to call out a

second time to get her attention. She was a deer in the headlights. "He's a woman hater. Killed his ex-wife for cheating on him and found out he liked it. Mock him."

Cowering in the corner of the room, she shook her head at Sim like he was mad. "What?"

"Emasculate him. Manipulate his ego."

She continued to shake her head, but slowly she turned to face Cruz, who continued to toy with Jason, punching him in the side of the head before ducking away whenever he swung his staff and tried to retaliate.

"Hey, Cruz," Gerry called out. "You sad little man. You snatch women because none would look at you otherwise. Pathetic! Your penis is so small and you do not know how to use it. You are a eunuch, *oui*?"

Cruz stopped dodging Simon's staff long enough to turn and glare at Gerry. "Shut your mouth, bitch!"

"Make me, you pathetic little boy. No wonder your wife started fucking someone else. She wanted a real man. Not a silly little boy like you. *Tête de noeud.*"

Cruz's smile disappeared. His face contorted with rage. His attention turned away from Jason, and he stalked after Gerry. From the floor, Lee Chen tried to grab Cruz's leg, but the man kicked him in the jaw and sent him rolling away without barely a look. He scowled demonically at Gerry. "I am going to fuck you all night long, red-headed bitch."

Gerry sneered. "I am French. I only fuck men with class, so take your tiny peepee someplace else."

"Bitch!" Cruz put up his hands and lunged for Gerry's neck, but before he reached her, Lee Chen reappeared and struck him around the head with an object. It was a plaster cast.

He'd yanked it off of Bundy.

Sim looked over and saw that the 'campus killer' was now missing an arm.

Cruz staggered, shaking off the blow. Chen swung for him again and clumped him in the shoulder, knocking him sideways. There was blood in Chen's mouth and he spat it out. "I will kill you, man," said Chen, his face a mishmash of bruises and cuts.

Cruz lunged forward, but before he reached Chen, Jason appeared and smacked the wooden broom handle against the back of the killer's head so hard that it snapped in two. It was a knockout blow, possibly even fatal, and it switched Cruz off like a light.

The Kraken flopped to the floor like a lifeless dummy.

Sim slumped back against the wall and tried not to pass out. His heart was almost beating out of his chest.

I was right. We can survive this if we use what we know. Every killer is fundamentally weak. A broken vessel. We just have to know where the cracks are.

Chrissy, I need to find you.

I have to survive.

Lee Chen dropped beside Cruz and smashed Bundy's cast down onto his head. Then he did so a second time. And a third. Until the Kraken's face was a bloody octopus of brain, bone, and tissue. Exhausted, Chen then rolled onto his back and lost consciousness, succumbing to his injuries. The attack had seemed personal. Perhaps the pent-up frustration of being wrongfully imprisoned.

Sim felt sorry for the man. *Innocent or not, he seems to be on our team.*

Gerry stepped over Cruz's body and crouched down beside Mike. She felt the big American's fatty neck for a pulse, but when she slumped down beside him with a defeated look on her face, it was clear that he wasn't getting up again.

Jason moved over to Sim and leaned against the wall. He shook his head sadly, but said nothing.

Neither did Sim.

There were no words.

CHAPTER
SIXTEEN

GIBBONS MET the others at the dock, but not before using the computer in the VIP reception lounge to unlock the rest of the Keep. That bitch taking his keycard had thrown a spanner in the works. He'd hoped to keep the inmates and low-level staff contained, rather than spread out around the prison, but it wouldn't matter in the end. They would all end up the same as Monroe, Jones, and Ballesteros by the end of the day.

The boat had left, leaving him in charge of nine heavily armed freedom fighters. He led them through the biting rain and took them around the back of the Keep where they could gain quick access into C Block. From there, they would clear out A and B blocks, and finally the high-security wing. They could mop up here and there wherever the inmates and staff had got free.

The Burning Dollar was the fastest growing underground movement in the world, filled with young and old alike. People who were sick of the one per cent and the WEF treating the planet and its population like it was theirs. Their nefarious plans to control every being on Earth would never come to fruition. The Burning Dollar would not allow it. Screw corporations like Everstech and Le Grande Mar. They were all due a fall.

Nealy was no different to any other member of the elite. The kind of man who tells the world how to act while doing whatever he pleases. *Don't use diesel cars*, they say from their private planes. *Don't support China and its inhumane working conditions*, they say from the floors of their Beijing factories. *Follow the green agenda*, they yell from their ships full of toxic waste, bound for India or Africa. It was the energy companies that created the term 'Carbon Footprint' in order to shift the economic burden onto the individual rather than take responsibility for it themselves. It was all one big game.

Nealy spoke of a better tomorrow from Ecohamlet's boardroom, while creating a theme park full of serial killers for paying customers to gawp at. He was a cupidinous beast, with billions to his name while half the world starved. Creating a better tomorrow was all fine, so long as he didn't have to live the same life as ordinary people.

Well, today he's going to die in the gutter like those he refuses to help.

This plan had been eighteen months in the setting up. Gibbons had taken a shitty job for a shitty man on a shitty island in order to get access to the Keep's operating systems and eventually launch a deadly coup. No one was leaving this island alive.

"Everyone, on me," he said, raising his MP5 and heading over to the fire exit at the back of the Keep. The sensor was green, unlocked like every other door now. He opened it carefully and gave a hand signal for his team to spread out inside.

They did so, immediately firing their weapons.

"I guess the party's starting early then," said Gibbons, and he pivoted around the door frame and hopped inside the warehouse. He instantly picked a shot and took down an inmate, but a dozen more were loose inside the themed 'Lair of the Boxcutter'.

At least there was no sign of the sick freak himself. Gibbons wanted to bag that one for himself. But that could wait.

Wild maniacs filled the warehouse, many of them half naked. He hadn't expected to see so many of them together in one place like this, and it made things a hell of a lot more urgent. Even before he picked his second shot, a female killer almost leapt on top of Gibbons. It was only because his teammates had him covered that the woman ended up riddled with bullets.

"There're too many of them!" shouted Riley.

"No," said Gibbons, shooting an orange-suited killer in the side of the head, a man he thought might have been Abdul Achebe, the Nigerian Blight. "We've got this. Put these monsters down."

"Sir, we can't—"

The first of his men screamed, quickly followed by a second. Gibbons peered through the throng of bodies and saw a scraggly, long-haired teenager leaping around like a monkey. The feral creature had leapt at one of Gibbons's men and had immediately torn a massive chunk out of his jugular before releasing him in a spray of his own blood.

Gibbons emptied half a clip at the freak but missed every shot. More of his men screamed around the warehouse, set upon by killers from every angle. Many of them attacked even after receiving bullet wounds. They didn't go down like normal men. They ran hot with fury and madness.

"Shit shit shit!" Gibbons sidestepped, trying to keep his back to the wall. The mission had gone to pot. Unlocking the entire prison had been an error. The plan had been to execute the killers in their individual cell blocks, but too many of them had congregated out in the open. "We need to retreat!"

He turned back to the door to outside, but a Hispanic man with a thin moustache blocked his way, grinning like he'd just eyed a massive meal after years of starving. Gibbons aimed to take a shot, but someone barged into him from the side. It was one of his men, bleeding from his throat and gargling in mortal panic.

This has all gone down the toilet. I can't help my men. It's too late.

Gibbons dodged into whatever spaces he could find and eyed the small cubicle with the glass tunnel entrance. The tunnel led into the waxworks, and then into the rear administration area of the prison. From there, he could grab a buggy from the garage and flee. Fuck the mission. He'd done enough damage just by causing a prison riot. Nealy would have no chance of opening this place up to the public after this. Too many people had already died.

Gibbons was just sorry his brothers of the Burning Dollar were amongst the casualties.

Good men, every one of them.

"Help me," one of his men called out, but it was hopeless. Gibbons sprinted to the partitioned cubicle and burst through the door. There was nothing inside to barricade the door with, so he wasted no time and carried right on into the tunnel.

He immediately barged into a glass panel, busting his nose and drawing blood. "What the f—?"

The moving glass compartment was usually set into a hidden compartment in the concrete, disguised by a wooden board and poster, but that access was currently open, revealing the shadowy holding area beyond. Obviously, the Boxcutter had got loose from his cell, its entrance hidden behind a fake wall at the back of the unlit space. Nealy wanted the deformed freak to terrorise his guests inside the glass tube, like some kind of shark attack, before upping the ante and appearing inside the tunnel itself, making the guests think he'd got loose. It was a stupid idea and in the worst taste. How did Nealy even hope to get the maniac to play ball?

"I need to get the hell out of here," Gibbons told himself. It was only a matter of time before the killers pursued him into the tunnel. He could still hear gunfire in the warehouse behind him, but only one or two of his men could still be alive. Once they were dead...

"Fuck this." Gibbons smashed the butt of his MP5 against the glass, but all it did was bounce off and injure his wrist. Growling, he reared back and levelled his weapon, pulled the trigger three times.

The hardened glass was tough, and for a moment it looked as though it might absorb the gunfire, but then, all at once, it shattered into a million pieces. There was another section of glass behind it – the other side of the moving compartment that kept the Boxcutter contained. Gibbons unleashed another five rounds and shattered it as well.

The way ahead was clear.

Gibbons broke into a sprint.

Time to get the fuck out of here. Nealy, I hope you're trapped somewhere right in the middle of all this. May your hubris be your end.

And Palmer, I got a bullet with your name on it if you're still breathing.

A body lay ahead. Someone had clearly died in the tunnel, but that was of no concern to him. Hopefully, it was Palmer or Nealy. It was right at the end of the tunnel, but as he got near, he saw it was no one he immediately recognised. In fact...

The misshapen lump rose slowly from the floor, like grains of sand falling in reverse. The man was seven feet tall and wide enough to fill the entire glass tube.

William Kendall White. The Boxcutter.

Oh shit!

Gibbons skidded to a halt, his heart in his throat. Terror turned him around and he sought to go back the other way, but the tunnel entrance was now filling up with the other maniacs.

He was penned in at both ends.

Raising his MP5, Gibbons sprayed bullets at the approaching mob. Three bodies hit the ground, their blood spattering the sides of the glass tunnel.

His weapon clicked, empty.

Gibbons reached a shaking hand down towards his belt and pulled free a magazine. But the bottom hit against his belt and it went tumbling out of his fingers. "Damn it."

He dropped to his knees to retrieve the magazine.

A shadow fell over him. He looked up.

The Boxcutter reached out for Gibbons with two massive hands, yanking him upwards before he could grab the magazine. His temples instantly ached with pressure. It felt like his eyes were going to pop out of his skull. Suddenly in a nightmare, he found himself face to face with the Boxcutter, feet dangling inches above the ground as two massive hands held him in mid-air by his head. Desperately, he swung his MP5, smashing the butt against the monster's face. He felt soft, spongy tissue where the nose bone should have been. The blow had zero effect.

The Boxcutter grinned, every tooth in his jaws stinking and brown.

The pressure on Gibbons's skull increased. It felt like his temples were closing in on his brain. "L-Let go of me, you freak!"

The Boxcutter stuck out his tongue and licked Gibbons on the cheek, foul saliva getting into his mouth. He gagged and then squealed as the pressure in his head increased. Hysterically, he kicked out with his legs.

And prayed to God.

Then, all of a sudden, his eyes weren't where they were supposed to be and his vision split in two. No longer could he feel his body, and as he flopped to the ground, he saw pieces of his own skull spattered on the ground. His dissected vision lasted only a second before fading to black.

And then there was nothing.

"What the fuck is with you, mate?" Jason asked Sim as he sat on the ground, staring at a spot of blood on his hands. He didn't even know where it'd come from. "You didn't fight or do anything. You just stood there while Mike died. What the hell? What the actual fucking hell?"

Sim shook his head. "I helped. I did."

"At the end. When it was too late. What happened to the guy who gave us all a speech earlier? What knocked the wind out of your sails, you... you goddamn coward?"

Sim glowered. "Back the hell off, man."

"No. Screw you, Sim. You act like Mr Integrity. Well, where was your integrity then?"

Gerry moved over to Jason and put a hand on his shoulder. It was stained with Mike's blood. "This was not his fault. He did what he could."

Jason shook his head in disgust. "Not enough."

Sim knew Jason was right. His dislike of the guy was still there, right at the forefront of his mind, yet he could find no reason for it besides pettiness. For all that he faulted Jason, he had shown no hesitation in trying to protect everyone.

Meanwhile, I froze and did nothing.

I'm a coward, just like he says.

"It's the Boxcutter," said Sim. "He does know me."

Jason shook his head, some of his anger leaving to make room for confusion. "What? How?"

Sim shrugged. "You already know my mum was murdered. When we met, you researched me and found that out, even though I don't share that with anyone. That's part of the reason I stopped working with you. It wasn't cool snooping on me like that."

"But... I didn't bring it up to upset you, mate. I wanted to be your friend. Guess I thought you'd want to talk about it."

Sim shook his head. "I never want to talk about it. It was the worst moment of my life. Not even Chrissy knows. She thinks my mum died in a car crash."

"Well... what really happened? Are you saying the Boxcutter killed your mum?"

Gerry covered her mouth and gasped. "This is terrible."

"The Boxcutter attacked my mum when I was fourteen years old," said Sim, willing his mouth to stop, but the words came out on their own. "He'd killed nine women by that point and he chose my mum to be number ten."

"Shit," said Jason.

Sim looked up and saw that Gerry and Jason were both gawping at him. So was Lee Chen, who had come to on the floor and rolled onto his side, clutching his ribs. "We were walking alongside the canal near where we lived," he continued. "My mum… she'd been drinking at the pub, and I'd been called by a family friend to come walk her home. She was a mess. Drunk pretty much every day that I can remember her. Sometimes, she used to say she wished I'd never been born. Anyway, that doesn't matter anymore because she died that night."

"But…" Gerry frowned. "How did you survive?"

"The same way as Sara Khan, by jumping into the water. I had gone into the bushes to take a leak, so the Boxcutter must have thought my mum was alone. When the Boxcutter came up behind her, she screamed. I tried to defend her. I said she was drunk and would vomit all over him if he tried to take her, and that she had a habit of wetting herself sometimes, too. I assumed he wanted to sexually assault her, so I was trying to disgust him into changing his mind."

"And did he?" asked Gerry.

"Not until what I said next. I broke down in tears and said she was a really bad mum, but that she was the only mum I had, and please don't take her from me. For some reason, that seemed to get through to him, and it gave me enough time to grab my mum and pull her backwards into the canal. The Boxcutter stayed at the edge. I don't think he can swim because of his deformities."

"I know all the victims," said Jason, frowning. "How come I never read about your mum?"

"Because she didn't die like the others. She drowned in the canal after falling in with me, and so the police didn't link her to the Boxcutter murders. In fact, they didn't even believe me. They decided I was a frightened kid, spooked by the recent news stories about grizzly killings, and that the perpetrator was really just some run-of-the-mill rapist or someone with a grudge against my mum – there were plenty of those about."

"I'm sorry," said Jason. "That sucks. No wonder you're so messed up."

"Thanks, and… yeah. After I saw William Kendall White earlier, I just… froze. I'm messed up, just like you said."

Jason winced. "I didn't mean it in a bad way. I just… understand you a little better now. Being on this island with the man who killed your mum… No wonder you froze. Sorry I got on your back. Gerry's right." He looked over at Mike's body. "This isn't your fault."

Sim shook his head. "No, you're the one who's right. I *was* a coward. I should've done something. Mike's dead because of me."

Gerry folded her arms and shivered. Unlike Jason and Sim, she wasn't wearing a jacket. "Failure builds us. Use it as a block to stand upon and lift yourself higher."

Jason nodded. "I think she means you can do better next time."

Sim stood up and brushed himself off. "I will. I'm sorry." He looked over at Mike again, wishing he could bring the rambunctious American back to life. The guy might have been filthy rich and a little crass, but he'd been all right.

"What do we do now?" asked Gerry, still shivering.

Jason pointed at Chen. "I think we decide what to do with him, yeah?"

Chen was propped up on his elbows, his face covered in bruises and his lip swollen. There was a pleading look in his eyes. Almost childlike.

"He saved me," said Gerry. "I think he's a good man."

Sim pictured Chen beating Simon Cruz's skull in with Bundy's plaster cast and shuddered, but he couldn't deny Chen had fought to protect Gerry. He had been their ally, and they needed every one of those they could get right now.

Sim walked over to Chen and offered a hand.

Chen took it nervously and climbed to his feet. Once up, he bowed respectfully. "Friend," he said. "No hurt."

Sim nodded. "Do you want to come with us, Lee? Um, follow us?"

"Follow? Yes."

Jason adjusted his baseball cap, which had somehow remained on his head all this time. "Guess he's with us, then."

Gerry started moving. "Let's go. More madmen could come through that door at any minute. I've been fondled enough for one day."

The door Chen had burst through must have led back to the cell blocks, which meant other inmates could be nearby.

So it's best we head in the opposite direction.

Sim patted Jason on the back. "My turn to take lead. You got my back?"

"Of course, mate. YouTubers need to stick together, right?"

"Right."

They followed the waxworks around a snaking path to the left. There must have been over thirty statues, and Sim poked several of them in the ribs.

We don't need any more surprises.

Fortunately, none of the statues turned out to be real, and they made it through safely. At the end of the pathway was a set of double doors, with a sign above it reading: WE HOPE YOU ENJOYED THE TOUR. STAB YOU LATER.

"We made it through," said Gerry, putting a hand against her breast and sighing. "This is the way out."

"Unless Nealy has any more surprises," said Jason. "Best we don't assume we're safe just yet."

Sim agreed. They might walk through these doors expecting

salvation, but instead of an exit, find... something else. So Sim turned sideways and pushed the door open cautiously.

It led into a gift shop, with serial killer puppets and glossy books about murderers. It appeared empty, and a shutter at the far end of the shop was raised halfway.

Tours always end at the gift shop. It's finished. It's over.

Sim turned back, almost too relieved to speak. "It really is the exit. There's a gift shop through here."

Jason put a hand on his back and gave him a gentle shove. "Then what are you waiting for? Let's not hang about and wait for someone nasty to catch up with us."

Sim nodded and shoved his way into the gift shop, with Gerry and Jason right behind him. Chen came a few steps behind.

Something *clicked* to Sim's left.

"Hold it right there!" said a voice.

Sim froze. He was unarmed, but he considered trying to turn and swing his fists. But before he could make a move, a second voice caused him to relax.

"Sim? Oh my God, you're okay!"

Sim moved, not even caring that Palmer had a gun pointed at his face. The sight of Chrissy, unhurt and smiling, was the only thing that existed to him right then. So he raced right past Palmer and grabbed Chrissy in an almighty hug, kissing her neck and feeling such relief that he almost fell over dizzy. "Y-You're okay," he spluttered. "I can't... I can't believe it."

"More like I can't believe you're okay. We saw on the CCTV. You were in the tunnel with the Boxcutter."

Sim felt his mouth dry up and had to lick his lips. "He wasn't able to get at us. It was okay. I'm okay."

She nodded. "I saw. But then we couldn't pick you back up on the feed. We were about to come and search for you."

"Probably best you didn't. It was rough in there."

"Down on the ground now!"

Sim turned to see Palmer aiming his gun at Chen. Chen had

his hands in the air and got down on his knees. "Please," he said. "No hurt."

"Leave him alone, mate," said Jason testily. "He's with us."

"He's an inmate," said Palmer.

"An inmate who fought to protect us," said Gerry. "He's not like the others. He's an innocent man."

"It's true," said Sim, nodding to Chrissy, who seemed shocked to hear it. "Simon Cruz attacked us and Chen helped us. He's okay."

Palmer lowered his handgun slowly, looking back and forth between Gerry and Jason. "Where's Mr Rondon?"

Gerry sighed. "Mike did not make it."

"Yeah," said Jason, taking off his baseball cap and letting it hang by his side. "He went down fighting like a true Texan."

Palmer cursed and punched the wall. "Damn it. Gibbons is going to pay for this."

"Who's Gibbons?" asked Sim.

"The fucking psycho who shot me," said Chrissy, uncharacteristically crass. Sim supposed being shot was a reasonable excuse for bad manners.

He suddenly realised her jacket was stained with blood and gasped. Underneath, her shirt was a sodden mess. "Oh my God. What happened? Are you okay? We need to—"

She put a hand up to stop him. "I'm okay. It feels like someone pumped hot acid into my shoulder, but I'm not going to die."

"Gibbons is a member of security," said Palmer. "I knew there was something off about him, but I didn't act soon enough. He sabotaged this place by letting every killer out of their cells."

"No shit!" said Jason. "Are you going to get us out of here?"

Palmer nodded. "Now that you three are here, we can plot an escape route. We have CCTV in the room behind us. Let's go take a look to see where's safe."

He led them towards a small room behind the counter. Jason had to stop, briefly, to go back and gather Chen, who had remained on his knees with his hands in the air, but then they were all inside.

Palmer stooped over a computer and brought up a collection of video feeds. "I've sectioned off the most important cameras," he said. "Let's see how bad things are."

He flicked through a few feeds, including those from the cell blocks. A few inmates were still in their cells, but most had fled. Then he flicked to the abandoned warehouse that Sim and the others had exited earlier. It had changed a lot since then. A dozen inmates were now inside, and multiple bodies littered the cement floor. In the corner, swinging empty rifles like batons, two uniformed men fought for their lives.

"Who are they?" asked Sim.

"I have no idea." Palmer shook his head. "They don't work on this island. Christ! Look at all those bodies. There must have been one hell of a fight."

"Looks like the uniformed dudes lost," said Jason. "I can see a few of their buddies."

Sim saw them too. Several uniformed men lay dead on the concrete. "We need to help those two men still alive."

Palmer shook his head. "It's too late."

And it was. They winced and held their breath as the CCTV turned bloody. One inmate – the Kissimmee Killer – ducked down low and came up underneath one of the soldier's swinging rifles. He picked the man up and heaved him against his colleague. Then the other inmates pounced.

They tore the two flailing men apart like a pair of cooked chickens, tearing off strips of flesh with their bare hands and biting into the most succulent meat. Most of the killers were not cannibals, but they were all animals desperate for a kill.

"Switch it off," said Chrissy, grimacing.

Sim shook his head. "If we had been in there a few moments longer, we might have ended up the same way."

"Check the waxworks," said Jason, letting out a breath. "See if anyone's coming."

Palmer shook his head. "We tried earlier, but someone turned the camera to face the wall. Must have been Cruz, if you say he was trying to hide."

Sim nodded. Part of Cruz's MO was lying in wait in back alleys and recessed doorways. He enjoyed leaping out at people and snatching away their lives as he drugged them and dragged them into the ocean.

Well, the Kraken is dead now. Good riddance.

"We need to find Nealy," said Palmer. "If anyone is still alive, he'll be with them."

And it was true. When Palmer brought up the feed for the Keep's panic room, they all saw Nealy and two dozen members of staff – mostly orderlies and some kitchen crew – hiding out. At least the inmates hadn't got everyone.

"We need to get those people out of there," said Palmer.

Jason puffed air out of his cheeks. "Why? It's a panic room. They're safer in there than anywhere else, surely?"

Palmer nodded. "You're right, but we have a problem."

"What?"

Palmer brought up another camera feed. It was some kind of VIP lounge, with a fully stocked bar, several deep sofas, and a massive television on the wall. It was also on fire.

"That's the Whitechapel Room," said Palmer. "The panic room is immediately next to it. Once that fire spreads…"

Sim groaned. "It'll cook everyone inside."

Palmer looked at him and nodded.

CHAPTER
SEVENTEEN

"WE NEED TO GO GET THEM," said Palmer, leading everyone out of the security office and back onto the shop floor.

"Screw that," said Jason. "*You* get them. You're the one with the badge."

Palmer frowned. "What badge? Look, if I go alone, I might not make it. We all need to go together. It's safer that way." He held up his gun, aimed it safely at the ceiling. "Stick close and I can protect you."

Sim nodded. "We can't let those people burn."

"Goddamn it," said Jason. "Why do we have to be the good guys?"

"Because we *are*. We're going to make it through this." He looked at Chrissy and smiled. "Now that we're all together."

There was a knock at the door. The one that led back into the waxworks.

Everyone spun around, startled. Palmer immediately went into an aiming stance, handgun out in front of him.

"Who the hell is that?" asked Jason in a shrieking yell. "Who is it?"

The knock came again.

"We need to block that door," said Palmer. "Somebody, help me to—"

The door opened. Gerry, standing nearby, ducked behind a display table. Chen moved beside her, a hand on her back as he glared at the doorway.

Sim grabbed Chrissy and pulled her behind the counter.

Something grotesque stepped through the door and entered the room.

Palmer yelled a threat, but his voice quickly tailed off into a whisper. Then, a few seconds later, he uttered a single word. "G-Gibbons?"

The man who staggered into the room should not have been alive. His skull was a misshapen mess, like an apple dropped on the pavement. His right eye dangled on his cheek, while the left bulged like a squid in the cave of its socket. A shattered lower jaw hung askew, mouth gaping. Like a zombie, he shuffled into the middle of the room, moaning.

Chrissy covered her mouth and looked away. "I'm going to be sick."

"Jesus…" Jason shook his head, unblinking. "What the hell happened to him?"

The zombie spoke. "Be… ide… me."

Palmer lowered his gun a moved towards the man. "Gibbons, it's going to be okay. I need you to lower yourself to the ground. You need to keep from moving any more."

"Be… ide… me."

Palmer put a hand on the man's shoulder and startled him. There was no indication that Gibbons even knew where he was, or who was there with him. He was a dead man walking, powered by adrenaline and dying organs. "It's okay, Gibbons. I'm going to help you."

"Be… hind me!"

The door burst open and the Huntsman appeared, snarling through his thick beard. Behind him, a dozen more maniacs chittered like excited monkeys. A mob mentality had taken over them, adding to their natural bloodlust, and each killer fed off the murderous energy of those around him. They had nothing to lose and were eager to make the most of their new-found freedom.

Palmer took a shot and hit John Woodward between the eyes. The Huntsman fell backwards, obstructing those trying to get in behind him.

"Behind me," Gibbons muttered, before collapsing to the floor and going into convulsions.

Palmer fired again, hitting an inmate in an orange jumpsuit, but two others quickly ducked around him and made it inside the gift shop. Palmer glanced over at Chrissy and yelled at her, "Get out of here! Go!"

Sim tugged at Chrissy, but she shook her head and pulled away. "Hey," he said. "What are you doing?"

"Hold on." She reached down beneath the shop's counter and produced something from underneath. It was some kind of tiny rifle.

Sim frowned, hoping she didn't plan on trying to stay and fight. Serial killers were flooding into the room, one after another.

"We have to go."

"I know." She slid out from behind the counter and aimed the rifle towards the doorway where the killers had started to bunch up in front of Palmer. The security man fired shot after shot, hitting body parts and torso. The falling bodies kept others at bay, but Palmer was slowly being overwhelmed.

Jason, Gerry, and Chen hurried over to the shop's half-raised shutter. Jason stopped long enough to call out to Sim and Chrissy. "Get over here. Quick!"

But Chrissy stayed put and yelled at Palmer. "Get back!"

Palmer turned just as Chrissy fired a whizzing projectile at the ground near the door. It struck the tiles and cracked open, unleashing a puff of yellow gas.

Sim's eyes stung almost immediately. *What the hell is that stuff?*

Chrissy aimed the rifle and tried to fire a second time, but nothing happened. There had obviously only been the one capsule inside, so she tossed the weapon and grabbed Sim's hand. "Now we can go. Palmer, come on!"

Palmer was half blind, spluttering and coughing, but he started after them with an arm over his eyes. Behind him, half a dozen serial killers dropped to the floor, rubbing at their faces and choking.

Except for one.

One figure stepped out of the spreading orange mist, their face a contorted, snarling mess.

Sim shoved Chrissy, begging her to join Jason. He then turned to help Palmer, who was staggering around, unable to see clearly.

The Boxcutter stepped out of the mist and grabbed Palmer by the back of the neck. He shook the man like a rag doll. Palmer cried out in surprise and began to struggle.

Sim moved as fast as he could, ignoring the others calling for him to leave, or the burning sensation slowly invading his sinuses. He couldn't stand by and watch anyone else die, so he threw his entire weight against the Boxcutter.

It was like hitting a brick wall.

Sim bounced off him onto the floor, his shoulder feeling broken.

It was enough to get the Boxcutter's attention.

William Kendall White let go of Palmer and move in on Sim. His foul breath was almost as pungent as the gas filling the room.

Sim could barely keep his burning eyes open.

The Boxcutter grinned and spoke with a voice like rustling leaves. "We meet again, boy. Two killers reunited."

Sim slid backwards on his butt, trying to gain purchase with the heels of his trainers. "I'm n-nothing like you. I'm not a monster."

The freak stooped over Sim, moving his obscene, barely human face closer. He was like an otherworldly titan, a man born of a snorting bull and a dying leper. He spoke in a whisper, his words floating on the fetid breeze of his breath. "Are you sure about that, boy? I saw the darkness inside you. You feel it, don't you? It runs through our veins."

Palmer tackled the Boxcutter from the side and brought up his handgun, but the Boxcutter threw out an arm and deflected him. He let off a shot but barely grazed the beast's shoulder. It summoned a grunt of pain, but that was all, and the Boxcutter grabbed him by both wrists, holding him powerless.

Sim clambered to his feet and moved to help, but Palmer turned his head and yelled at him to go. "G-Get to the others before this whole place... argh... burns down."

The Boxcutter let go of Palmer's left wrist and plunged a massive, twisted thumb into his eye socket, wrenching a blood-curdling scream out of the man. The gun went off two more times, but both shots buried themselves in the ceiling.

"Run!" Palmer cried through his agony. "Go!"

Sim took two steps backwards, turned, and then left the man to die. He joined the others and they ducked beneath the shutter, coughing and spluttering as the peppery gas assaulted their airways.

Palmer's screams tore through the air behind them.

"Where are we going?" Jason asked as they ran aimlessly through an open plaza. There were shuttered shops and empty restaurants to either side of them, some of them lacking interior furnishings – still works in progress.

"We follow the smoke," said Sim, blinking and rubbing at his eyes. A thin, grey veil swept across the floor ahead.

"R-Running towards a fire?" said Jason, clearing his throat. "Great. Toss me your phone!"

Sim frowned. "What?"

"Like you said, I'm an opportunist. Let's get this on film. For posterity."

"Whatever." Sim reached into his pocket and grabbed his phone, tossing it to Jason as they ran. Jason almost fumbled it, but he got a grip and entered the PIN that he still remembered from before.

They discovered the flames nearby, coming from the same lounge they'd seen on the monitors. The fire had spread since, chewing at the carpet a few feet from the entrance. Fortunately, they didn't need to go inside.

"Where's Nealy's panic room?" asked Gerry, looking back and forth.

Sim hadn't expected a blinking sign reading PANIC ROOM, but he had expected to find a door or a hatch. All he saw was smoke billowing out of the lounge, filling the nondescript hallway.

Then he saw it. He rubbed at his eyes again and pointed. "There!"

Jason saw it too. His nose was running, and he used the back of his arm to wipe it.

There was a sliding door, made to be almost invisible. It was only because Sim knew what he was looking for that he spotted the parallel grooves demarcating the two sides of a six foot panel.

Jason pressed his hands against the panel and it popped out a couple of inches, allowing him to slide it along the wall. Behind was a thick metal door. Of course, it was locked.

"Bang on it," said Sim, wiping sweat from his forehead. It was getting hot. "Nealy's inside. He might hear us."

Jason thudded both hands against the door but barely made a noise. "Hey! Hey, Nealy, get the hell out of there. You need to come out. There's a fire."

Everyone yelped when a tiny compartment opened at the top of the door and a pair of eyes stared out at them. "Mr Dreadful, is that you?"

"Yeah, mate. You need to get out of there, pronto."

"It's safer in here. I'm attempting to call for help."

Gerry stepped up to the door and frowned. "Attempting?"

"Yes, it… appears all communications are currently down."

"Gibbons," said Chrissy, folding her arms and sneering. "He sabotaged everything, didn't he?"

"Yes," said Nealy grumpily. "When I get hold of him, he'll wish he'd never been born."

Sim sighed. "He's already dead. Palmer, too. Pretty much everyone that isn't in that room with you right now. Listen, there's a fire in the VIP lounge. You need to get out of there."

"What? No… No, no, no. The sprinkler system will take care of it."

Jason groaned. "Which part of 'sabotaged everything' didn't you understand, mate? Gibbons has switched it all off. If this place wasn't a death trap before, it is now. We need to get our arses onto the ferry and off of this island."

Nealy cursed behind the door. There was the sound of chattering behind him. Frightened chattering. "Okay, we're coming out. Stand back."

Sim and Jason stood back, along with Chrissy and Gerry. Chen had wandered away but was still with them, about fifteen feet away from the fire. By now, they were all sweating from the heat.

The door clunked and opened outwards. Nealy appeared, jumper sleeves around his elbows and slick blond hair dishevelled. He looked nothing like the man from the business pages or the cover of *Time* magazine. "I'm glad you're all still alive," he said. "Where's Mike?"

Gerry shook her head.

Nealy almost toppled over. "Oh… Oh, no. That's… Mike was a good friend. I considered him more than a colleague." He slumped against the wall as others spilled out of the panic room behind him. Many of the faces were sweaty and stained, showing that the heat had been slowly rising inside the panic room.

Sim sniffed back a wad of peppery phlegm and coughed. It cleared his sinuses and allowed him to open his eyes fully as he grabbed Nealy and shook the man by his arm. "You're going to get us all out of here, Nealy. You should never have built this place. What were you even thinking?"

Nealy grunted, but instead of anger, he showed only remorse. "I don't believe I *was* thinking, Mr Barka. When all you know is success, failure becomes inconceivable."

"Well, I'm sorry that it took so many innocent victims to humble you. People weren't put on this Earth to help you learn a lesson, Nealy."

"You're right. Come on, let's put an end to my mistakes and leave this godforsaken place. Follow me."

The group headed off down the hallway, but Nealy soon skidded to a stop. "Wait, is that Lee Chen?"

"He's with us," said Jason, rubbing at his eyes with his forearm. "Long story, mate."

"Oh, okay, very well." Nealy shook off his confusion and started leading them again, back past the empty stores.

They didn't see Montez Sidwell until it was too late.

The huge athlete charged out of an adjacent hallway and barrelled into Jason, sending him skidding on his back along the polished floor. He was so stunned that he didn't even make a sound, besides a dazed grunt. Sim's phone somehow remained in his hand and his cap was still on his head.

Some people in Nealy's group split off, running down the hallway in terror.

Sidwell looked around, a sleepiness to his expression. "W- What the hell is going on in this place? Who the fuck are you people?"

Nealy put a hand up and shushed the gigantic man. "Easy there. I need you to stay calm and—"

Sidwell smacked Nealy's hand away. "Yo, don't tell me to

stay the fuck calm, man. Hey... I know you. You're the piece of shit that bought me like a fucking slave."

"No. No, no. I rescued you from rotting in a maximum-security prison."

"Rescued me for what? To wave at the crowds and eat fried chicken while you and your rich pals can point and laugh? 'Lordy, look at the big old negro locked up where he belongs.'"

"Hey," said Sim, hoping his mixed-ethnicity might buy him some goodwill, seeing as Montez was seemingly going to take things there. "It ain't like that, man. This place was built to exploit *everyone*, not just black people. Nealy's an egotistical prick, but I don't think he's racist."

Montez shrugged his massive traps. "Maybe not, but he still drugged my ass and locked me in a goddamn box." He shoved Nealy so hard that the man flew clear off his feet. Sim caught him before he landed. "So I think I might just kill a bitch."

Montez charged Nealy again, but Sim shoved him out of the way. Montez was so quick, though, and so heavy, that it was hard for him to slow down. He piled right into Jason just as he had got back to his feet and knocked him straight back down to the ground again. Gerry fell with him, and Chrissy nearly, too. The three pleaded for Montez to stop, while more of Nealy's people sped off in fear.

Sim stood on the other side of Montez, next to Nealy. The murderous athlete was in their way, separating them from the others. "Please stop," he begged. "You're not a psycho, Montez. A lot of the monsters in this place are stone cold killers, but not you. You made a bad decision, and it led to something terrible, but at least you can claim you weren't in your right mind. It was the drugs."

Montez sneered. "You sound like my lawyer." But then his expression suddenly changed. "There ain't no excuse for what I did."

"No, I guess not," said Sim. "But you don't need to hurt us.

Help us get out of here and I'll make sure people know you did the right thing. It's not much, but it's something."

Montez was breathing heavily. Smoke billowed down the corridor behind him.

The Boxcutter roared from the adjacent hallway. Death itself was coming.

"The hell is that?" asked Montez.

Jason raised Sim's phone to film. "That's Count Dracula, and this is his keep."

"Please, help us," said Chrissy, staring imploringly at Montez.

William Kendall White appeared at the end of the adjacent hallway, a dozen maniacs bunched up behind him, none brave enough to do anything but follow the gigantic beast. Even amongst monsters, the Boxcutter was a freak.

Montez shook his head. "Jesus, that is one ugly motherfucker." He turned his head to look at Sim, and he sighed. "Get out of here, bro."

Sim nodded in thanks. He reached out to Chrissy and she rushed into his arms. Gerry, Jason, and the other survivors from the panic room quickly crossed the hallway.

"Are you going to stop them?" Sim asked Montez.

"What? Hell, no. I might not want to murder your ass, but that don't mean I give a shit about you."

"Oh. Understood."

"Come on!" Jason yelled.

Everyone took off along the widening plaza, passing by yet more shuttered-up shops that would now never get a chance to accept customers. William Kendall White bellowed from the hallway, closer now.

Nealy skidded up ahead, turned, and waved a hand at everyone to follow him. There was a staircase leading upwards.

"Hey," said Jason. "Why are we heading up, man?"

"Because we're not going to outrun those maniacs," said Nealy. "None of us is fast enough."

The remaining survivors from the panic room ignored their boss and kept on running, heading past the stairs and towards the Keep's exit. Nealy called for them to come back, but their panic had taken control of them and running was all they could do. Sim considered going after them.

But then he looked back and saw that the maniacs were indeed gaining on them. Some of the inmates were lithe and muscular, in far better shape than the likes of Sim and Nealy. The man was right: they would never make it outside.

The group reached the top of the stairs and entered a long hallway with windowed offices and a staff toilet. Nealy rushed ahead, his tennis shoes screeching against the floor. Sim shoved Chrissy in front of him and glanced back over his shoulder. Footsteps sounded at the bottom of the staircase. "We need to get somewhere safe," Sim shouted. "Now!"

"In here," said Nealy. "It's the control room. It has a manual lock inside. Get in! Get in!"

Lee Chen rushed inside first, seeming confused about what the plan was. Gerry and Jason were behind him. Sim ushered Chrissy forward, hurrying her inside. He was about to follow her, but Nealy grabbed him by the shirt and yanked him back. For some insane reason, he slammed the door closed and leaned against it.

Sim glared at him. "W-What are you doing?"

Chrissy cried out from inside and tried to open the door, but Nealy held the handle from the other side.

Hooting lunatics appeared at the top of the staircase, their leering mouths contorted into hungry grins.

"Let me go in," said Sim, attempting to push Nealy aside. The man was unexpectedly strong.

"No," said Nealy. "You and I have got a different mission, son." He put his face against the door and yelled. "Mr Dreadful, barricade this door and keep those ladies safe. Sim and I will be back soon with help. Do not open this door until you hear from us."

Sim shook his head, utterly aghast. Once again, he was separated from Chrissy.

The killers were racing down the long hallway.

A *clunk* sounded, and Jason yelled from inside the control room. "I locked it, but what the hell are you doing, Nealy?"

Chrissy was calling out, and it sounded like she was being restrained and reassured by Gerry. "Sim! Sim, what's happening?"

"I..." He looked back down the corridor. The inmates would be on them in another five seconds. "I'm okay. Stay inside. We'll be right back."

Nealy grabbed Sim by the arm and they started running. The killers were twenty metres behind, yelling and swearing, promising to do the most barbaric things to them. Somehow, rising above their hysteria, was William Kendall White's rasping whisper. "I see you, boy."

"We're fucked," said Sim. "They're going to catch us."

"No," said Nealy, sprinting beside him. "We're going to get weapons and kill every one of these maniacs."

Sim was huffing with exertion, wondering how long he could keep this up. "If anything happens to Chrissy, I'll kill you."

Nealy glanced back and seemed to panic. He pumped his arms and dug a little deeper, went a little faster. "That's fair, son. I'd kill me, too."

"He left us!" said Chrissy. "He left us!"

Jason stood with his back to the door. He had turned a manual bolt on the inside and was now standing in her way. She tried to move him, but he was too strong, and then Gerry was pulling her away.

"It's okay," said Gerry. "Nealy sounded like he had a plan."

"What? That idiot hasn't had a plan since the moment John Woodward shit his pants."

Jason nodded. "You're right, but if I hadn't got this door locked when I did, we would all be dead. Those maniacs are right outside."

Lee Chen caught their attention. There was another door at the back of the room. He raced over and bolted it, too.

Chrissy didn't need to be told that. She could hear them out there, yelling and whooping. "You locked Sim out there."

"I did what he would have wanted. I kept you safe. If… If he'd been hurt, we would have heard him. Nealy and Sim got away."

Chrissy could hold herself up no longer. Her legs seized and the pain in her shoulder reignited. Gerry had to ease her down onto a swivel chair, and it was then that she noticed three dead guards under one of the desks. She screamed.

"Oh, flip!" said Jason, looking away.

"This is a nightmare," said Chrissy. "Or Hell. That's it, we're all dead, and this is Hell."

Gerry rubbed Chrissy's back as she slumped in the swivel chair. "You are a good person, Chrissy, so why would you be in Hell? This is… a crisis, but we are not yet dead. I intend to keep it that way, *oui*?"

"Me too," said Jason, still standing by the door. He lifted Sim's phone and started filming around the room. "Hey, Lee, you doing okay?"

Lee Chen was crouched near an open locker. There were weapons inside, and he was examining them. He turned back to Jason with a pistol in his hand. The top of it seemed to be missing. "Broken," he said.

Jason sighed. "Gibbons really took care of everything, didn't he? Psycho got what he deserved."

"He was worse than a psychopath," said Gerry. "He was a man who replaced his morals with beliefs. A terrorist."

"I'm all aboard for giving capitalism a great big kick in the nuts," said Jason, "but not until someone comes up with something better."

Chrissy was still shaking her head. If not for the fact she'd puked already today – thrice – she would have done so again. "We won't make it out of this. Listen to them out there. We can't get out."

"Look," said Jason, moving in front of her. "If I know one thing about Sim, it's that he's smart. He'll find a way out of this."

Chrissy huffed. "I didn't know you were a fan of his."

"I've always respected Sim. It hurt me when we stopped being friends." He shook his head. "Or when I realised we were never friends in the first place."

"I'm sorry," she said, amazed that she could even feel such a thing at that moment, considering how much danger they were all in. "Sim and I have been so critical of you and your channel... We forgot you're a human being with feelings. You're not as bad as I thought you were, Jason."

"Gee, thanks."

"Hey, I still don't like your content. It's exploitative."

"Yeah, maybe you're right. I suppose we could all do with a little self-reflection."

"*After* we leave this island," said Gerry. She moved around the room to stretch her legs but ended up hissing with pain and lifting her foot.

Jason frowned at her. "What's wrong?"

"*Zut*! I stepped on something." She started picking at her foot, which was now bleeding, and produced a small red shard. "Looks like... a piece of ceramic."

Jason reached out and took her hand, helping her hop over to a chair.

There was a slight odour in the room, which caused Chrissy to glance down at the dead guards. Had one of them defecated upon death? Apparently, it was quite common.

She noticed Lee Chen moving across the room. He still held the broken handgun, its insides exposed by the missing top piece.

"Lee?" she called. "Hey, Lee, what are you doing?"

Jason turned away from Gerry and went to say something, but Chen cut him off by smashing the butt of the pistol grip against the side of his head. It knocked him out cold.

Chrissy leapt up out of her seat, her shoulder flaring with white-hot pain. "Lee! What the hell?"

Chen turned towards her, his face suddenly different.

He's a predator. How did I miss it?

Chen backhanded Chrissy across the face and sent her to the ground. Her mouth filled with copper pennies. Her vision blurred.

Gerry cried out as Lee turned and grabbed her. She immediately clawed at his face and drew blood from his cheeks, but he seemed to enjoy the pain. He grinned, but the expression didn't reach his eyes.

Gerry screamed as Chen threw her to the ground. She attempted to kick out at him, but he caught her bare feet and dragged her along on her back.

Then he raised her bare right foot towards his face and opened his mouth.

Gerry moaned as Lee Chen started sucking her toes.

Chrissy crawled across the floor, trying to shake the cobwebs free of her brain. She spat a mouthful of blood and felt an empty gum pocket with her tongue.

Gerry squirmed and kicked herself free, then planted a foot in the centre of Chen's chest. The blow caused him to ignite into a rage. He yanked on her leg violently and went red in the face. "Whore!"

"Fuck you," Gerry yelled back at him.

Lee gripped her foot tightly. And then wrenched it.

There was a loud *snap,* and Gerry shrieked in agony.

Chrissy leapt to her feet and shoved Lee away from Gerry, but he only turned around and grinned.

Then he came for her.

CHAPTER
EIGHTEEN

"THIS WAY, THIS WAY," said Nealy, wheeling around a corner.

The maniacs were right behind them.

"We need to get out of this hallway," said Sim. "We need…"

"In here!" Nealy yanked open a door and shoved Sim inside, then turned and slammed the door shut. "Grab something to hold this door."

Sim looked around. He was in some kind of locker room, with three rows of metal cabinets and long wooden benches. There was a dead man lying in the middle of the floor, a thin black rope tied around his neck.

"Who the hell is that?" asked Sim.

Nealy groaned. "That's Frank. Gibbons must have murdered him."

"You really should have hired better staff."

"Frank was a good man. Unfortunately, it only takes one bad apple to spoil the pot."

The door rattled as the maniacs threw themselves against the other side. Nealy put his back to it and shouted, "Come on, get something to block this bloody door! Hurry."

Sim grabbed one of the benches and was relieved when he

found it to be heavy yet mobile. He dragged it over to the door, his strength enhanced by his panicked nervous system. Once he reached Nealy, the two of them lifted the bench up onto its end and leaned it against the wall. They wedged it diagonally just underneath the door handle to keep it from turning.

Both of them stepped away nervously.

"It won't hold," said Sim. "Not for long."

"We only need a minute," said Nealy, and he rushed to the rear of the locker room where there was a separate, caged-off area. "Gibbons might have sabotaged the Keep," he said bitterly, "but I wanted to make sure there was a place or two that only I could access." He reached into his pocket and pulled out a small set of keys. He unlocked the mesh cage and unlocked the door.

Sim stepped up beside Nealy while the man opened a double-width locker. Inside was exactly what they needed. Guns.

"You ever fired one of these before, son?"

Sim shook his head. "I wouldn't know where to start."

Nealy grabbed a modern-looking black rifle along with a stubby magazine and raised them both in front of Sim. "JTS M12 something or other. Besides a little clay pigeon shooting from time to time, I'm not really a gun guy. Anyway, it's an automatic shotgun with a nasty kick, so you need to hold it firmly against the inside of your shoulder. Don't press it against your collarbone. Magazine loads by pressing it into the receiver here and giving it a bit of a waggle. To take it out, just press the paddle switch here." Nealy shoved the magazine in with a bit of back and forth wiggling and then slid it out again by pressing on a little thumb release. It seemed easy enough.

"Okay, I think I've got it."

"Good lad." Nealy slammed the magazine back into the receiver and handed the weapon to Sim. "First time you shoot a shotgun, it'll scare the bejesus out of you. Just be ready for the kick and the noise and you'll be fine."

Sim nodded, holding the shotgun against his shoulder for practice and feeling both unnerved and empowered. This slick black chunk of metal and plastic was going to determine whether he lived or died.

And whether or not he made it back to Chrissy.

Nealy grabbed a matching shotgun for himself and loaded it. Then he grabbed a spare pair of magazines and handed one to Sim. "This gives us ten shots in total. A hit anywhere will do the job, but try not to let anyone get up close. Once they're inside the range of your barrel, the weapon becomes a hindrance, not a help."

Sim nodded, understanding that guns were better when there was space to fire them. "Okay. So, we just… shoot our way out of here?"

"Think it's time the hunted became the hunters, don't you?"

"Why did you build this place, Nealy? And why did you bring me here?"

"Not really the time for it, eh? But I suppose I owe you some answers. You did a video on Geoffrey Evans once. Do you remember?"

Sim frowned. He immediately knew the episode to which Nealy was referring. "Yes. Evans and John Shaw raped and murdered two young women in Ireland."

Nealy nodded. "County Wicklow. Elizabeth Plunkett and Mary Duffy."

"Okay, but how does that relate to you?"

Nealy put a hand on Sim's shoulder. "There were other women, son. Other victims of Evan's vile impulses. Let's just say I happened to have a connection with one of those women. The reason I chose you to come here is because of the compassion you showed when reporting on those crimes. It spoke to me on a personal level, and I wanted to meet you."

"Then I really have to ask, why Jason?"

Nealy tittered. "Because he has a talent for trivialising the extreme. I needed to normalise the existence of the Keep if people were ever going to accept it. To tell you the truth, my investors were getting cold feet. I needed to build a buzz on a shoestring budget."

"So you chose YouTubers?"

"Influencers. The cheapest exposure you can buy. Most of you will whore yourself out for pennies on the dollar. Anyway, we need to get out of here. I promise I'll make this up to you later, Mr Barka. I pay my debts."

"So long as you're alive," Sim added.

"There is that."

A crash sounded at the front of the locker room.

Sim realised he was shaking, so he steadied himself. He pressed the shotgun against his shoulder and prepared for the fight of his life. "Time to take back the Keep, I guess."

"Screw the Keep," said Nealy. "It can burn."

The bench fell away from the door, no longer jamming the handle. With the automatic locks disengaged, the maniacs outside were easily able to open the door and rush inside.

Nealy shot first, and the noise was startling. A red shell leapt into the air and a trail of smoke puffed out of the barrel.

Miguel Reyes, the old, demented serial killer, went down screaming, his entire left arm detached, bar a few strands of gristle. The smell of his blood filled the air as more maniacs flooded in behind him, snarling like wild dogs.

Here goes. Sim pulled the trigger and unleashed a bellowing fury from his shotgun. It kicked backwards against his shoulder, a solid punch, but he kept it under control. He saw nothing exit the barrel except smoke, but a raving lunatic went down like God had punched him.

Sim fired again and opened up a bloody hole in the chest of the Cali Cutter.

I just killed two notorious serial killers. What the hell is happening?

Nealy moved shoulder to shoulder with Sim as they advanced, leaving the cage behind them and crossing the locker room. Half a dozen maniacs had made it inside, but the doorway caused them to bunch up into a group. Together, Sim and Nealy dispatched them easily. In fact, it was shocking how easily taking a life became when your own depended upon it.

For the first time since coming to the Isle of Durne, Sim felt hopeful. He felt in control.

He felt powerful.

They moved out of the locker room and back into the hallway. There were not as many inmates as Sim expected, and one in particular was missing.

Where is the Boxcutter?

Sim's fears turned towards Chrissy. Although he'd had no choice, he had left her, and he had no idea if she was okay. Ironically, he had to rely on Jason, of all people, to protect her, a man he had hated less than a day ago.

I don't hate him. I'm jealous of him.

He faces evil with a smile on his face. He doesn't let it win.

"I won't let it win either," Sim said out loud, and then emptied his last shell into Francine Mescal. The French poisoner went down screaming, clutching her shattered shoulder as it bled all over the ground. There were a couple more inmates in the hallway, but Sim needed to reload. He pressed the magazine release and let the metal ammo container fall to the floor. Then he slammed in the spare. But it wouldn't click into place. "Come on, damn it!"

An inmate leapt at Sim, but Nealy moved in the way and smashed the shotgun's breech against the man's snarling mouth. His teeth went airborne, tinkling to the ground. Nealy tossed the shotgun down, empty.

Sim wiggled the magazine and clicked it home.

He raised the shotgun and pulled the trigger.

The broken-toothed maniac went airborne like his teeth.

Slipping quickly out of his bloodlust, the final inmate turned and ran. Sim aimed and prepared to pull the trigger. But he didn't. He couldn't shoot a man in the back. Not even a horrific killer.

Nealy snatched the weapon from Sim, raised it against his shoulder, and fired.

The inmate flopped to the ground. A hole in his back.

Sim looked at Nealy and took a step back.

Nealy shrugged. "Time to take charge, son. You can leave it to me."

Sim nodded and leapt around the bodies in his way. The hallway was clear, and so was his route to Chrissy.

But where the hell is the Boxcutter?

Sim, with Nealy beside him, beat at the control room door and begged to be let inside. When there was no answer, Sim assumed the worst. He started kicking at the door, sending plaster flakes raining from the ceiling above.

A scream sounded. Chrissy.

Sim bellowed and threw himself against the door. It rattled but stayed in place. "Open the fucking door. Jason!"

"Stand aside," said Nealy. He aimed the shotgun and fired off a shot that left the metal area around the lock scorched and pitted. Sim kicked it again and the door rattled a little more in its frame.

Nealy fired again. Then again.

Then the shotgun was empty, so he started beating at the handle with the weapon's stock. The handle started to bend and break free.

Heavy footsteps sounded on the stairs. William Kendall White appeared on the landing, another six inmates at his side, and a plume of black smoke rising behind them. In the massive freak's hands was a fire extinguisher. Had he gone to find something to help break down the door?

"Nealy, hurry." Sim kicked at the door. "Come on!"

Chrissy screamed again.

But who's in there with her? The door is still locked, and William Kendall White is out here.

Nealy smashed at the handle again. It finally fell to the ground. "We're in!"

Sim barged open the door and forced his way into the control room. He was astonished by what he saw.

Gerry was in the corner, lying next to three dead guards. Jason was unconscious on his back.

And Chrissy was screaming as Lee Chen tried to tear off her clothes.

Sim launched himself at Lee. He knocked the killer sideways and then immediately checked on Chrissy. She was gibbering in fear but didn't seem hurt.

Nealy slammed the door and put his back against it. The Boxcutter was right outside. "We need to get the hell out of here," he warned.

Sim looked over at him. "And go where?"

Lee Chen launched himself at Sim and knocked him onto his back. He was different from before – a sly fox with a toothy sneer. A predator. Even the wounds on his face seemed to have receded, as if he'd been playing at being an injured lamb.

Chrissy screamed as Sim fought to keep Lee from beating him. The man was bony and awkward.

Jason stirred nearby, spouting confused gibberish.

Nealy groaned as the door rattled behind him.

Sim grabbed Lee's wrists and tried to keep the killer's fists away from his face. He was strong for his size, but not as big as Sim, which meant the fight was nearing a stalemate. The problem was that every second they fought was a second nearer to the Boxcutter getting inside.

Gerry let out a moan and started dragging herself over to the dead guards. Sim didn't know what she was doing, and he was further confused when she started to crawl under the desk with them.

Lee Chen struggled to pull his wrists free of Sim's grip. He gnashed his teeth and tried to bite.

The door sounded like it was going to give way at any moment as bodies threw themselves against the other side.

Sim gritted his teeth and fought to keep hold of Chen.

I have to do something. I can't talk my way out of this.

I have to fight.

Trapped on his back with Lee on top of him, Sim lifted his head off the ground. He opened his mouth and clamped down on Lee's shoulder, feeling muscle and fat splitting between his teeth.

Lee Chen bellowed and pushed himself away, losing a thick clump of flesh as it tore free.

Sim spat the morsel out and tried to keep from gagging. He looked over and saw Nealy about to lose his battle with the door. They locked eyes, a shared moment of panic.

"Hold on!" Sim clambered to his feet and threw himself against the door just as it was about to open. Nealy nodded at him but was too disturbed to speak.

Jason crawled to his feet nearby, now awake enough to recognise the danger they were in. He, too, clambered forward and settled against the door, adding his own weight to the effort.

But that left no one to deal with Lee Chen.

The Shanghai Spike produced a length of sharp metal that he must have been concealing inside his prison jumpsuit the whole time. Grinning, he sneered at Sim, and then turned around and leered at Chrissy. She was still lying on the floor, dazed by her own energy-sapping fear.

"No," Sim shouted. "Don't you touch her."

But Lee didn't listen. He stalked after Chrissy. She put up her hands and screamed.

A gunshot rang out.

Lee Chen cartwheeled and crashed against a bank of CCTV

monitors, then crumpled to the ground, clutching his thigh. Blood flowed between his fingers.

At the back of the room, Gerry held a smoking handgun. She must have taken it from one of the guard's bodies.

Thank God for the French, thought Sim.

One danger dealt with, Sim now refocused on what was happening at his back. He turned towards Nealy. "What do we do now?"

"We need to go through that door," said Nealy, pointing to the room's other exit.

Jason shook his head. He was down on his butt, pushing at the bottom of the door with his feet. "Soon as we move away from this door, they're coming in."

"How many?" asked Chrissy. "How many maniacs are left out there? I heard shooting."

"That was us," said Sim. "We thinned the herd, but there's still half a dozen of them out there, not to mention…"

No one needed to mention William Kendall White.

The door continued to rattle behind them, opening half an inch after every blow. There was a metallic clanging that must have been the Boxcutter smashing the fire extinguisher against the door.

"I'm so sorry," said Nealy, shaking his head in shame. "I'll never be forgiven for my sins. Not after this."

There was a moment of silence. No one could offer solace against a statement that was so obviously true.

"I killed my mum," said Sim.

Everyone stared at him. Chrissy gasped.

Sim nodded to let them know they had heard him right. "What I said about the Boxcutter is true. He attacked me and my mum next to the canal, but when we jumped into the water, he ran away. I had never learned to swim, and I went underneath the water. For sure, I thought I was going to die." He took a moment, placed a hand over his heart. "I can still feel that pressure in my chest now. But, right when I was about to lose consciousness, I came up on the other side and managed to pull myself out. It was like a miracle, a second chance, I couldn't believe it. Then I turned around and saw my mum still struggling to keep herself above the water. She was right in the middle of the canal, drowning. I could have jumped in and saved her, but…"

Chrissy shook her head, confused. "Why didn't you?"

"Because she was a selfish drunk. I spent my entire childhood cleaning up after her, being embarrassed by her. When I was really young I used to go entire weekends without food while she drank herself stupid or disappeared on a bender. Sometimes, she used to hit me." He shrugged. "And in that moment by the canal, watching her struggle to keep her head above the water, it was just so easy to do nothing. All the anger – all the hatred that I didn't even know I had inside – bubbled up inside of me and I let her die. She understood what I was doing towards the end. I saw her eyes change the moment she realised she was going to die. She knew."

Jason shook his head. "Fuck, man, that's…"

"Evil?"

"Nah. It's… sad. Just sad. I'm sorry that happened to you, Sim, and I'm sorry that you had to do that."

Sim nodded to himself for a moment and then looked up again. He wanted to see Chrissy's face, to see the horror she must have felt. "The thing that stays with me the most," he carried on, "is that when my mum was gone, swallowed up by the dirty brown water, I looked across to the other side of the canal and saw William Kendall White. He was watching me – and smiling. It was like we shared something. He thought we were the same. I suppose we are."

Gerry used a desk to pull herself up. She still held the gun, and she used it to point to something on the ground. "We need to stop talking and get out of here. Chrissy, grab that piece of metal and jam it underneath the door. It might buy us a few seconds, no?"

Chrissy glanced down at the length of sharp metal that Lee Chen had been intending to stab her with. It looked like part of a cheap chair leg. Chen was still alive in the corner of the room, clutching his leg with gritted teeth.

Chrissy picked up the length of metal and shoved it underneath the door, shoving it back and forth and needling it further and further until it stuck tight. To everyone's relief, it stayed there, wedged beneath the door, even as inmates threw themselves against the other side.

"Okay," said Nealy. "Get that door open. We'll make a run for it together."

Chrissy opened the door on the other side of the room, flinching as if expecting to be attacked.

"Okay," said Nealy. "After three."

He counted, and they ran.

The door burst open behind them but caught against the wedged metal bar. The inmates shoved at the door, scraping the metal shard along the ground and sending up sparks.

It bought them only a handful of seconds. Not enough.

"Shit," said Sim, and he rushed back to slam the door closed again. An inmate got an arm and half of his chest through the gap. Gerry fired the handgun and struck the wall a few inches away from him. It was enough to send the inmate back out into the safety of the hallway.

Jason rushed to help Sim keep the door closed.

But Nealy stood in the middle of the room, looking back and forth.

"Mr Nealy," came a rasping voice beyond the door. It was William, a beast that could somehow whisper and shout at the same time. "You killed so many of my fellows. That makes me very angry. You need to be punished."

Nealy stood, stiff like one of his waxworks.

"That's okay," whispered William. "We all need to be punished sometimes. You get used to it. Hey, do you want to make another one of your deals?"

"Go away," said Nealy, no longer in control of himself. Suddenly full of fear. "I thought we had an agreement."

"Things have changed."

Jason glared. "What fucking agreement, mate?"

Nealy shook his head, as white as a sheet. "I agreed… I agreed to let William escape if he gave me two years. Two years of cooperating and scaring guests, long enough to get this place established, and then…"

Sim could barely believe what he was hearing. "You were going to help him escape?"

"No, of course not. It's just what I told him."

"You've got issues, mate," said Jason, shaking his head.

"You lied to me?" said William, having obviously overheard. "How disappointing. Mother doesn't like liars. I'm going to have to punish you very badly now."

Nealy wobbled, his lower lip quivering. "J-Just go away. I… I…" He turned and ran, rushing through the open door at the back of the control room. Chrissy stood there, holding it. She hadn't thought to close it.

The other door rattled behind Sim and Jason. They wouldn't be able to hold it for long.

"Go on," said Sim, gritting his teeth between words. "Both of you, get out."

Gerry shook her head. She was standing on one leg and wincing in pain. Her raised ankle was red and swollen. "I'm not going anywhere without help."

"I won't leave you," said Chrissy, clutching the desk behind her.

Sim shook his head, tears in his eyes. "So what do we do?"

"Dead," said Lee, laughing and wincing. "You people dead."

Gerry pointed the gun at him, but then decided not to waste the bullet.

"The plan hasn't changed," said Jason. "We need to make it out of that door and hope we can get the hell out of here without dying."

"I can barely walk," said Gerry.

"But you have that gun," said Sim. "It might be enough if you hit them as soon as they come through the door."

Gerry groaned and raised the gun. "I suppose we have no choice."

"Okay then," said Sim, taking a deep breath. "So… after three."

CHAPTER
NINETEEN

"TWO... THREE." Sim launched himself forward, away from the door. A split second later, Jason did the same.

The door burst open behind them, the metal shard coming loose and clattering across the floor.

There was no time to look back.

Gerry fired her gun.

Sim grabbed Chrissy and pulled her through the door. Then he stopped and waited as Jason took Gerry by the arm and helped her limp backwards while continuing to shoot at the open doorway.

The inmates ducked, taking cover in the hallway. Gerry's shots went wild, but they were dangerous enough to keep the inmates at bay. Only Lee Chen remained in the room as she backed through the rear exit with her arm wrapped around Jason's shoulders.

"Where do we go?" asked Chrissy, looking back and forth down the corridor they were in.

"This way," said Sim pointing. If his bearings were correct, it led towards the front of the Keep – and hopefully a way out. "Everyone, stay together and—"

The Boxcutter appeared from a recess and grabbed Sim by the throat.

Everyone screamed, and Sim felt himself about to freeze. Instead, he thrust out an arm and poked the beast in his one good eye. It caused the Boxcutter to let go of Sim and clutch at his face, bellowing and cursing.

"Go," said Sim, shoving everyone ahead.

The corridor looped back around to the other side of the control room, which was not where they wanted to be, so they slipped inside a door several metres ahead. Inside, they found an open-plan office with computers and desks. Sim imagined it full of accountants and customer service people, the notion now absurd. To slow the Boxcutter down, everyone grabbed office chairs and shoved them into the aisles as they hurried. Jason had to almost carry Gerry to keep her moving.

The intercom hissed to life overhead and Nealy's voice drifted through. "I'm so sorry. If you can hear this, you have five minutes. I'm going to log into the system and activate a full lockdown. I can't risk any of the inmates escaping. My duty is to contain them."

"Fuck you, Nealy," Jason shouted. He pulled off his baseball cap and tossed it at the ceiling angrily. "You can't do this."

"You have five minutes," Nealy said again. "Get to the shower block if you can. There's a plumbing access tunnel in one of the cubicles – I think it's number six. It can take you down to the public toilet block on the first floor. It's right near the exit. I'll be waiting for you outside in case you make it. I'm… sorry."

The speakers hissed, and an urgent alarm sounded. Sim didn't even know when the last one had ended. It had become background noise – a nightmarish motif.

William Kendall White burst into the office behind them. He stalked the aisle, launching the chairs out of his way in a rage. His right eye was puffy and red. Sim had pissed him off.

Gerry fired her gun three more times. Only one round hit,

striking William in his shoulder, but he reacted as if it were nothing more than a bee sting.

Then the gun clicked empty.

Gerry swore in French and tossed the gun away. Everyone turned and hurried for the door at the side of the office, with no idea where it led. Sim hoped it was the shower block Nealy had mentioned. William continued tossing chairs out of the way as he came after them, a charging beast.

Sim stopped in the aisle and called out to the others, "I'll be right behind you."

"No," cried Chrissy. "Sim!"

William slowed, seemingly confused, or maybe just pleased by Sim's apparent willingness to fight. "I need to know," said Sim. "I need you to answer me."

William sneered, his plump lips parting beneath a fleshy squid of a nose. He came to a stop ten feet away. "What is the question?"

"Were you born this way? Or did your mother make you like this?"

"What does it matter?"

"Because I need to know if evil exists, or is it just a label that we apply to pain? What makes you hurt people?"

William laughed, a spluttering sound like a motorbike engine starting. "Why not ask yourself? Why did you watch your mother drown?"

Sim licked his lips. It was a question he had asked himself every day for twelve years. Perhaps it was finally time to answer it. "Because I was afraid that if I didn't I would become like you, that my soul would twist so much from the pain and anger that I would lose sight of all the goodness inside me. I let my mum die because she was a monster, and I was one of her victims."

William nodded, a perverse smile on his face. "You became a killer to escape being a victim."

Sim nodded. "It terrifies me to the core, but I'm not sorry I let her die. I'm... just not." He looked back and saw Chrissy waiting by the door, listening to his words. "I wanted a different life, and I got one."

William nodded his oversized head, a thick, creamy tear forming beneath his irritated eye. "I gave you a gift, boy. I gave you a chance to stop being her victim."

"You did. Thank you for that."

"But where was my gift?" he suddenly roared at Sim. "I lived in darkness so long that it crept inside me. It swelled my bones and twisted my muscles. After a while, I wondered if sunlight was something I'd dreamed of. You want to understand evil, then look no further than those who call themselves 'mother'."

"I'm sorry for what happened to you, William."

"Be sorry when I send you to the darkness and tear your soul apart."

"No thanks." Sim dropped to the floor and rolled beneath a desk. He stretched into a crawl and pulled himself out the other side. William, with all his deformities, wouldn't be able to follow. He would have to drag the table out of the way or go around.

"You can't escape the darkness, boy. It surrounds you."

"But I have a light to keep it away." Sim leapt to his feet and sprinted to join Chrissy. She grabbed him with both arms and they rushed out the door to where Jason and Gerry were waiting for them. Shouting echoed nearby, and when they looked, they saw the remaining inmates racing down a hallway towards them. Lee Chen was at the rear of the mob, limping and bleeding but fuelled by rage.

"Over here," Jason shouted, and to Sim's delight, he saw his friend standing next to a sign reading: SHOWER ROOM.

Five minutes, he told himself. *Five minutes to find our way out of this damned place.*

He grabbed Chrissy's hand and squeezed. "We're not dying in this place."

She looked back at him and nodded. "Let's get the fuck out of here."

The shower block was dripping wet. Members of staff must have been using it that very morning, with no inkling of the horrors to come. How many of those people were now dead?

The tiled floor was vast, with dozens of showers to either side. Rather than cheap shower curtains, every cubicle had a thick glass door. No expense spared.

"He said shower number six." Jason was still propping up Gerry, so he nodded at Sim to check it out.

Sim and Chrissy stuck together as they raced over to the sixth cell on the left. They yanked open the door, but there was nothing on the floor except tiles and a small drain. "Shit," said Sim. "There's nothing here."

"It's the numbering," said Chrissy. "It must go back and forth rather than up one side and down the other." She let go of his hand and hurried across the room. When she opened up the third shower cubicle, she whooped with joy.

Everyone rushed to join her.

There was a large grate set into the floor. Chrissy reached down and grabbed a pair of recessed handles. The grate was clearly heavy, so Sim had to help her lift it. Once they got it out of the way, they found themselves staring into a black hole.

The door to the shower block opened.

"Come out, come out, wherever you are," one of the inmates called.

"The darkness is coming for you, boy," William whispered. "Close your eyes, accept it."

Nobody inside shower cubicle six spoke, not wanting to give away their hiding space. Already, Sim could hear the inmates yanking open shower doors.

Only seconds left.

Jason held onto Gerry and helped lower her quickly into the

hole. They sent Chrissy next. Sim ignored Jason's attempts to get him to go down before him and instead insisted he go last. There was no time to argue, so Jason leapt down after the women.

Sim glanced towards the door and saw shadows darken the glass. He dropped onto his butt and sat at the edge of the hole, legs dangling. Then, when the door began to open, he slid down.

The tunnel entrance dropped three feet and then snaked off ahead. It was a cramped space, but easily large enough for a person to crawl through without risk of getting stuck.

Unless that person is a seven-foot freak. Good luck following us, William.

But William wasn't the only danger.

As Sim clambered through the tunnel with Jason's rear end in his face, he felt the tunnel vibrate behind him. He glanced back over his shoulder, but there was no light. The darkness had swallowed him whole. Suddenly, he felt a little of what William Kendall White's childhood must have been like.

The inmates behind him in the tunnel called out to him, threatening to eat his heart. Their scurrying hands and feet clanged frantically on the metal as they crawled.

"Hurry if you can," Sim yelled into the shadows ahead.

"I am doing my best," said Gerry, and it was clear she was in pain. Sim didn't know how badly her ankle was injured, but it hadn't looked good.

Jason's butt dissolved into darkness as he picked up speed. Sim increased his own crawl to keep up. He had no idea how close the inmates behind were.

Eventually the darkness lightened up ahead, the black turning to grey.

Gerry let out a scream, followed by the sound of crashing.

"Whoa!" Chrissy shouted. "The tunnel drops here. Careful."

"I'm okay," said Gerry. "It's just a few feet."

Sim bunched up against Jason, who was stretched out over a

gap, slowly sliding his legs inside the hole. Chrissy called upwards, already below. She was okay.

Sim felt his heart beating in his chest. He glanced back at the darkness behind, waiting for a grimacing ghoul to appear. The frantic vibrations of his pursuers were getting closer. They couldn't be more than a few metres behind.

"Come on," said Jason, and he disappeared downwards.

Sim groped forward, feeling the edges of the hole and spreading himself across the gap. Once he was secure, he pulled his legs over the edge.

Someone grabbed his ankle.

He turned his head and saw a familiar face in the dark, scowling at him.

"I kill your bitch," said Lee Chen, his lip split and bleeding. "I make it hurt."

Sim snarled. "And I thought you were innocent. You can rot here with the rest of them"

He kicked out the leg that Chen was holding and connected with his face. It was enough to free himself, and suddenly Sim was falling into the hole. He landed on his hip, and for a second the gloom exploded with stars. Then he felt Jason gripping him by his feet and trying to drag him along.

"You good, mate?"

"Yeah," said Sim, shoving his legs away. "I'm coming."

They got going, Lee Chen right behind. The tunnel rocked and rattled as they hurried on their hands and feet. The shadows ahead continued to lift. They were nearing the end.

"There's something here," said Gerry. "I see… I see a way out. *Oui!*"

Sim let out a relieved breath. His heart was beating faster and faster, and the tunnel was feeling narrower and narrower. It was like crawling through the bowels of a beast.

There was the sound of hinges squeaking ahead. The tunnel suddenly lit up.

Gerry and Chrissy cheered.

"We're out of here," said Jason, bounding forward.

Sim glanced back into the grey shadows and saw Lee Chen hurrying after him, as well as several inmates behind him. It filled him with panic, and he started shoving Jason.

"Hey! Hey, man, just hold on a—"

Jason's body slid out of the way, falling out of the tunnel and into whatever lay ahead. He cried out in pain, but when he swore, it became clear he was all right. Sim didn't have time to feel guilty. He propelled himself forward and through the gap. He fell head first into Chrissy's arms, but his weight sent both of them tumbling against a partition wall.

Sim got his feet on the ground and caught his balance. They were standing inside a toilet cubicle, having exited through a hatch eight feet up on the wall.

Lee Chen's scowling face emerged from the hole.

Sim grabbed the hinged panel that Gerry had opened and swung it closed, smashing it against Chen's face. It sent the man back inside the tunnel, howling.

Jason yanked open the cubicle door and told everyone to make a run for it.

Gerry almost fell as they bundled their way out of the cramped space, but Sim and Jason grabbed her and lifted her off her feet. Together, they raced across the tiled floor and exited the toilet block.

And found themselves in a burning hell.

The fire had spread everywhere, and the entire room was full of choking black smoke and an unbearable heat. Rising from the smog, Jack the Ripper had his back turned to them, staring out of the large stained-glass window.

They were standing on the balcony in the main entrance hall.

But the lower floor was engulfed in flames. The inferno was

climbing the walls and super-heating the floor, ceramic tiles cracking like popcorn in a microwave.

"Where do we go?" said Jason, looking around urgently. "We're trapped."

"This way," said Chrissy, and they hurried across the landing towards the double doors that led to the ride station, where this whole nightmare had started.

But Seth Markle, the Kissimmee Killer, stepped out and blocked their way. Two other killers stood behind him. More smoke billowed out of the room behind them. The entire Keep was on fire.

"Okay," said Sim, turning Gerry around. "This way."

They raced in the opposite direction, not knowing where it would take them.

Lee Chen burst out of the toilets with another three inmates.

"There's nowhere to go," said Jason, skidding to a halt and almost dropping Gerry. "We're cut off."

Sim looked around, but there was nowhere to go. Killers closed in on them from both ends of the landing. Smoke and heat rose from below.

Maybe he could find something to defend himself with. But all that was nearby was the balcony railing and a giant statue of a Victorian Killer.

We're rats caught in a burning building. Where the hell do we go? Up!

Sim grabbed Gerry under the arms and hoisted her up. "Get on the railing and leap."

"What? Are you mad?"

"Quickly!"

Gerry must've known it was either jump or fall into the fire below, because she gripped the railing with her feet and leapt. She landed on Jack the Ripper's back and clung on. Thankfully, his cape was made of real material.

The inmates saw what was happening and raced to stop them.

Sim helped Chrissy onto the railing. Then, he and Jason leapt up either side of her, wobbling and fighting to keep their balance.

"After one," said Jason, and then shouted, "ONE!"

The three of them leapt onto the giant cloak beside Gerry. The French psychologist almost fell, but she clung on for dear life. Flames licked the air ten feet below them.

The inmates amassed on the balcony.

"Climb," Sim shouted. "Climb."

It was a crazy plan, with no promise of success, but it was either that or stay put and be murdered. Or burned.

They clambered up the cloak, moaning with exertion. Their bodies had been on high alert for the last two hours. It was only a matter of time before their tired muscles gave out. Maybe even their hearts.

Lee Chen leapt from the balcony, but the other inmates thought better of it and disappeared back into the Keep.

"I will eat your pussy," the Shanghai Spike promised. "I will wear your skin."

Everyone climbed higher and higher, scaling Jack the Ripper's back. Sim prayed they would find some kind of lighting rig to climb on, or maybe a ceiling access, but if there was nothing at the top except open air, then...

We'll die up here.

The statue wobbled under the onslaught of scrambling humans, and as they got higher, the movement became more severe. Jack was solid, but there was no telling how heavy the waxwork was. Several tonnes, at least.

Several tonnes of wax currently sitting in the middle of an inferno.

Sim glanced down and saw Lee Chen right below him. He was struggling because of his wounded thigh, but he still kept up. It was incredible that the killer had even managed to pursue them this far. Bloodlust was a powerful thing.

They reached Jack the Ripper's shoulders, and the climb became easier as the vertical eased towards the horizontal.

Gerry pulled herself up beside the statue's giant neck and nestled beneath Jack's ear. Chrissy joined her and they both held on.

Sim stared upwards, but all he saw was the bright red pentagram painted onto the ceiling.

The pentagram moved.

No, not the pentagram. Us.

Jack the Ripper leaned forward. Somewhere in the flames below, his legs were melting.

"The statue's going to fall," said Sim. "Hold on to something."

"What?" Jason looked down at Sim, having made it onto the shoulder with the women. "What are you— Look out!"

Sim's left hand slipped as something seized his leg and pulled him down.

Once again, Lee Chen had caught up to him and was grabbing at his ankle. This time, there was no way to kick the man away.

I'm going to fall.

Chrissy called out to him, terror filling her voice. "Sim!"

"Hold on," he shouted, feeling the statue lean further. "Just... hold on."

Jack the Ripper bent forward, his scalpel lengthening and liquifying. The bottom of his fabric cape shrivelled and smoked.

Chrissy screamed, holding on to the giant wax ear with Gerry. Jason clung onto the cape. Sim held on with everything he had, but his fingers felt like they were about to snap off at the knuckles. Lee Chen yanked harder on his ankle, trying to wrench him free.

"Hold on," Chrissy yelled down to him. "Sim, don't let go!"

"It's okay," he said. "I love you, Chrissy. You're the best thing that ever happened to me."

"Sim!"

Sim could hold on no longer. His fingers were seizing up. The heat wafting up from below was waiting to devour him.

Jason reached down and tried to grab him, but he couldn't lower himself enough without falling. Lee Chen pulled himself higher and started pulling at Sim's belt.

"I love you, Chrissy," he shouted again.

"Sim! Don't!"

His left hand came free.

And then he was falling.

But he fell forward not down.

Jack the Ripper collapsed forward, his stovepipe hat tipping towards the front wall of the grand entranceway and shattering the stained-glass window. The air turned to ice as biting rain and blistering wind rushed inside.

Sim realised he was still clinging to the statue. In fact, he was almost lying flat. The heat intensified, and when he looked over the edge, he saw an inferno burning right below him.

Chrissy and Gerry called for help. Gerry was hanging from the fabric over Jack's shoulder. Jason had to crawl over and grab the back of her blouse to pull her back to safety. The grey sky was visible through the broken stained-glass windows. It was surreal. Burning flames below, and cold, stinging rain above.

Lee Chen was still behind Sim, clinging to the cape. Now that Jack the Ripper was lying face down, it was possible to stand up. Sim was the first one to make it to his feet, and as Lee Chen tried to do the same, he lashed out and kicked the man in his bloody thigh.

Lee Chen wailed in agony and collapsed onto one knee, clutching at his thigh and unable to bear the pain. The expression he gave Sim was one of pure evil, and probably the last thing dozens of innocent Chinese women had seen before they had died grizzly deaths. Chen was a monster. A serial killer without remorse.

"Burn in Hell," said Sim, and he booted Chen in the shoulder and sent him tumbling off the statue. He went screaming into the flames below.

Sim staggered across Jack the Ripper's back and rejoined the others. As he did so, the statue dropped again, melting faster and faster in the heat of the flames. Beneath the fabric cape, the surface they walked upon became soft and uneven, more like sand than wax. It sent Sim tumbling, but Chrissy and Jason caught and steadied him.

"We're going to burn," said Chrissy. The sweat was pouring out of all of them, and the smoke was so thick that it coated their skin and made their voices hoarse.

"We need to jump," said Jason, pointing to the end of Jack's stovepipe hat. It was hanging over the cobbled courtyard outside, having smashed through the stained-glass windows.

"It's too high," said Gerry.

The floor went out from under them as Jack plummeted another foot.

"A little less high now," said Jason.

Sim was getting lightheaded, either from the smoke or the heat, or both. "We have no other option. Come on."

They stepped through the remnants of the stained-glass window and entered the downpour. The dark wax beneath their feet changed colours and started to run, the chemicals separating. A few more minutes and it would be more liquid than solid.

"Hold on to us," Jason told Gerry, and along with Sim, they lowered her over the edge.

"Aim for the flowerbed," said Chrissy, pointing to a raised bed of soil and flowers directly below.

Jason and Sim swung Gerry a little right and then let go. She dropped like a stone, her legs folding. When she collapsed onto her rump, she groaned in pain and rolled back and forth, but then she gave a thumbs up. Nothing else broken. The best they could hope for.

They lowered Chrissy next, and Sim was relieved to see her land a little less awkwardly. She was straight back on her feet and brushing soil from her butt.

Jason turned to Sim. "I'm thinking we might actually make it off this island, mate."

"Yeah." Sim reached out a hand. "I'm sorry for being a dick. Maybe when we get through all the therapy, we can be friends again."

"I'd like that. After you."

Sim shook his head. "After you, Mr Dreadful."

Jason lowered himself alongside the melting stovepipe hat and let go. He landed in the mud and almost stayed on his feet, but then he went sprawling onto the courtyard cobbles. A painful fall, but he made it back to his feet and seemed more or less okay. "I meant to do that!" he yelled up at Sim.

"Sure," said Sim, and he then performed the manoeuvre himself, feeling more than a little proud when he landed perfectly on his feet, and only fell forward onto his hands and knees to terminate his momentum. It didn't hurt at all.

They had made it.

They were finally out of the Keep.

But when Sim looked up, he saw someone speeding towards them.

CHAPTER
TWENTY

THE KEEP COLLAPSED BEHIND THEM, metal groaning, glass shattering, roof tiles falling from the sky. Burning embers hissed in the air as they fought against the rain. Soon, the entire building would implode, but that wasn't what concerned Sim.

Nealy sped around the side of the Keep in a golf buggy. He beeped a cheerful horn, which was obscene concerning the circumstances, but it was almost drowned out by the sheer force of the rain hitting the cobbles.

Chrissy threw her head back. "Thank God."

Gerry put her arm around Jason and said something in French that might have been a prayer.

They headed across the courtyard.

Montez Sidwell stepped out from behind one of the small food huts. He was covered in blood, and his jumpsuit was tied around his waist, leaving his massive pecs exposed. In his hand was a kitchen knife. "You folk getting outta here?"

Sim nodded. "Yeah."

Sidwell took a step forward. "Then I'm coming with. I ain't asking."

"Fine." Sim didn't care. The authorities could deal with Sidwell later. "Let's go."

Nealy's golf buggy came to a stop about twenty feet ahead. He looked up at the flaming Keep behind them and shook his head. His dreams were burning, and for him, the strife was only just beginning. Dozens of deaths were on his shoulders, and there would be hell to pay.

But at least he waited for us.

Nealy's expression suddenly changed. He yelled out a warning.

Sim turned his head and saw a stream of bodies racing around the side of the Keep. Seth Markle led the pack: the Kissimmee Killer, famed for strangling nine tourists in Florida. A big man with recorded brain damage caused by an industrial accident.

Sim and Jason grabbed Gerry and started hurrying, but even working together, they were too slow.

Thunder rang out across the English Channel. The rain was relentless, beating, beating, beating.

Montez Sidwell stopped a little ahead of them. It looked like he was going to help, but then he surprised Sim by smashing him in the face with the handle of the knife. "I'll let you play defence," he said without remorse.

Sim's vision flashed. One minute he was standing, the next he was flat on his back with rain hitting his eyes.

Chrissy raced over, trying to get Sim on his feet, but he was a boneless lump. Jason held onto Gerry nearby, seeming unsure what to do. All of them looked like drowned rats. Meanwhile, Sidwell sprinted towards Nealy.

Nealy stomped his foot down and sped off.

Sim looked towards the Keep and saw the last of the inmates rushing along the cobbles.

Jason shook his head. "We were so close."

Chrissy helped Sim get to his feet. They would have to fight. A standoff against half a dozen crazed killers. No other option.

"Eyes wide open," said Sim, and he reached out and held Chrissy's hand.

She smiled at him. "Eyes wide open."

The Kissimmee Killer raced towards them through the hammering rain. He raised a length of wood over his head, a charging Viking.

But the Viking suddenly toppled sideways.

Feral Fred landed on Seth Markle's chest and tore at his face. He was small and skinny but attacked like a screeching eagle. Markle tried to dislodge him, but as he opened his mouth to roar, Fred reached his entire hand into his throat and yanked out his tongue by the root. The Kissimmee Killer choked and spluttered, choking on his own blood and insides.

One of the other inmates rushed towards Fred, but Brenda Bates appeared and slashed his throat with a scalpel. Her wounded wrist was now wrapped in a clean white – rain-soaked – bandage. Standing behind her were two other inmates, James Sachs and Edward Gotz, two of the world's meeker murderers.

Sim wiped the water from his eyes, not sure if he was imagining things.

Feral Fred leapt at another inmate, but this man was able to wrestle the smaller killer to the ground. He beat at Fred's face, smashing him with a hard right fist. Brenda tried to help her friend, but she was blocked by a second inmate. Edward Gotz. The Composer turned and fled. James Sachs went with him.

No honour amongst killers.

Sim struggled to his feet.

"What are you doing?" said Chrissy, reaching out to grab him when he started to move away from her.

"I'm taking a leaf out of Jason's book and getting involved. No more spectating." He staggered over to Feral Fred and booted the inmate on top of him. The man fell backwards onto the cobbles but immediately leapt back up. He charged at Sim, but Sim grappled him and tripped him back down to the ground. The killer's head struck the cobbles and it left him momentarily dazed.

Fred leapt on top of his chest and tore him apart.

Brenda slit the other inmate's throat.

It was over. Only two killers left – Brenda and Fred.

Both killers glared at Sim, madness in their eyes – a love of murder.

Sim took a step back, hands in the air. Again, he felt like turning his back would be a bad idea.

Brenda moved, but only towards Fred. She reached down and took his hand, like a mother with a child. They stared at Sim a moment longer, but then they turned around and left, Fred scurrying beside Brenda as they continued holding hands.

Sim had no idea where they might go to. He expected they had no idea either.

"We need to make it to the dock," said Gerry, further down the cobbles.

Sim rejoined the others, and they hurried across the remainder of the courtyard. They reached the top of the hill, and when they looked down at the dock, they saw a single orange ferry bobbing in the unsettled water. Halfway down, Sidwell sprinted after Nealy in the golf buggy.

"If Sidwell gets on that ferry," said Chrissy, "he'll leave without us."

"Then we better get moving," said Sim.

Jason grunted, adjusting his hold on Gerry. "We're going to slow you down."

Sim looked at Chrissy and she gave him a tiny nod. He then turned and patted Jason on the back. "Then we'll meet you at the bottom."

Sim and Chrissy were only halfway down the hill, running, falling, and slipping in equal measure, when Sidwell and Nealy made it to the dock.

The golf buggy almost tipped over, Nealy brought it to such a sudden stop, and when the man leapt out, Sim feared he might get on the ferry and leave without them. But he didn't. Instead, Nealy turned and faced Sidwell.

"They're waiting for us," said Chrissy, scooping her soaking blonde hair behind her head. "They're going to wait."

Then, to their horror, Sidwell sliced the air with his kitchen knife and Nealy toppled to his knees, clutching his neck.

Sidwell rushed for the ferry.

"No!" Sim shouted. "No-no-no!"

They raced down the hill, desperate to keep their only way off the island from departing. If they were left behind…

Most of the inmates might be dead, but somewhere behind us is William Kendall White.

Sidwell got on the ferry, searching the deck and no doubt trying to figure out how to pilot it. It brought Sim and Chrissy a little more time and allowed them to reach the bottom of the hill.

Nealy was lying face down on the ground, his beige trousers darkened by the soaking rain. He was still moving, but his blood was mixing with the muddy puddles. Sidwell had dropped the kitchen knife on the ground beside him.

Sim picked the knife up and examined it. The rain had washed off most of the blood, but not all of it.

"What do we do?" Chrissy knelt beside Nealy and put a hand on his back. "Sidwell's an animal."

"No," said Sim. "He's weak. Wait here. Trust me."

She nodded. "Always."

Sim stepped forward, hiding the knife behind his back as he did so. He reached the edge of the floating dock and stopped. Sidwell was clomping up the metal stairs to where he would find the bridge. Sim yelled out over the downpour and got his attention.

"Hey, bro! What do you think is waiting for you out there? It's all gone. You're done. Whatever mediocre career in the NFL you had waiting for you is down the toilet. No more of the high life for you, dawg."

Sidwell turned around on the steps and frowned. "Yo, are you crazy? I will fuck you up, boy."

"Nah." Sim snickered. "You only take on pregnant women, right? No wonder your friends were only interested in your money – you suck! As a player and as a human being."

Sidwell bounded back down the steps. "You got a death wish, player? Say one more word to me and I will come over there and crush your skull."

"If you can catch me. You were never that fast on the field."

Montez stepped off the ferry and onto the floating dock. He shook his head and smirked like he couldn't believe what he was hearing. The rain running down his face made it look like he was melting. "Boy, I used to hit thirty-k's every game. Ain't nobody that could run like me. They used to call me the M-Train."

"Bullshit," said Sim. "You couldn't tackle a goat."

"Oh, you want to see me tackle? Boy, you about to lose your teeth."

Montez took off like a rocket, picking up speed at an unbelievable pace.

Sim planted his feet in the muddy gravel. His bladder threatened to release what tiny amount of liquid filled it, and his soul wanted to escape his body. But he stood his ground. He faced his fears.

He faced a killer.

Montez reached what was no doubt thirty kilometres an hour, pumping his limbs like the pistons of an engine. A charging bull. A stampeding rhino. An unyielding block of testosterone-soaked muscle.

Sim held the knife behind his back.

And brought it around in front of him right at the last moment.

Sidwell ducked into a tackle and hit Sim like a train, just as he'd promised. Their bodies crunched together, a hard shoulder against a soft stomach, and Sim heard the air escape him like a widow's wail. He saw only the dreary grey sky above him as he flew backwards through the air.

He came down hard on his back with Sidwell's colossal bulk pounding him into the earth. It felt like he might never take a breath again. The rain assaulted his face, almost seeming to mock him.

Sidwell rose up onto his knees, clutching at his neck with a mad panic in his wide brown eyes. The kitchen knife had buried itself so deeply into his windpipe that only the handle was showing, and when he tried to yank it out, he couldn't. His brutal charge had impaled him. Sim had used the killer's own brutality against him.

Sidwell's face darkened. He couldn't breathe. More and more, he panicked, trying to pull the knife free, trying to suck wind through his obstructed throat. Perversely, he almost seemed to beg Sim with his eyes.

He wants me to help him.

"No one will remember you," said Sim.

Sidwell collapsed onto the gravel and began to convulse.

Nealy moaned on the ground nearby.

Sim collapsed on his back and struggled to take a breath. His ribs felt like searing hot spikes.

Chrissy raced over to him and started patting him down. "Babe! Babe, are you okay?"

He couldn't breathe. He tried and tried, but he couldn't. He couldn't.

I'm suffocating. Montez broke my insides. I can't catch a breath. I can't...

A strangled gasp took over Sim as his diaphragm suddenly expanded and allowed his lungs to suck in air. It was the most exhilarating, yet painful, inhalation he'd ever taken. Life in its purest form.

I'm not going to die.

It took almost two whole minutes to get his breathing back, and there was no doubt about him having multiple broken ribs, but he was alive. Alive and with Chrissy.

Nealy was still alive, too. The man was clutching his neck and looking at them wearily. For some reason, he hadn't bled out. He must have got lucky, the knife missing his artery.

Sim got gingerly to his feet, aching all over his body. He limped over to Nealy and, along with Chrissy, they got him on his feet and helped him on to the ferry. There, they lowered him down on the outside deck and propped him against a metal bench.

Nealy pointed towards something, and Chrissy spotted a first aid kit on the wall. "I'll try to take care of it," she told Sim. "You go check on Jason and Gerry."

Sim nodded and left her. He hopped off the ferry and back onto the bobbing dock. He looked up the hill and saw Jason and Gerry more than halfway down.

William Kendall White was with them.

The gigantic killer was limping down the hill with a massive hand wrapped around each of their necks. With a snap of his wrist, he could break Gerry and Jason's necks like twigs.

When he spotted Sim, the Boxcutter grinned.

Sim looked back at Chrissy, but she was stooped over Nealy, seeing to his wounds.

I could leave right now. Run up into the bridge and get us the hell out of here. I only met Gerry today. Jason isn't my friend. I could leave. If I don't, Chrissy could die. She might end up as another of the Boxcutter's victims, and I can't let that happen. She deserves a full life, one filled with wonderful experiences.

Experiences I've been keeping from her by refusing to put the past behind me. I could leave now and make everything right.

Sim turned back and looked up the hill. Jason and Gerry were drained of all colour. They weren't even making a noise. They were silent, like gazelles caught in the jaws of a lion.

I could leave.

Sim moved away from the ferry and headed up the hill.

William Kendall White glanced at the muddy ground and noticed Sidwell's body. The sight made him laugh, the sound like angry wasps. "You were the only person to escape me, boy," he said, raising his head to look at Sim. "The only soul who ever looked upon my true self and lived to tell the tale. Do you think this is fate? A chance for me to right a mistake?"

"I'm not a mistake," said Sim. "I survived because I manipulated you. I hit a nerve and caused you to hesitate."

"I was younger, then. Whatever ounce of humanity I might once have possessed has long since departed."

Jason and Gerry closed their eyes. Both were waiting for death.

"Let them go."

"How about I keep them? It'll be just like before. All you have to do is nothing. Get on that ferry and float away. Watch them die while you live."

Sim shook his head. "Not going to happen."

"Then I'll slaughter every one of you."

"Perhaps. But I won't abandon my friends. I'll make *you* an offer instead."

William smirked. "I'm all ears."

"Let them go and I'll stay. You think I'm the one that got away? Well, you can have me in exchange for Jason and Gerry, as well as Chrissy and Nealy. Let them all leave on the ferry, and I'll stay."

Chrissy had realised by now what was happening, and she yelled out hysterically from the ferry. "Sim, get on the boat!"

He turned back and smiled at her. "I can't do that, babe. It's time for me to face my past. You can't kill someone and hope it just goes away. Eventually, you have to own up to what you did, what you are. I'm a killer."

"Yes," said William. "You have no idea the pleasures that await when you unburden yourself of humanity."

"You're not a killer, Sim," Chrissy yelled. "You're the kindest person I know. It's not your fault that your mother was unfit to have children. All you did was protect yourself. The difference between you and that monster over there is that once you freed yourself from abuse, you never killed again. You didn't develop a taste for it. Because you're not a monster. You were a victim."

Sim swallowed a lump in his throat and managed to smile. "I think you might be right. It's why I can't leave Jason and Gerry to die."

"You have a deal," said William. "You stay behind and I'll let them go. Step over to me."

"No," said Chrissy. "Don't do it."

But Sim ignored her and started up the hill. For the first time in hours, he no longer felt his heart beating. His panic was at an end, and all he felt now was a numb determination to survive.

I've come too far to fail.

William shoved Jason and Gerry forward. They staggered down the hill, still silent, still dazed. Having been seized by such foulness, such wickedness, had left them shellshocked. All Jason could manage as he passed Sim was a vacant nod.

Sim stood his ground, ten feet from death personified. He looked upon the face that had haunted his dreams for the last twelve years and felt... nothing. "You deserve to die on this island, William. At some point, you stopped being a human being and became a virus. You need isolating and stamping out."

William stepped to the side and reached down. He yanked the knife from Sidwell's throat, kicking the corpse away to wrench the blade free. Once he had it, he held it in front of him like it was a piece of fine jewellery. His right eye flickered excitedly in its socket. "First, I'm going to take away your light. Then, once you understand true, endless darkness, you'll welcome your end."

Sim glanced back towards the dock. Jason and Gerry had staggered onto the ferry. Nealy was still slumped against the bench on the outside deck. Chrissy stood at the rear railing, staring out at Sim and shaking her head. He couldn't tell if it was raindrops or tears on her cheeks.

Thunder clapped like a starting pistol.

"Start the engine," Sim yelled. "Get the ferry out of here."

Jason clomped up the stairs to the bridge. He acted drunk, but Sim could see he was trying to get a hold of himself.

The ferry was attached to a post via a length of rope. Chrissy grabbed it reluctantly and started to untie it. She shook her head as she did so. "Sim, we're not leaving without you."

"Just tell Jason to start the engines."

William glared at him. "If you try to run, I'll catch you. You'll never make it."

"I know. I reckon I can get close, though." He took a step backwards.

"What are you doing?"

"Running away from my fears." Sim turned and sprinted for the dock, ignoring the agony in his ribs. Chrissy cried out a warning, and he knew William was right behind him, propelled by awkward, bounding strides.

The ferry rumbled as Jason succeeded in switching on the engines. In a few seconds, he and the others would be away from there, finally safe. That was all Sim wanted. A chance to rescue people from a serial killer. If he saved Chrissy's life, it would make up for the one he had taken.

I killed my mother.

But I'm not a monster.

Sim made it to the edge of the dock and leapt for the ferry.

The Boxcutter grabbed him by the back of the neck and yanked him backwards so hard that his entire spine shuddered. His broken ribs stabbed at his insides.

The water was right in front of him, but he was pulled away from it. Chrissy reached out to him from the back of the ferry, terror etched all over her face.

"Nice try." Sim gasped as a knife appeared in front of his face, pointed towards his eyes. "But I warned you."

"Y-You're faster than you look."

William placed his chin over Sim's right shoulder, pressing the sides of their heads together like a pair of embracing lovers. He moved the knife closer, the tip hovering back and forth. "Which eye should I take first?"

"How about yours?" Sim grabbed the knife and pulled it towards his own face. At the same time, he lurched to his left and dropped his head. As William had been pressing his temple against Sim's, it caused his head to follow.

The knife plunged into the Boxcutter's only good eye. He let out a bellowing wail, grabbing at his face and trying to stop the bleeding. "Noooo!" he cried out. "Nooo!"

Sim took a step, preparing to run for the safety of the ferry, but William snatched out and grabbed him. The two of them staggered to the edge of the dock. Chrissy stared at Sim, bug-eyed, and begged him to get onboard. As if he wasn't already trying.

"Y-You blinded me!" William yelled. "You blinded me!"

"Now you know what darkness really is, you fucking freak."

"I'll kill you." Despite his blindness, William managed to wrap both hands round Sim's throat. His strength was insane, and Sim felt himself losing consciousness almost immediately. Stars invaded his vision like tiny flying saucers.

I escaped you once. I'll escape you again.

This time for good.

Sim wrapped both arms around the Boxcutter's waist and drove himself backwards. Both men went tumbling over the edge of the dock and into the freezing cold water.

Sim quickly discovered that he still couldn't swim.

CHAPTER
TWENTY-ONE

SIM WENT UNDER THE WATER. Bubbles and currents disorientated him, the water churning around the ferry's propellers. It was impossible to see, even with his eyes wide open, and the only thing he could make out was darkness below and light above.

He flapped his arms and kicked with his legs, the motion instinctual, like some encoded part of his DNA contained the secret knowledge of swimming. He felt himself rising.

I'm not going to drown. I won't.

Sim broke free of the freezing water and felt the icy air bite his cheeks. The ferry was only a few feet away, but when he reached out his arms he slipped back beneath the water. He kicked his way back up again and saw Chrissy peering out at him. So close.

I just need to make it a few feet. I just need to swim.

He crawled through the water, drowning slowly but then catching a breath. His panic kept him afloat, but the problem was how long he could keep it up for. Already his legs were stiffening. The pain in his ribs made every sucking breath a struggle.

Like a shark, William Kendall White broke the surface of the water. He swiped his arms around and backhanded Sim across the skull. Then he grabbed hold of Sim and started dragging him down.

Sim did everything he could to stay afloat, kicking with everything he had. "L-Let go of me."

"I'll swallow your soul. We'll spend eternity in Hell together. You're bound to me, boy. Don't you see?"

Sim choked on water, spat it out. "I see. My eyes are... wide open." He reached out and grabbed William's misshapen head with both hands, pushing down on him. The two of them sank beneath the water, stinging salt assaulting Sim's flesh. He kept his hands on William's head, pushing the man down beneath him. In the water, their size difference no longer mattered.

They continued to sink. Lower and lower.

The light overhead got darker. Life fading away.

Sim glanced down and could barely see William beneath him, but he continued to push down on his head, fingers wrapped around bony skull plates. The lower Sim sank, the lower still that William went. They were back at the canal, only this time they were drowning together.

Then Sim let go, kicking himself away from William with both legs.

William tried to grab at his ankles, but Sim kept thrashing and kept himself from being caught. He started to rise, to swim away. William Kendall White, with his misshapen limbs and misaligned joints, could only sink like a rock into the murky depths.

Sim saw a tiny sliver of light overhead – the tiniest promise of life. He kicked with everything he had left inside of him. Pain and agony and fear went into every movement, all of it coming out through his legs and propelling him upwards. His entire body was numb, his mind a broken mess. The only thing he could do was focus on that light above.

Chrissy.

Chrissy.

Chrissy.

The light began to fade. His chest began to burn. Pressure. It was the only sense he had left. Pressure. Growing. Increasing. Taking over him. Darkness crept in around the edges of his vision. Death whispered in his ear.

He wasn't going to make it.

Drowning had always been his destiny.

His legs finally gave out. His upward momentum faded and then stopped completely. The water became unbearably heavy. His lungs turned to stone, and every regret became a thorn in his brain. So many regrets.

I never left the country.

I never ate calamari.

I never asked Chrissy to marry me.

Sim's entire body seized. His limbs refused to obey. His body had suffered enough.

A strange, unwanted peace fell upon him.

He was exhausted, but finally he could sleep.

It was okay to give up.

And so he did.

Sim's senses swirled, a confused maelstrom as the darkness exploded into light. The grey sky rained down on him, stinging his face with its onslaught. Thunder boomed, rattling his chest.

"Oh no you don't," said Jason, yanking Sim by the back of his shirt. Leaning out beside him were Chrissy and Gerry. All three dragged Sim through the water and up onto the deck. There, he lay on his back, gasping for breath.

Chrissy's face was an unsymmetrical mess of pain, panic, and fear. Her emotions pulled at the tiny muscles like competing puppeteers. Sim knew then how much she loved him.

And how much he loved her.

"E-Eyes... wide... open," he said.

Chrissy smiled and dropped to hug him.

When he turned his head, he saw that the ferry was bobbing on the water, slowly floating away from the dock. At the top of the hill, black smoke rose into the darkening sky. Night would arrive soon, but the burning Keep would light up the sky until morning. It took a long time for evil to die. It never gave up easily.

Nealy moaned from nearby.

Chrissy helped Sim to sit up, and he saw the Irishman still propped up against the bench. He had a pad taped to his neck, and it looked like he might pull through. Even so, he was as pale as porcelain and utterly miserable. "What the hell was I thinking?"

"I dunno," said Jason, wringing the bottom of his T-shirt out. "It wasn't one of your best ideas, mate."

He shrugged. "Suppose I was due a downfall. I might never recover from this."

"Sorry," said Chrissy, and then she shrugged. "Also not sorry."

"It's fine. I'm surprisingly okay with it. Getting your throat cut gives you a different perspective on what's important. I've learned many things about myself today, not least that I'm a coward."

Chrissy nodded. When she spoke, her teeth chattered. "S-So, what's next for you?"

"I'm going to do everything I can to make up for what happened here. I have debts to pay. Debts that will take a lifetime to even half pay off. Other than that, who knows?" He smiled at Chrissy. "Perhaps I'll find a good woman and get married. Seems like a man is much stronger with someone who loves him by his side."

Sim reached out and squeezed Chrissy's hand. It was ice cold. "I'm only half a person without her."

Chrissy looked over at Gerry and chuckled. "Maybe there's hope for them yet."

"*Oui*," said Gerry, sitting on the bench and clutching her ankle. "But Evers hasn't seen the size of my bill yet. He might be less hopeful then."

Nealy laughed. "Whatever number you've got in your head, double it. All of you. I'll make this right. I give you my word."

Chrissy groaned. "We took your word once before."

"Yeah," said Jason. "Maybe next time you should just open up a freaking petting zoo. Goats and shit, yeah?"

"I accept your wise advice, Mr Dreadful."

Everyone chuckled, although it was a tired and broken sound. They were all soaking wet and shivering, their hands shaking with the cold.

Sim got to his feet and leaned over the railing. He watched the dock disappear into the distance, glad to see it go. He also saw figures on the shore, maybe five or six. Inmates or staff, he didn't know, but now that they were on the ferry, they could call for help.

He found himself worrying about Fred and Brenda. They had escaped the Keep but had chosen not to kill Sim when they could have. Was it because they owed him for his earlier kindness? To think that such a simple thing as kindness could mean so much told of how tortured some souls were. When you knew only suffering, a friendly smile could mean the world. He hoped they didn't get hurt in the aftermath of all this.

"Hey," said Jason. "You want this back, or should I just toss it in the water?"

He was referring to Sim's phone. Somehow, he had kept hold of it.

"No! Start filming. This will make a great outro for our channel."

"Yours and Chrissy's?"

"No, *ours*. You, me, and Chrissy are going to start something new, something better than both our channels. We're going to go after active serial killers and put a stop to them. You were right. It's better to do something to help rather than just report on things when it's too late. Even if you make a few mistakes along the way."

"I'd make fewer mistakes with you onboard, mate."

Sim nodded. "And maybe you can teach me how to lighten up." He glanced back at Chrissy and smiled. "It's time for me to let go of who I was and start being the man she sees in me. I spent so long worrying about what—"

Jason patted him on the back. "Yeah, this is a moment where you need to lighten up. Stop thinking and go be with her. Dickhead."

Sim chuckled. "Thanks. Anyway, get filming. I'll give you an interview once I catch my breath."

Jason unlocked the phone, but he didn't start filming. He just stared at it thoughtfully.

Sim walked over to Chrissy. She was shivering against the railing near the back of the ferry and rubbing at her face with a dirty right hand. When she sensed his approach, she looked up and smiled. "You okay?"

"I don't even know how to start processing an answer to that question. But I have you, so nothing can be that bad."

She shook her head and looked off towards the island. "I can't believe this happened. How many people died today?"

"I don't know. For once, I don't want to think about it. Maybe it's time to take a break from death for a while?"

She frowned at him. "What do you mean?"

"How about we go on a safari? For, like, a whole year?"

"I think… that sounds like the most amazing thing ever. You sure you're ready?"

He raised an eyebrow. "After what we went through today, I'm ready for anything. I love you, Chrissy. It's why I'm alive. Without you, I wouldn't have been able to fight so hard. I spent so long worrying about the darkness inside me that I ignored all of the light. All of the love. You fixed me, Chrissy. You made it so—"

"Lighten up!" Jason shouted from the bottom of the staircase. "Chrissy, I told him. He needs to stop with the monologues."

Chrissy erupted in laughter. Once she'd caught her breath, she smiled at Sim and nodded. "He's right. Stop thinking." She leaned forward and kissed him.

And they held each other until the coastguard pulled them apart and wrapped them up in thick blankets.

They had their whole lives ahead of them. Sim was going to face it with his eyes wide open.

Feral Fred fought like a man twice his size, but he wasn't so vicious with a trank dart in his arse. Same with his carer, the skanky women with the knotted hair.

There were only nine killers left on the island, which would infuriate Conner's employers at Le Grande Mar. He didn't know why they wanted a bunch of maniacs, but they had been very clear about containing them without lethal force. Every inmate was to be captured alive.

Problem was, the prison had burned to the ground. Conner couldn't even tell what it had looked like. He'd set a few fires in his time, usually to cripple a rival of whoever was paying him, but this scene was odd. A thick carpet of wax covered the front part of the ruin, while charred skeletons littered the rear. In one corner of the building's footprint, the remains of a glass shark tunnel cluttered the ground. It was the strangest prison he'd ever heard of.

The fire had occurred five days ago, but Le Grande Mar had been obstructed by the coastguard until today, when the island had finally been released from custody. No one had stepped foot on the island in that time, and it was only Evers Nealy's intervention that had kept it out of the papers for the time being.

Conner's orders were to find any surviving inmates and destroy anything not burned in the fire. He had brought a specialist arson team with him for that purpose, but right now, everyone was scouring the island for survivors. There weren't many.

Right now, he was walking the coastline, theorising that any survivors would want to be on the beach trying to signal for help. Well, help was here, wielding a hunting rifle and a multi-use Taser. He had brought fourteen men with him to the island, equally armed with non-lethal firepower, but they had opted to spread out to cover more ground. His team was one of the best in corporate espionage, but this gig was on the boring side. No inherent danger, and no requirement to kill. A dud of a mission.

At least it paid well. Le Grande Mar always paid well for this shit. And often. If life was a chess game, Le Grande Mar was the biggest cheat going.

The island was a wretched place, full of grey stone and weedy patches of grass. The drizzling grey sky only made things more depressing. It led Conner to decide that he was due a holiday after this mission was over. Maybe he would visit the Seychelles. He'd killed a man there once; it'd been nice.

There was a dark lump on the pebble beach ahead. Conner crunched his way over to it, figuring it was a dead seal or maybe a clump of seaweed. But when the lump moved, he realised it was a person. If it were a member of the island's staff he was to escort them to safety, where a shithead lawyer and a thick envelope full of cash would be waiting for them. If it were an inmate…

Conner raised his rifle and lowered himself into a crouching walk. "Identify yourself, friend."

The person on the beach rose slowly, like a python uncoiling. Except this person was the size of an upright cow. They wore a grubby brown jumpsuit the colour of dogshit. An inmate, for sure.

"Yikes, you're a big fella, huh? I'm going to need you to stay right where you are."

Whether the person hadn't heard him, or was just plain

ignoring him, they turned around to face Conner. They were as ugly as the day was cold, with a face like rhubarb crumble. For some reason, the ugly son of a bitch was smiling.

"I'm here to help you," said Conner, "but for both our safety, I need you to put on some handcuffs for me." He reached to his belt and unclipped the cuffs, then tossed them towards the stranger. But the stranger didn't react and allowed the cuffs to fall onto the pebbles at their feet.

"Fuck sake!" Conner rolled his eyes and snorted. "Have it your way."

He pulled the trigger and sent a tranquilliser dart right into the big man's chest, near the heart. It would take a minute or two, but the effects would start in only a few seconds.

"Stay calm and everything will be okay. You're going to feel a little woozy, so I suggest you sit dow— Hey! Stay right where you are!"

The large stranger marched towards Conner without fear. *The freak must be retarded,* was the only thing he could think as he pulled his Taser free and fired it from the hip.

The electrified barbs clung to the stranger's dirty jumpsuit. Conner pulled the trigger and sent a current down the line. The reassuring *click-click-click* always made him smile, and he always liked to try to make the target piss themselves.

But this target didn't even flinch. The gigantic freak rose up even taller and picked up speed, charging Conner like a bull. The jumpsuit was smoking where the barbs had attached themselves.

"What the fuck?" Conner reached for his belt, but he had nothing to defend himself with. He'd even been told to leave his knife on the boat. Le Grande Mar had screwed him over with their stupid parameters.

Conner absorbed the charge, but it was still too much to resist. The massive freak lifted him off his feet and threw him into the air. He landed hard on the pebbles, but at least they cushioned the worst of it. Like the trained fighter he was, Conner rolled onto his feet and raised his fists.

He gave the freak his best right uppercut, landing it right beneath the chin. A knockout blow, for sure. But the freak grabbed Conner by the throat and snarled. Right then, he realised who he was up against.

This is the freaking Boxcutter. He was supposed to have drowned. Shit!

"P-Please, don't. I can pay y— ARRRRGH!"

William Kendall White poked out both of Conner's eyes. It was a transcendent experience, well above simple agony, and by the time it was over, he no longer felt human. The pain had transformed him, and all he knew was darkness. Then his tormentor dragged him some place, cold and quiet, and started taking pieces of him away. He lost track of the days, but he hoped to die soon. END.

WANT MORE HORROR? GET 'WITCH' NOW HERE FOR ONLY 99c / 99p!!!

WANT FREE BOOKS?

Don't miss out on your FREE Iain Rob Wright horror pack. Five terrifying books sent straight to your inbox.

No strings attached & signing up is a doddle.

Just Visit IainRobWright.com

ALSO BY IAIN ROB WRIGHT

Animal Kingdom
AZ of Horror
2389
Holes in the Ground (with J.A.Konrath)
Sam
ASBO
The Final Winter
The Housemates
Sea Sick, Ravage, Savage
The Picture Frame
Wings of Sorrow
Hell on Earth (6 books)
TAR
House Beneath the Bridge
The Peeling
Blood on the bar
Escape!
Dark Ride
12 Steps
The Room Upstairs
Soft Target, Hot Zone, End Play, Terminal
The Spread (6 books)
Witch
Zombie
Hell Train

Iain Rob Wright is one of the UK's most successful horror and suspense writers, with novels including the critically acclaimed, THE FINAL WINTER; the disturbing bestseller, ASBO; and the wicked screamfest, THE HOUSEMATES.

His work is currently being adapted for graphic novels, audio books, and foreign audiences. He is an active member of the Horror Writer Association and a massive animal lover.

www.iainrobwright.com
FEAR ON EVERY PAGE

For more information
www.iainrobwright.com
author@iainrobwright.com

Copyright © 2022 by Iain Rob Wright

Cover Photographs © Shutterstock

Artwork by Carl Graves at Extended Imagery

Editing by Richard Sheehan

All rights reserved.

No part of this book may be reproduced in any form or by any electronic or mechanical means, including information storage and retrieval systems, without written permission from the author, except for the use of brief quotations in a book review.

❦ Created with Vellum

Ingram Content Group UK Ltd.
Milton Keynes UK
UKHW011957120623
423315UK00005B/334

9 798367 732856